A WINDOW IN THE EARTH

By Matthew Fish

Edited By

Stephen Mathis

May 18th, 1997

James Janes
The Cave at the Janes House
Pine Hallow, Missouri

Dear James,

Where do I begin? Where do I even start? There are things that I have thought long and hard about pretty much each and every day after everything that has happened. I promised you that I'd keep in touch, and this letter, although hard to write, is the first of many more I plan to write to you. Honestly I don't know where to begin, so I'll just go with whatever comes to mind, I guess.

You know, the other day I tried to look up Pine Hallow on the internet (you know what that is, right?), and I found no mention of it anywhere. This letter should really be a huge pain for the postal service to get to you. I still plan on coming by someday and visiting. Lord knows that I want to; it's just that everything has been so crazy. Sometimes I'm not even sure of what really happened that summer. I really wish things were different, but I guess it's just as father used to say, "Things that change change because we are people who have no authority to change them."

I'll write more when I get the chance. Hopefully, I'll be coming down there soon. I deeply hope that we can meet again, and just talk about everything.

With much love,

Christopher

Chapter 1: A Home for New Hopes

Seven steps from the front porch, sixteen steps to the road, thirty more to the first turn, and then five-hundred miles to home.

It was late summer in 1993 and both of Christopher Janes and James Janes' parents were dead. The two were told that it was an "unfortunate car accident" involving a drunk driver; however, neither was given many specifics about it. Christopher was closer to fourteen than thirteen and James had turned fifteen a few months ago. Given their young ages, the rest of their family had felt that it was way too early and far too messy to get in to the finer details of how it exactly had happened, so they were spared the play-by-play of how the drunk driver in the other vehicle had crossed over the median on I-55 heading south and hitting them head on, killing their father instantly, and how their mother, who had survived the initial collision, ended up fighting for three hours in the ER before finally slipping away. Later in life, Christopher, when finally told, would not refer to it as an unfortunate accident at all, yet a sad, careless form of murder.

It was decided that the best place for brothers would be with their grandfather, Mathias, out in the Ozarks. Although born Mathias Janes, he was commonly known among family and friends affectionately, if not strangely, as “Grandpa Bones.” He was a good-tempered man in his early seventies who had two red hunting dogs and had served his country in the often-forgotten Korean War; at least, those were the only two qualities that Christopher and James knew him by. Upon further questioning by Christopher, he deemed it very likely that this small bit of information was the only thing that his aunt actually knew about Grandpa Bones. That, and as their aunt put it: “He has himself a nice little place out in the country—a *beautiful* place out there in the country. Pretty isolated, though, pretty well cut off out there.”

Their Grandpa Bones lived alone in a two-story cottage-style house about eighty-odd miles from Springfield, Missouri. After the Korean War he longed for a peaceful, quiet life out in the country, something he had missed throughout all those noisy years of war and service. Bones’ wife, Catharine Shultz, had unfortunately passed away in the fall of 1989 to lung cancer. Unlike her husband, Catharine had been slightly reluctant to move out into the country. Having been born a city girl herself and grown up in Saint Louis, she was accustomed to a more modern lifestyle. However, it did not take long out there in the country to convince her to stay. It would be those quiet moments, out in the woods, when the sun was high above and the shadow of the leaves shimmered all around her, like the reflection of sun on water, that a calm, cool breeze that would break the silence of the leaves and promise to steal you away with it, if only you would just let it. She grew to love the woods, and she loved looking at the clear sky at night and seeing the stars, and the sounds of a world that wasn't diluted and stamped out by man or machine. When she died, Bones buried her alone at the place she loved most, atop a large hill where the two would often sit and look out at the world. It was a nice spot where the trees broke just enough to frame out the hills around them. It was where Bones planned to be when he died as well.

It was late at night as Christopher and James rode with their aunt to their new home, the road ahead of them as black as the road behind. Without the van's lights, Christopher believed they would be lost to the darkness completely. "Are we much farther now?" he asked, gazing out the side window into the blackness.

"Not much farther…about a half an hour more or so." Aunt Lynn shifted her eyes to the rearview mirror and back to the road ahead. "I think you'll really enjoy it there," she added, not really knowing if they would indeed enjoy it, yet just saying it to be saying something. In all honesty she felt rather uncomfortable with the situation at hand. She, like most of the family, had not been close with the children or their parents. In all severe honesty, she felt that she had much better things that she could be doing at the moment than driving eight hours into the wilderness, and one of those were watching her late night shows on Cinemax. However, doing this did make her feel a bit better about everything, or at least made her look better to the rest of the family, and to her that was what *really* mattered.

Christopher tried to think of some kind of reply, but then quickly decided otherwise. It was awkward for him as well. Too strange, too soon; things were just way too confusing and there was way too much to figure out. He looked over to his brother James, who was sleeping in the seat next to his. It seemed that James was always sleeping since their parents' accident. Perhaps life was better in dreams, and so James was taking up a more permanent residence there. He was a year and a half older than Christopher. He was more artistic as well, and much more outgoing; however, his school attendance and marks seemed to suffer as a result of spending much of his school time engaging in sports. He was, after all, quite an accomplished soccer player. On the other hand, Christopher was much more booksmart and logical. He'd do much better in school, if he didn't love videogames and Nintendo as much as he did. It wasn't just too much *Mario*; it was too much *Zelda*, and way too much *Final Fantasy*. What reason was there to care about this one tiny real world, he supposed, when countless videogame worlds were out there and in need of justice, in need of a great man, in need of a hero? It was just so appealing to him, and so convenient that the hero was always Christopher. It made sense to him in a strange way: James slept and went into his dreams to escape reality; Christopher could be lost happily in the game world. At least there he could be an all-powerful white mage and cast "Holy", toasting the asses off of everyone that offended him. Then he could cast a quick revival spell, probably "Life 2", which would bring his parents back as healthy as they had been before the accident, and it would be guaranteed to work. *If only it were that easy,* Christopher thought to himself as he glanced once more at his dozing brother. *I wonder what his dreams are like?*

"I do believe that we are here!" Lynn exclaimed with more than just a bit of relief. Christopher had been daydreaming again and the last half-hour had flown by amazingly fast. They cornered a sharp turn through tall pine trees, pulling into a rough driveway made of dirt and rock. The van bumped and rocked against the weathered, makeshift road as the air was filled with the sound of grinding gravel. "Well this is fun isn't it?" Lynn remarked, being much more annoyed than amused.

It was a bit of fun, actually, or at least Christopher thought so. Much more fun than the first eight hours or so of this trip had been. He was even a bit amused at Aunt Lynn's annoyance; she had seemed rather uptight through the trip. She even managed to seem pretty uptight at the funeral. Secretly, he disliked her, although he'd never say it aloud. Christopher was a good judge of character, or at least he always felt that he had been. In a way he knew that Aunt Lynn didn't care for him much either. So, in a way, everything evened out, even if it was unpleasant.

"Shit," Lynn muttered angrily at the loud, tinny rattle of rocks striking the undercarriage of the van. She shot a quick look into the rearview mirror to see if anyone had noticed this little slip of obscenity. Content that the brother's possibly had not, she turned her fierce gaze once more to the road.

Christopher chuckled quietly for a moment, making sure that he kept it to himself. He was getting more and more amused with each passing moment. What surprised him most about everything that was going on was that James had managed, and was still managing, to sleep through this whole noisy, bumpy series of events. James' mouth was agape and he was drooling, his whole body seeming to vibrate as his head bobbled up and down on the backseat cushions. He was completely oblivious, like reality didn't matter or even exist.

How do you do it? Christopher thought. Since their parents had died, it seemed that the two had been much more separated than before, as if James had become a distant stranger. Christopher had always meant to ask just how it was possible that James was able to deal with everything—he just never seemed to make time to be with his little brother.

"Finally!" Lynn brought the van to a jolting stop. Dust kicked out from beneath the vehicle's tires, churning out a brown fog that billowed out behind them, making the night look all the more creepy.

"You awake?" Christopher asked. He gave James a short nudge on the shoulder.

"Yeah…."

"We're here." Christopher slid the van door open, carefully stepping out onto the earthy stone driveway.

“Yeah...,” James responded once more. He pushed himself up with one hand, violently attempting to rub his remaining fatigue from his bloodshot eyes with the other. He crawled out of the van on Christopher’s side and slid the door closed.

“Here, take these,” Lynn said, handing four suitcases to the brothers, one for each hand, and returned once more to the vehicle to collect a large box from the back. She ran ahead of the two brothers, dropping the box next to the front door. She turned toward the door and began banging on it. “Come on, come on, answer….”

Christopher and James stood behind their aunt, uneasily looking over their new surroundings. The air around them was filled with the sounds of crickets and frogs. A faint light shone through the small, dirty glass slits on the front door. It was definitely farther from any place they had ever stayed before. Not a streetlight or another automobile in sight. There were no familiar sounds of traffic—no honking horns, sirens, or stomping feet. No eager hums of electricity either, save for the van’s headlights, though they could barely be heard over the busy chorus of the creatures of the night.

“Maybe he’s not home,” Christopher said, feeling really uncomfortable at the thought that this was going to be his new home.

“I don’t believe this!” Lynn exclaimed. Her annoyance with the entire situation was slipping out more and more with each little test. “I spoke to him before we left; he said he’d be here.”

"He's here," James said sleepily. He was straining to keep his eyes open.

"You don't know that, honey. He's probably out drunk somewhere." Lynn shook her head in disbelief. "This is why no one ever talks—"

With that, the front door was flung open and the porch light flickered on, illuminating the darkness around them. There, clad in a red-striped and mostly stained set of pajamas, stood the venerable "Grandpa Bones", in all his bedtime glory. Now, Grandpa Bones wasn't your typical old grandpa type of person. Although at the ripe age of seventy-two, he kept himself in good shape and still might be considered handsome and fit, for an elderly sort of guy. He had a firm white smile he commonly wore, and had two tattoos: a beautiful lady on one arm and a black cat on the other. "Sorry, must have nodded out for a bit," he said; "been waiting a while."

"Yeah, well, it's been a long drive," Lynn retorted, purposely showing her impatience.

"Oh, of course, of course!" Bones reached over to help with the Janes brothers' luggage, ignoring Lynn's rudeness. He paused for a moment, suitcase in each hand, flexing his arm muscles. "See here, kids? Picked these up in the service of our country. Got myself a bullet in this one. Probably still there!"

Christopher chuckled as he and James helped bring a large trunk into the house. His first impression of Grandfather Bones was a favorable one. Bones had a warmth and kindness to him that just seemed to radiate. In fact, for the first time in a long time, Christopher actually felt some faint sense of hope for everything, that maybe things were going to be okay after all.

"I told you he was here," James said as he lugged in his two heavy trunks.

"Yeah, yeah...," Lynn muttered as she fumbled through her purse. It was readily apparent that she had no intention of stepping inside. It seemed as though she was eager to get far away from the three of them and return to her life as soon as possible. Pulling out her keys, she turned to the others and nodded for no reason in particular. "Well..."

"Of course!" Bones said, placing the luggage onto the floor. "Let's say our goodbyes before we get packed in, right?"

"It's just that I've got a long way to go. You understand."

"Oh, definitely." Bones reached into his pajama pockets and pulled out a small wad of cash. "For the gas and getting 'em here safely." He handed Lynn the money.

"Thanks," Lynn answered plainly, as if she expected the handout.

"I'll take these suitcases up. Have a good trip back," Bones added with a smile.

"Right...." Lynn placed the money in her purse and looked to Christopher and James. "It was great seeing you guys again, I know that things have been real bad with—you know—everything that has been going on. I know we don't really know each other well and all that. Well...you know."

"Yeah...," James answered back, seeming apathetic.

"Yeah, we know," Christopher said. He didn't exactly know how James felt about her, but he suspected James didn't really care much for Aunt Lynn either, or rather, for as much as they knew of her. She was probably a nice person. Perhaps it was just that the situation at hand had brought them all into a place that neither one really wanted to be in. Even though her actions seemed selfish, it's really hard to gauge someone on actions alone when dealing with uncomfortable situations.

"Right...," Lynn repeated as she readied herself, keys in hand. "Also, this probably isn't permanent, you know. Everyone has a lot to work out on what to do with you two, you see?"

"We get it," James said, sounding pretty annoyed.

"Right...," Lynn said once more as she made her way back to the van. "I mean, he's pretty old, so don't give him too much trouble. And try and have some fun. I mean, that's what is best for both of you right now."

"We'll behave, don't worry about us," Christopher said. He watched Aunt Lynn crawl back into the van. *Like you'd actually worry about us,* he thought, watching as James completely ignored Lynn's departure and entered the house. Christopher waved once to her and smiled. It was, after all, the polite thing to do.

Christopher stood alone on the porch as he watched the red glow of the van's two rear lights shrink into the night. For a moment, he thought about his old home back in Bloomington, Illinois. He thought about how completely different it was from this new home-to-be. It wasn't a completely bad change, just a very different one, a change he hadn't expected at all. It was just so strange to be somewhere and not see lights off in the distance, or to not see traffic on the roads. All in all, the silence of the woods was actually a little creepy, a little disorienting. There was one good point here that Christopher did enjoy, and that was the smell. It's a funny thing to think about, but it definitely did smell much more pleasant here. The air just did not seem to be as crowded or tainted.

Christopher was lost in thought; he had not even realized that James was back outside and standing behind him, looking off in the direction of the road they had followed there.

"She gone?" James asked, knowing the answer but wanting to hear it anyway.

"Yeah."

"She really sucked," James said, smirking.

The two chucked for a moment, for the first time in forever, or so it seemed to Christopher. At least James was able to find some sense of humor in all of this. After everything that had happened, Christopher had been worried that they might never have the ability to laugh at anything ever again.

Chapter 2: The First Night

Grandpa Bones gave his short, "time-constrained" tour of the place he proudly considered home. The main room, or living room, looked rather cluttered. It was as though Bones wasn't that much of a fan of dusting and had something of either a habit or hobby for keeping old copies of *TV Guide*, as well as newspapers, around well past their expiration date. The main room also contained the only television set in the entire house, and it was an old black and white set, much to Christopher's disappointment. The kitchen, also located on the main floor, was like stepping into a whole other world when compared to that of the living room; it was white and clean and almost painfully bright to Christopher's adjusting eyes when he crossed between the two rooms. Also on the main floor was Grandpa Bones' bedroom, which was "Far too untidy to tour this night, maybe next week," he said, ushering the brothers past the door and up the stairs.

The upper floor of the house contained two

bedrooms set aside for the Janes brothers. Each was tidy in the sense that Bones had decided a few hours before the brothers' arrival that it needed some emergency attention. It was a quick and somewhat short fix, yet it was workable. Each room had clean sheets and plenty of room for each brother to express their specific decorating style whenever they were comfortable enough to give it a chance. There was also a small room across the hallway from the bedrooms, which was mostly used for storage. It was full of wartime memorabilia and other non-daily use items that probably hadn't seen the light of day in a quite a spell, and probably wouldn't any time soon. This room also led up into the attic; another area that Bones claimed was far too unpleasant for an evening exploration.

Back on the main floor of the house, and just past the kitchen, was the entrance to the basement cellar. It was a pretty typical place as far as basements and cellars go, having a slight earthy smell and dampness to it. The three rushed through that area pretty quickly, as they were a bit creeped out by the feel of a basement at night. They figured many people were, regardless of age.

Christopher felt very hopeful about his new surroundings. It was a definite change from what he was used to. Just like the surrounding country, it was a completely different world. However, Christopher was slowly learning that sometimes different doesn't always have to be a bad or good thing. It's just a different thing, a different way to be.

After the tour, James decided to go ahead and go to sleep, although it was only eleven o' clock, and he had definitely been sleeping a lot more since the accident, as Christopher had noticed before. He had hoped that tonight he would finally get a chance to speak to James about how things were unfolding, and these new unfamiliar surroundings. Yet, it seemed that once more that they would not get the chance—at least not this night.

"You staying up for a bit, then?" Bones asked Christopher. He kicked his feet up and lay back on the dusty gray couch, scratching the salt-and-pepper-colored growth of hair beneath his chin.

"If it's okay…," Christopher timidly replied. He wasn't sure as to what any real ground rules were, since so far none had exactly been laid out. "I don't think I can sleep, at least not right now."

"If it's okay?" Bones repeated as he clicked the TV over to a *M*A*S*H* rerun. "Of course it's okay. Hell, I just figured I'd let you guys have the run of the place for a few days, you know, get used to everything around here, then maybe we'll see what goes and we'll do the figuring of what is okay and what's not."

"Thanks," Christopher said, feeling even more relieved. Bones' demeanor was quite a comfort to him. He had been desperately worried that Bones might end up being someone unpleasant like Aunt Lynn, but he honestly didn't believe he'd be that bad. After all, out of everyone in the family, Bones had been the one who agreed to take the two Janes brothers in. "I mean, I really appreciate it. Everything."

"How old are you, Christopher?" Bones asked, taken aback for a moment by Christopher's politeness. "Thirteen, right?"

"Yes, sir," Christopher answered. "Fourteen this September."

"That's far too young to worry as much as you do. Hell, after all you've been through I think you should be able to do just whatever you feel like for a while."

"If you don't mind…," Christopher began as he sat down on the couch across from the TV set, beside Bones, "…could I ask why you decided to take us in?"

"Shit…," Bones said suddenly, as though the matter bothered him immensely, but then quickly recomposed himself. "Oops. Crap, I mean, or whatever. Truth be told, I never really stayed in contact with your father and mother as much as I think I probably should have. It's not that we ever had any kind of disagreement; no, it's just that I choose to live out here, and you know everyone else lives very busy lives. I bet you don't even remember the last time you guys were here before."

"We were here before?" Christopher asked, desperately trying to remember something he hoped he had not forgotten.

"I think you were probably two back then."

"I don't remember," Christopher replied, feeling a bit sad.

"Well anyway, no matter; no one remembers stuff like that when they're two," Bones said with a deep chuckle before he went on: "Like I said, I never stayed in contact, and I should have. I always meant to, and then this happened. The rest of the family, they were all talking about splitting you two up, and who would take whom. Seems as though your parents weren't that close with any of them either. I can't say I blame them. I think the whole rest of the family is a bunch of snobby bastards. That's just what I think though, okay?"

"Okay," Christopher said quickly, and smiled.

"Okay, well hell." Bones reached into a dark, filthy crevice between the cushions of the couch, pulling out a small silver flask and a healthy plume of dust. After taking a deep drink and grimacing momentarily, he placed the container back in between the cushions. "Like I said, they were talking about splitting you up, and I didn't think that was right. They were all talking like you were some damned liability. You're kids for Christ's sake."

"I see," Christopher said as he let out a deep breath of discouragement. "Did you have to pay Aunt Lynn for her to get us here?"

"Yeah," Bones answered bluntly as he repositioned himself more comfortably on the couch. "But don't let it bother you, not one bit. Don't even waste one moment of your life worrying about what she thinks, and, as far as the money goes, it was worth it. She doesn't know you, and she isn't even trying to get to know you, that makes her worth about as much as a turd in a ten dollar blender to me."

"Thanks, I mean, really thanks," Christopher said, laughing a bit at the 'turd in the ten-dollar blender' part, even though he didn't really get it. If there was even anything to get, he wasn't exactly sure. The part about his family bothered him deeply, but he was glad that Bones was here and he was happy for all that he had done for both him and James. The conversation made him feel just that much more comfortable with the entire situation. "It has been really confusing lately—I mean, with everything. I do worry a lot, too; I worry a lot about James as well."

"He's been pretty quiet since he got here," Bones said, nodding in agreement. "I did notice that."

"He wasn't like that before; he was so much more outgoing. He loves to talk and make jokes and stuff. That's why I was worried. He's changed I think," Christopher said, looking down toward the floor. "Can people just change like that?"

"Well, I reckon he has quite a few demons in his head he needs to chase away. Painful events affect everyone differently. I've noticed with my experience in the war, that when you go through something that changes your life, it's very, very difficult to really get back to the place you once considered normal," Bones said, a faraway look in his eyes, a look of being somewhere else, somewhere in the past. "I lost a brother in the war, and it was really hard. I mean it took quite a bit of working out in my own head just to get back to who I was. I know it probably doesn't make much sense, but yeah, in the end he'll work it out and be back to normal. It'll just take time."

"I understand," Christopher said with a yawn. He wished that James would just be back to normal now and that there wasn't anything to work out, yet he had a good idea of what James was probably going through. It was just so strange for their parents not to be around. Strange that he and James were somewhere new and their parents weren't even here with them. It was such an unsettling, depressing thought, to think that he'd never see them again, or talk to them again. A feeling like being locked in a black room with no way out and no one to ever come and let you out. That was a place that Christopher was afraid of: someplace where you were alone and miserable and no one would ever come for you.

"You look pretty tired there, son," Bones observed as Christopher's eyes got heavier and heavier, slowly losing their battle against the almighty gravity of sleep. "Besides, tomorrow I'll introduce you to the rest of the family."

"I almost forgot the dogs!" Christopher exclaimed. How could he forget? It was, after all, one of the only things he was really excited about when he had been told. Their house back in Bloomington was far too small to allow him to have dogs, let alone two dogs!

"Yep, Poppy and Kate. I'll properly introduce the both of them to you in the morning, and, if he's around, you'll make the acquaintance of Stinky as well,"

Bones said, a big grin on his face.

"Stinky?"

"Yeah, he's a gray-and-white tomcat that hangs around, and he's pretty stinky. I don't know what exactly the hell that cat gets into, but yeah."

"I can't wait!" Christopher rose from the chair, now excited for the next day to come. Actually, more excited than he had been in a long, long time. "What time do you want me up?"

"Whenever you feel like it," Bones said, still smiling.

It was difficult at first for Christopher to get to sleep that night. It was that sense of just being in a new place, a place that wasn't at all familiar, that did not even feel remotely the same. It didn't smell like home did either, and this bed didn't feel the same way that his old bed did. He was happy at least to have his same pillow, and that his faithful friend Fred, a small, white stuffed dog, was along with him. Still, everything just felt too strange. It was like when they went on family vacations and stayed in hotels. They were comfortable, yet just not comfortable in the same way that being in your own bed is just so perfectly comfortable. Comfortable and familiar, that was it. This place seemed to be neither of those two things.

Eventually all the unpleasant thoughts drifted away, carried off by the faint chirps of crickets and songs of frogs croaking faintly in some distant pond.

That was another thing that Christopher was not used to, yet he was glad for their company as well. As his eyes grew heavier and heavier, he eventually let himself go, and the darkness came into his mind and calmed him as slipped away into sleep. He was having some kind of strange dream, something he couldn't really wrap his mind around. Then, for no particular reason at all, he was awake again.

"What am I doing awake?" Christopher thought to himself, his mind racing. He wasn't quite sure what had awoken him. It was just a sudden shock. Like when it's dark and your going down a set of stairs and you forget about that last step, where you think you should be stepping down onto solid ground, only to find air and uncertainty. That strange way your stomach seems to plummet during a large dip in a roller coaster. "Was it a bad dream I was having, one that I can't remember?"

Christopher shot quick glances in every possible direction, hoping to find something familiar to fix his gaze upon, momentarily forgetting where he was in this unfamiliar place, and being overcome with a sickening sense of panic. A hot, burning feeling slowly swelled up from his stomach, and he felt like he was going to vomit.

There was a loud *pop* somewhere out in the dark, followed by what sounded like a door slamming. Terrified, Christopher shot up in bed, his eyes searching desperately around once more for something familiar, something to calm him down.

Then he thought *What if it's something as simple James just taking a leak? He's been louder than* this *before…on many occasions.* It was perfectly logical, or so he hoped. What was it exactly that had him feeling so illogical? It's not like he was the only one in the house, after all. "Just need to calm down, I'm just not used to this place yet," he muttered to himself in the dark, eyes firmly shut. "I just need to calm down. It was probably just Bones."

He didn't think talking to himself was too weird if he didn't do it all the time, and besides, he could feel the fear subsiding inside him, little by little, just because he heard someone say the words. He wasn't sure as to what had caused this heightened state of panic, but he was glad that with every passing moment it was actually leaving him. "I just need to calm down," he repeated, clutching onto Fred the dog, remembering once again that this was something, this was familiar. Fred was comforting.

This method of thinking did seem to help, as slowly Christopher felt himself start to relax more and more. He let himself lie back down in bed. Moments passed and nothing seemed to really be happening, although he was sure there *was* something happening, couldn't see it. No scary monster had come to claim him, and no ghost seemed to wish to torment him further. "I'm okay," he said to himself.

"You'll be fine," a voice spoke from right below Christopher's chest.

Christopher was in that moment of time right before the disconnect, right before sleep, when he found himself scared and startled anew. In his half-awake state he swore that Fred, his stuffed dog, had just told him he'd be fine.

"Did you just talk to me, Fred?" he thought, far too tired to actually say the words. It was as though he had been suddenly drugged, like that heavy feeling he got when his parents gave him NyQuil. "I think Fred just talked to me."

Chapter 3: Pine Hallow

Little feet, little voices—distant sounds echoing through the chambers of summer's heart.

Christopher awoke the next morning unable to picture with much clarity what had happened the night before. Perhaps it was the thrill of a new morning, or the fact that this new bright day was filled with all kinds of new noises to which he was unaccustomed. Back at home in Bloomington, Christopher would often awaken to the sound of nearby construction and passing vehicles flooding the busy street a few feet outside his window, which was next to the head of his bed. Here in this new bed, the noise outside was gentler, yet the urgency was the same. He didn't think that the sounds of birds could be so loud, so interesting.

Christopher slowly rose from the sheets and stretched his arms, and then, yawning, slid out of bed and shuffled over to the window. Outside it was a beautiful summer day, one of those cloudless days where the sky seems so bright and blue that it's almost painful to look at, yet too nice to actually keep yourself from trying. Christopher remembered something that his father had told him a few years earlier: "A new, cloudless day is like a clean, blank sheet of paper, able to accommodate to any dream you can come up with, in whatever way you choose to bring it alive." He was never exactly sure what his father had meant, something about the world being open to those who dream to make it different. Something like that. All he knew is that it seemed so relative to times like this one, and the thought, of course, brought him to his father, a subject he was definitely not comfortable with yet.

As he beheld it, he found the view the window afforded him of the house's backyard was quite an intimidating one. With no road, no building, nor any sign of other people in sight, Christopher was left with a rather isolated feeling—that strange, empty contentedness you feel if you've ever been out in the woods alone at night, or stopped by the side of the highway on a lone desert road. All around him were views of green, rolling hills covered with trees, some of them as tall as buildings were back home. Christopher imagined for a moment that each hill was the tomb of some dead colossus, now overgrown with vegetation and long forgotten. Off in the distance he could vaguely make out what he thought was a lake and made a mental note of it, intending to ask Grandpa Bones. It had been years since he had been fishing and he would greatly appreciate the opportunity to do so again.

After retrieving one of his suitcases from underneath the bed, Christopher rummaged through both of them and picked out some of the clothes he would wear for the day. It was a strange thing, to have everything he owned packed away. He wondered for a moment what had happened to the rest of his stuff back at home. He had heard something about it all being stored, but where? He was only allowed three suitcases; a lot of things had to be left behind. He remembered that James had a much easier time with it than he had—it was almost as if James no longer cared for a lot of the things that he had used to. In a way, Christopher could see why.

Dressed and ready for the day, Christopher made his way downstairs, smelling some sort of breakfast being cooked, and judging by the scent it was most likely sausage or bacon. He wondered if James was up yet. Hopefully today he would have a chance to talk with him.

"Mornin', Christopher!" Bones exclaimed, dragging a seat out from under from the kitchen table, which was quite a feat since he held a spatula in one hand, and the other covered in a comical pink oven mitt that had white jalapeño pepper-themed embroidery on it.

"Morning…," Christopher answered, taken aback a little by the situation. Here was Grandpa Bones, cigarette dangling from his mouth, trying to juggle all these different morning chores that he was obviously not accustomed to doing. It was not that Christopher did not appreciate the attempt; he was actually impressed a little. "Is James up yet?" he added, glancing at the half-eaten meal of scrambled eggs, sausage, and bacon across the table.

"Yeah, he was up earlier. He ate a bit and then just kinda took off," Bones answered, almost dropping the skillet filled with the eggs he was attempting to scramble in the process. "I think he just wanted to kinda explore the area on his own. I let him go; figured it might be good for him."

"Did he say anything?" Christopher asked, reaching for a glass of water.

"Say anything?" Bones asked back, pulling a plate out from the shelf and placing it before Christopher.

"Yeah, you know, about what's going on?"

"Oh, about that…," Bones said as he laid out the breakfast on the table. It was a fairly nice spread, especially from one who was so obviously out of practice. There was some bacon, not all of it was burnt, and eggs with a few black specks of the pan here and there, sausage that looked and smelled peculiarly like regular hamburger, yet was caringly shaped into the appropriate appearance that one would normally expect from sausage. "I didn't really do much askin'—it was more of the usuals."

"'The usuals'?"

"Yeah, you know, how did you sleep, how do you feel, how was the room—the usuals," Bones said while he sat and assembled a plate of his breakfast creations. "His answer was, 'Fine.'"

"To which question?" Christopher asked, poking

at the hamburger sausage. It was a little greasy, but not so bad taste-wise.

"Oh, all three," Bones answered. "Sorry, I probably should have pressed him more. I didn't know what to say."

"It's okay; sometimes I don't know what to say to him either. Lately, at least," Christopher said. He finished up the partly burned bacon. "I wish he would have waited though; I would have liked to go exploring around too."

"No big problem there, then. After you meet the dogs I'll show you around a bit." Bones pushed his plate aside and poured a fair amount of whiskey into his tall glass of orange juice. "When James gets back, maybe we can take the truck out, and I'll show you some more of the local sights."

"Maybe you shouldn't," Christopher said, his words emerging as a whisper. His eyes were fixed on the glass of orange juice that had just been spiked with whiskey. It wasn't uncommon for him to see people drink; his parents used to have a few during nights out at the movies and such. It was just how the thought of Bones getting behind the wheel after a drink brought back memories of how his parents had been killed. "If you're going to take the truck…."

"Right," Bones whispered in reply. His lips and cheeks sagged, and he lowered his widened eyes in grim realization. It was like that brownie you were eating really being dog shit, and someone had just told you the end of the world was right around the corner, he thought with a sigh. "I'm so sorry," Bones said, pushing the glass aside. "I wasn't thinking, you know, it's just…"

"No, it's okay; it's just that…I don't think we should drive," Christopher quickly added, trying to put words together when he wasn't even sure exactly what he was trying to say. "I don't mind that you drink. Just…maybe we shouldn't take the truck out."

"You're very right!" Bones said, attempting to steer the conversation in a more desirable direction. He felt so embarrassed about it—honestly, he felt downright awful. It was just one of those morning things he did every now and again; after all, before the kids got here he didn't have much company, or even that much of a daily agenda. "I promise, never on days when we are driving."

"Thanks," Christopher said with a smile. He was glad that Bones agreed, although Christopher felt a bit out of place at having to tell Bones how he should act; however, getting his opinion out did make Christopher feel a lot better. He was even a little proud of himself. When he was younger he hardly ever expressed his opinion about things; he was always the quiet one who would sit back and just keep his thoughts to himself. He kind of let others go on ahead with their views and opinions, since it never seemed very important, at least until now.

After breakfast, Bones opened a door in the corner of kitchen that led outside. "Well, here's the rest of the family," Bones said as he led Christopher around the house where the dog cage was located. The cage itself was quite spacious and surprisingly clean and well-kept, save for the occasional stray leaf or branch that managed its way into the cage. It was lined with potted plants that looked very well-cared for. The cage was attached to part of a large shed which appeared to be the real home of the dogs, and that the cage was merely for when they felt like being outdoors.

"Where are they?" Christopher asked. The cage was empty.

"Poppy! Kate!" Bones shouted with his hands cupped around his mouth, yet there was no reply, and the dogs simply did not show. "Poppy! Kate!" Bones shouted, louder and more urgently this time, only getting the same result. "Can't you whistle?"

"Yeah," Christopher answered, puzzled. "Can't everyone?"

"I can't," Bones admitted as he shook his head. "Sometimes they only come when you whistle for them; it's something they learned from Cat."

"Cat?" Christopher asked, though he had a pretty good idea who exactly Bones had meant—he just wanted to be sure.

"Cat, Catharine: your grandmother."

"That's who I thought you meant. Anyway, how do you call them since they only want to come to someone whistling?" Christopher asked. He was slightly amused that Bones was unable to whistle; he had believed that everyone in the whole world possessed at least a limited ability to do it.

"I don't. Sometimes they just don't listen, and so sometimes I don't bother trying," Bones answered matter-of-factly. "So, go ahead, give us a whistle then."

Christopher chuckled for a moment as he knelt down, placed a hand to his mouth and belted out a loud, undulating whistle.

Within a few seconds two very large dusty red dogs bounded through the opening in the shed. They were much larger than Christopher had imagined that they would be: they were very strong, sturdy-looking dogs. Their ears drooped down as they sniffed frantically about, very aware that they were in the presence of someone new.

Christopher was overjoyed at the sight of the two hounds. He placed a hand into the cage and the pair began licking his hand repeatedly. "Which one is Kate, and which one Poppy?" he asked.

"Well..." Bones scratched at his chin. "If I remember right, the one with the red collar is Kate, and the one with the black collar is Poppy. Honestly, it's so hard to tell—they are sisters, you know—and they look pretty much just alike."

"I thought Poppy was a boys' name, though," Christopher said. He petted Kate through the cage as Poppy continued to lick wildly at his hand.

"Yeah well, we thought we were getting a boy-'n'-girl sort of deal, but I guess there was some kind of misunderstanding." Bones placed a hand on Poppy's head. "They've been great, though—great old dogs to have around. I believe they'll be eleven this year. That's like fifty or so in dog years, I guesstimate."

"Yeah, they're great dogs," Christopher said. He continued to pet Kate and Poppy through the cage, his hands sopping wet with dog slobber—but that bothered him very little. He had wanted dogs as far back as he could remember, and since this was to be his new home, it was almost as if he had finally gotten his wish. "I've always wanted dogs. I mean, I've really, really always wanted to have dogs."

"I'm glad. So, that means you won't mind helping me take care of them then, eh?" Bones said with a deep chuckle. "Besides, it's good to have someone around here that can whistle decently."

"I'd be happy to!"

"Great, it's decided then." Bones fished through his pockets, pulling out a ring of keys. "Later on we'll take 'em for a walk, but right now let's go ahead and take the truck out and I'll show you a couple of the sights around here, okay?"

"What if James comes back?" Christopher asked, excited to get out for a bit, yet still worried with what was going on with James.

"Well, I'm hopin' we'll run into him somewhere. I imagine that he'll stick to the road around here at least," Bones said, nodding his head toward the driveway. "Let's get out there."

Grandpa Bones pulled back the dirty tarpaulin covering his old white Ford truck, leaving Christopher to puzzle over why the truck was even covered up to begin with. Whatever foul fate that could have befallen the truck, if left unprotected, had already come and passed long ago. The paint was peeling, filthy and gray in some parts and just plain rusted red, brown, and orange in others. It was colorful in a cloudy-fall-day kind of way. The front window had a few hairline cracks and the upholstery bore numerous cigarette burns on its stained surface, which could have, at one time, been soft and comfortable. Christopher climbed in, noting that the inside smelled like a nursing home, or a hospital, mixed in with a little bit of gasoline and cigarette smoke. It took Grandpa Bones quite a few turns of the key to start the engine, and a few more to start it up again after it sputtered and died shortly after. Once the truck got going, things seemed even worse. Once on a weekend vacation to the Science Center in Saint Louis, Christopher had gotten the chance to stand on a platform designed to simulate the different stages of an earthquake. He would have to guess the vibrations coming from the truck's engine would've been completely off the charts.

"Do you get many radio stations out here?" he asked, hoping to listen to something other than the obvious death throes of the truck's sputtering engine.

"Not many. Then again, none, due to the fact that the truck radio's been busted," Bones said as he backed the truck out of the driveway. "Got an emergency weather radio in the back, though, but it's only good for the weather reports. Not much else."

They made their way down the road; it was then that the isolation really set in for Christopher. On both sides of the street, as far as he could see, were simply long stretches of wood: large, confined spaces of trees where the sunlight cut through the canopies and dappled the earth below. It really, truly was so much different than Bloomington. He had visited places like this before, but it looked so much more different, so much more impressive now that it was to be his new home. It was like he was no longer just a tourist in a pretty new place, but a new resident in a whole new world.

"We're really out here, aren't we?" he asked, suspecting that the answer was very much so.

"Yeah, pretty much." Bones had his eyes fixed on the road ahead. "There are a few places around our place though. Let me see…there are the Scolts, a nice old couple like less than a mile from us. They pretty much keep to themselves though, not really much going on with them, ever. A little uptight, even."

"Sounds great."

"Yeah," Bones said, chuckling. "Then probably about a mile out is Ms. Leiter. She lives out there with her daughter, Kylie, should be about your age, I think. Ms. Leiter—Janice is her first name—she and her daughter come over every now and again. They play with the dogs, borrow some of my tools. Janice's husband, he ran out on them some time before. Left a mess and just disappeared."

"That's horrible about the dad, although that's pretty cool there's someone my age around here," Christopher said, a little uplifted at the fact. It didn't hurt the situation at all that the kid that was his age was a girl. Hopefully she was attractive, and interesting.

"Yeah, plus she's a girl, right?" Bones said with a sly little smile. "Let me see. Then there is Jack Olen, and Bill something-or-other. They've got a cabin about a mile and some change away. I think they mainly just use it for hunting or something or another. They are a couple of ass bandits, not that there's anything wrong with that though."

"'Ass bandits'?" Christopher asked with a hearty laugh. It seemed like something that should be spoken more out in the schoolyard by his friends and not his grandfather.

"Yeah, ass bandits—nicest guys though. This one time, it was dark and stormin' like all hell, and Poppy had managed to break loose of her cage. I was worried, you know, but I'm not built like I was, say ten, twenty years ago, so I'm out there in the worst god-forsaken downpour ever. Lightning flashing, thunder booming all around…made me think I was back on the battlefield. I'm out there with this junk-made Wal-Mart flashlight, made in, like, China out of five cents' worth of some kind of plastic substitute, or whatever, right?"

"Right."

"Anyway…" —Bones paused for a moment to catch his breath— "…so I'm out there in the woods trudging in mud coming up to my ass, and I slip on the root of a tree, twistin' my damn ankle. I'm like three hundred feet or so from home, and in no condition to get back home. Well, it turns out that Jack Olen had found Poppy barking outside his house just moments before I fell on my ass, and was out there in the storm, well on his way to bringing her on back to me. So he helped me back home and returned Poppy. Nicest man I ever met."

"That's amazing," Christopher said, shaking his head in disbelief. "I mean the timing—that's just amazing—and to go out in the storm like that, I've never heard of anyone ever doing anything nicer."

"Yep, nicest ass bandit I will ever meet," Bones said with a deep, throaty laugh. "Sorry, I know I shouldn't."

Christopher struggled to contain his sudden need to laugh. It was moments, just like this, that made him happy again. There was a time when Christopher thought that he might never be happy again, never really get a chance to laugh at anything again. He was glad that he was wrong about that. He wished so much that James was here to enjoy this with him—this was exactly James' kind of humor, and besides, it would be nice to see him happy again. He turned to Bones. "Where do you think James went to?"

"Oh, I saw him take a left from the house," Bones said. He lit up a cigarette with the car lighter and rolled the window down. "Really, the only place that you can get to around here going that way is the general store. It's about two miles or so away, so I wonder if he'd got that far or not, I'd suspected we might run into him along the way. Yeah, anyway, about the area…this whole area is called Pine Hallow. It's not got a whole lot of people livin' in it, and we are all pretty much spread out. The general store is mostly an overpriced grocery and bait 'n' tackle shop, set up mainly for some of the vacationers who come down this way to get to Wakanta Lake."

"Oh, the lake!" Christopher exclaimed, remembering that he had wanted to ask if that was a lake he had seen off in the distance from his room.

"Yeah, we'll go up there 'n' go fishin' soon," Bones said. "There really ain't no hotel or any place like that to stay around here, so the people who travel down here are more the outdoorsy camper type, and thusly stay out of our area. Which is a good thing, 'cause sometimes crowded can be…well…crowded."

"Where do we go if we need something? To the general store?" Christopher asked, thinking for a moment on exactly what he would do for entertainment around here. Bones didn't mention anything about a theater or bowling alley, or even a mall that he could hang out at.

"Well, if it's something small we need, that'll probably be it. Usually about once a week I'll head out to Springfield. It's about an hour or so drive, but I usually stock up on whatever." Bones tossed his unfinished cigarette out the driver side window. "If you need anything just let me know in advance, okay?"

"Okay."

"Well, here we are, and it looks like James already made it," Bones said as he steered the truck into the store's tiny parking lot.

Christopher hopped out of the truck when Bones finished parking it, making his way around the vehicle's bulk and running to the store. He was surprised to see James sitting on an old dirty brown bench under the building entrance's archway, looking tired and drinking a can of Coke. The really surprising part, though, was that he was not alone. Sitting next to James was a girl who looked to be about the same age. *This must be Kylie,* Christopher thought. *And what a good thing, too.* Kylie wasn't just pretty; she surely exceeded any picture he had composed in his mind. She had medium-length, dark, almost black hair, piercing blue eyes and very tan skin that seemed to embody summer itself. He had seen lots of pretty girls at school, but in his opinion, they were rather stuck up-looking, or just not his type. Christopher wasn't aware that he was staring, but everyone around him was very much aware of his gawking, including Kylie.

"Well then," Bones said, clearing his throat and breaking the steadiness of Christopher's somewhat creepy stare. "I'm going in to pick up a few things. You guys hang out here."

"How are you?" Kylie asked as she and Bones briefly exchanged glances.

"Oh, I'm great. How's your mother?" Bones said as he opened up the door to the general store.

"She's fine, thanks," Kylie replied, letting a brief smile slip from her lips.

Christopher slowly made his way up to James and Kylie, a little apprehensive as he had realized that he was staring, and was recently made aware that she had realized this as well. He nodded at James for a moment and then decided to introduce himself: "I'm Christopher."

"I know," Kylie answered with a half smile, holding out her hand. "Nice to meet you. James has told me a bit about you. I'm Kylie, by the way."

Christopher immediately shot his hand out, shaking her hand rather comically. He had shaken hands before, yet he had never found the gesture so interesting. It took him a moment to realize that he should let go. "I'm pleased…," he muttered.

"You're such a dork sometimes," James said, laughing and shaking his head.

"Sorry," Christopher said, more out of a need to respond than anything else. He sat down besides James on the bench, much too uncomfortable with the idea of sitting next to Kylie. "So, you walked all the way here?"

"Yep." James drank the last bit of his soda and tossed it into the trash bin nearby. "Was a good walk—you should have come with me."

"I walked here, too. I walk out here when I get bored sometimes," Kylie said.

"I would have come along!" Christopher exclaimed, almost coming across as offended. Besides, James had not even tried to wake him up or anything.

"Hey, don't blame me." James folded his arms, feigning grumpiness. "Someone was sleeping."

"I didn't sleep very well, so I slept in." Now that Christopher thought about it, wasn't there some specific reason that he couldn't sleep so well? It seemed as though something had happened, something strange, although now he couldn't remember whether or not it was a dream. It seemed strange to him.

"I couldn't blame you, for not sleeping well," Kylie said, brushing her hair out of her eyes. "Not out where you live, anyway."

"Yeah, you're going to love this," James said, shaking his head. "She's been telling me all sorts of things…."

"What am I going to love? Stories about what?" Christopher asked.

"Well, you see…," Kylie said, a serious look washing over her face, "…located near your Grandpa

Bones' house is an old Niutachi Indian cave. It's supposed to be some kind of holy place where it's said they would do rituals and all kinds of strange things way back when."

"Like, bad things?" Christopher asked, deeply concerned. It wasn't that he was very superstitious; honestly he didn't really believe in ghosts, UFO's or anything like that. Maybe Bigfoot, but that was a big maybe. He loved scary stories, and had read Stephen King's *It* at the age of twelve; however, he never quite slept well during that time. That and after watching *Aliens* late one night—that movie creeped the holy hell out of him—he didn't want to be alone again in the dark for the entire month of June.

"Like spooky, *ghosty* bad things?" James asked, mostly just to mock Christopher's obvious concern.

"No, no, no…," Kylie said, sounding a touch annoyed. "It's just a cave that was sacred to them, and the area is supposedly haunted by their spirits."

"That doesn't sound so bad," Christopher said, knowing that there just had to be a 'but.'

"But…," Kylie added, her voice growing more grim and serious. "About fifty years ago, long before even Bones moved in, a family lived in that same house. They had a daughter, about my age or so, and one day she just disappeared."

"Maybe she just ran off," James said, sounding a bit less sarcastic than he had probably intended.

"That's what everyone thought for a while, so everyone in Pine Hallow and a few folks from surrounding towns came out and searched for her. Like, a hundred people or so all covered the area from the house all the way to Wakanta Lake. Some of the people even searched the lake area, because she could have drowned, you see?"

"Did they find her?" Christopher asked, deeply engrossed in the story.

"Nope!" James added, attempting to spoil the moment before Kylie could answer.

Kylie shook her head disapprovingly at James' interruption. "I'm serious here!" she cried, clearing her throat and then continuing again in her grim voice. "Alena, the missing daughter, was never found—just up and disappeared! The only clue to her disappearance was found in the Niutachi Cave."

"What did they find?" Christopher asked.

"Just her shoes…and her silver necklace." Kylie let out a sigh of relief, thankful that she had gotten through the story so well. "They never found her, and then about two years later her parents just up and left. They never returned, and they say that the ghosts drove them out. That, or losing Alena. Either way."

"Is that true?" Christopher asked.

"It's probably just some folklore: urban legend

junk," James quickly answered. "I wouldn't let it bother you."

"Well, it's the story I've always heard. We should all check it out sometime," Kylie said with a nod and smile.

"Yeah, sounds like a real good time," James said, turning his head away from them.

"You'd really want to go?" Christopher asked.

"Sure, I mean, I'd like to know, you know?" Kylie replied.

"Yeah…," Christopher said, although he was very unsure about any of this. He didn't really want to know, but in a way it was intriguing enough that he might want to know.

"You boys ready?" Bones asked, startling the group. "Unless you guys feel like walkin' back?"

"I'm ready," James said, standing up. He had been more than eager to go for a walk to the general store this morning, but he was not even near the quota of motivation he needed for a return trip.

"I'm ready," Christopher answered, though he would have much rather have stayed behind and talked to Kylie more about, well, anything really. To him it really didn't matter; he could sit there and listen to her read from a dictionary and it would be interesting. The fact embarrassed him a bit as well.

Christopher watched out of the side mirror of the truck as the three drove back toward home. Kylie remained on that dirty old brown bench beneath the store's archway. He watched as she shrank as he went farther and farther away. Their eyes met for a moment as she was disappearing from sight and he quickly glanced away, his face growing hotter.

"I can see why you like her," James said, playfully pushing up against Christopher. "She's not my type, but I can see why you like her."

"I don't like her."

"I bet."

"So, Alena's Cave," Bones said. "I haven't heard that one in a while."

"You heard?" Christopher asked, glad that he didn't have to talk about Kylie anymore. It wasn't that he wouldn't like talking about her; it just made him rather uncomfortable.

"I walked in at the very end, but I knew," Bones said. "I don't want you guys to worry."

"I'm not worried. I don't really believe it." James folded his arms underneath his chest.

"Good," Bones said. "It's true, at least historically, about Alena, and that the cave was a Niutachi cave, but Catharine and I had lived there for such a long time. Never had any problems at all. Didn't ever really go fooling around in the cave or anything like that, but the whole area's supposed to be haunted, since the family who lived in the area before disappeared after their daughter went missing and all. But I don't think the superstition part holds any weight to it, though."

"But the cave is there, and the shoes and the necklace and everything?" Christopher asked. He was a bit relieved that there wasn't anything to worry about, and yet found himself a bit more concerned when Bones confirmed the story.

"Yeah, it's a short stretch from the house, right by the creek, don't know if you saw the creek or not," Bones said. "Don't think the shoes and the girl's jewelry are still there though; I'm pretty sure the family went and reclaimed that stuff."

"Before they ran off," James added.

"Yeah, before they disappeared," Bones agreed. "I doubt anything bad happened to them. I'm pretty sure they just couldn't stand to be in the area. Sometimes being somewhere where you've lost someone you love is hard. Sometimes even I think about leaving Pine Hallow, and I've always loved this land."

Once the three had returned, James, tired from the walk, decided to head up to his bedroom for a short nap; Christopher, making good on what he had agreed on earlier, helped Bones take the dogs out for a short walk. Christopher was much happier today, and it seemed as though a lot of good things had happened.

Things felt better, and when they pulled into the driveway to the old house, it felt like home. It was a strange thing to think about, but it really did feel like that. It was a good feeling, he decided, even if it was an uncertain one. He felt good enough to help with dinner; he had helped before with his parents, so even that was a nice return to something familiar. Throughout dinner James had remained silent. It was strange that he seemed to go in and out of these "moods." He had seemed a little happier earlier, and had even joked around with Christopher and Kylie.

Christopher finished bringing the dinner dishes into the kitchen, and was returning to the dining room, hoping for a chance to talk with James. To his surprise, however, James' seat was already empty.

"Where's James?" Christopher asked, stepping back into the kitchen.

"I think he just stepped out. Why don't you go check?" Bones said as he scrubbed a pot in the sink. "It could be a good chance."

Christopher nodded once and headed toward the door.

Night had fallen already and the air was full of the sound of crickets. It seemed so much louder here than back home.

"Fireflies," James whispered, nodding to Christopher.

"Really?" Christopher asked, excited. It's not that there weren't fireflies back in Bloomington, it was just that there was scarcely a chance to see them. He loved fireflies, and when he was little he would keep the few he could find in a jar in his room and stay up as late as he possibly could to watch them.

"Yeah, they're everywhere," James whispered, as if he were to speak any louder the fireflies would flutter away and never return.

"Beautiful," Christopher whispered back. All around him and farther out in the woods were hundreds of glowing, flashing green orbs of light. It was like being in space a million miles from earth, with every star in the universe shining back at you. "I've never seen so many."

"I know."

"How are you? I mean…" Christopher fumbled around with the words for a moment. "…are you okay?"

"I don't know. I don't think so."

"What's wrong?" The concern growing in Christopher's heart was so great he thought it would explode. He knew that something was wrong after all. He could tell, ever since the funeral James had been so distant.

"I don't feel like myself anymore." James fidgeted around with his hands. "I don't…well…I don't know what's wrong."

"You don't act like yourself sometimes. I mean, back at the store you were okay. We don't talk, but I know we haven't really had a chance."

"I know; it's okay though. I just miss mom and dad. I mean, well..." James hesitated for a few moments. "It's silly. I should be better. Really, how are you? You're the one I'm concerned about."

"I don't know," Christopher said, surprised at how this had turned back to him. He had been so worried about James that he had only given it some thought about how he was holding up. Perhaps that was his way of hiding how upset he really was, by being so concerned with James. "I don't know, James; I don't know how I'm supposed to feel."

"I know what you mean," James said. "I don't know either. Do you miss them?"

"Of course. Then again, sometimes I don't know how to miss them, or if I'm doing it right. I feel bad when I'm happy and guilty when I'm sad. I don't know...I just don't know."

"I'm sorry," James said, shaking his head. "I should have been more supportive. I don't know if anything is right anymore. Last night, I thought I was going crazy. Seriously, I thought I had completely lost it.

"Last night?" Christopher asked, vaguely remembering the night before. Something had happened, hadn't it? It was something out of a dream, this something involving weird voices. If only he could put his finger on it. "What happened?"

"Well...," James began, seemingly very hesitant to do so. "I don't know whether I was dreaming or not, but there was a girl in my room. She was just sitting there in the dark, crying."

"Was she a ghost?" Christopher shuddered for a moment.

"She was beautiful—really, really beautiful. She made me feel so sad. I had been feeling crazy all day, and that just made me feel worse. I don't know if she was a ghost or not."

"What did you do?"

"Well, I talked to her. I think I talked to her. I felt so crazy...I mean, I was so upset about mom and dad, I just thought I was going crazy."

"What did you say?" Christopher asked, growing more and more uncomfortable with each word that passed from James' lips.

"I asked her what was wrong. Shit, I was scared; really, really scared." James wrapped his arms around his body as if to comfort himself. "I thought I had completely lost it. I still think I did."

"Did she answer?" Christopher placed an arm around James. He knew this wouldn't be much comfort, but he had to do something. "Did she talk back?"

"Yeah…she said she was sorry about my parents, and that she knows what it's like to feel alone."

"Oh my god…."

"Yeah, if it wasn't a dream, then I've lost it, Chris. I've really lost it," James said, whimpering, and almost driven to tears. "I'm afraid of losing my mind. I don't want to not be myself; I don't want to be crazy."

"You're not crazy," Christopher said, squeezing James tightly as he hugged him. "Something happened to me last night, too—I thought it was a dream or something. I don't know."

"Something happened to you, too?" James asked, struggling to keep his composure. It was already apparent that he felt like crying—he just didn't want to do it in front of Christopher.

"I don't know. I wish I remembered—then it would prove to you that you aren't crazy," Christopher said, his mind racing through the events of the night before. There was something, but he was just so upset that he couldn't remember it.

"I want to go to the cave…," James said, hugging his brother back for the first time since the funeral. "Just to see."

"I thought you didn't believe in any of it."

"I don't, but maybe it will clear my mind. I feel that it's something I need to do. Will you come with me?"

"Of course," Christopher said. He didn't even have to think about it. He was so happy to talk with James again, and even happier to finally be able to help. "Let's go check it out."

"Tomorrow?"

"Yeah, we can go tomorrow."

That night Christopher and James slept in the same room. The fireflies danced and played outside their window, and the crickets slowly lulled them to sleep. Christopher squeezed Fred the stuffed dog closer to his chest, and for a moment he almost remembered something—something he was sure was important—but before he could think on it much more he was asleep.

Chapter 4: A Wind through the Mill of the World

Into the mouth of the world, the echoes of all we hear. At the base of the throat, our losses being all we feel.

"No, no…," Christopher protested, waving his hands. "Cereal is fine today; you don't have to cook."

"Are you sure?" Bones asked, sounding somewhat disappointed. "I really don't mind; don't think that you'd be putting me out or anything."

"No, we have…um…," Christopher said, his words tapering off as he poured himself a bowl of Cheerios, hesitating in his search for something to say that wouldn't come off the wrong way. "We have a real busy day today; me and James are going out exploring."

"Alena's Cave, right?" Bones said as he bent over and rooting through the refrigerator, his rump raised high in the air.

"How'd you know?" Christopher asked between bites of Cheerios.

"James was already up, probably even up before I was this morning," Bones said as he continued rummaging through the fridge, clanking glass bottles and occasionally making displeased grunts with each wasted discovery he encountered in its unexplored depths. "Yeah…he asked if he could borrow some flashlights, packed up a few things he got out of the fridge, then he asked what the best way was to get down to the creek."

"We were supposed to go together…," Christopher said, shaking his head dejectedly. When he had woken up, James wasn't in the bedroom, so he had just figured that James was getting an early start on breakfast or getting things ready, since they had agreed to go together.

"I think he just wanted to scout out the area. He said he'd be back for you." Bones pulled some form of meat out of the fridge, sniffing it cautiously. "I may have to go into town soon; we're not holding up so well on supplies here."

"What's that?" Christopher asked of the meat as he placed his cereal bowl in the sink.

"I'm not sure anymore," Bones said, fear slowly seeping into his voice. "That's not a good thing is it?"

Christopher laughed and shook his head, replying, "Probably not."

"Anyway," Bones said as he placed the mysterious meat assemblage into a trash bag, being careful as to not let any of questionable mass escape, "be careful out there. I told James, too, but I don't think he was too keen on the listening part."

"We will."

"Caves can be fun places to explore and all that, but just make sure you don't fall into a hole, or trip on something, or…" Bones paused as he tied up the scary meat package, tossing it at the nearest trash can and missing, where it made a nauseatingly wet plopping sound once it hit the freshly mopped floor. "Well, you know, just use good sense."

"Okay, don't worry."

"Oh, and take one of the dogs with you. It'll be really good for them to get out, and plus they'll help scare the snakes away from yuh."

Outside the air felt a lot more heavy and hot than it had the day before. The sky was crowded with clouds, and the sun peeked out from between them intermittently, causing the world to flicker faintly from light to darkness with every passing moment. Christopher hoped that it wasn't going to rain today, although it might help with the heat. He made his way to the dog cage, leash in hand. Once he was at the fence he crouched down and let out a short, shrill whistle, causing both Poppy and Kate to come bounding out at once. Christopher pondered for a moment as to which dog he should take. He couldn't remember. Was Poppy the one with the red collar, and Kate the one with the black collar? Practically, he figured it didn't matter. He opened the cage door and was immediately assaulted by two overjoyed and overexcited dogs, each one struggling just that much harder than the other to vie for Christopher's complete attention. Careful to not let the both escape, Christopher quickly hooked the leash to the dog with the black collar on. "Kate, right?" Christopher said as he gently ran his hand across the red dog's head. "Or is it Poppy?"

"I'm pretty sure that's Kate," James said, making Christopher jump slightly. "The one with the red collar is Poppy, I'm almost sure."

"I thought it was the other way around," Christopher said, shrugging as he led the excited dog over to James.

"Sit, Kate," James commanded.

The dog cocked his head for a moment, showing a possible moment of recognition; however, it did not even attempt to do what it was commanded to.

"Hmm…" Christopher gave a short tug on the leash. "Sit, Poppy!"

The dog's head came around to face Christopher, her ears perked up and once again there was that same look where it cocked its head sideways. However, just as before, the dog did not sit.

"Figures," James said as he removed one of the

two backpacks he had resting upon his back. He rummaged through the sack for a moment, checking to make sure everything was there before throwing the pack over to Christopher. "I managed to find a couple of flashlights. Grandpa Bones let me down into the basement. There's all kinds of junk down there. There should be enough food in the pack for lunch, too. I didn't know how long we'd be out, but it should be everything we need for this trip, anyhow."

"Thanks…." Christopher maneuvered the pack over his shoulders while maintaining his grip on the leash that held either Poppy or Kate. "Did you find the cave earlier?"

"Yeah, it's real close." James pointed out into the woods. "Took me like fifteen minutes or so to walk there earlier, so it's cool."

It didn't look as though there was any kind of trail or anything to go by, just a general direction. Christopher could make out the sound of a creek or stream up farther ahead, in the distance, remembering that Bones had spoken of it being down by the creek. The two brothers started off into the woods, James leading the way with the dog following closely at his heels. Christopher spent most of the walk looking at the things around him, wondering if he had spent too long living in the city. It was a strange thing to think about, given how young he was. Yet, he wondered how and when he had become desensitized to the appreciation of a natural, beautiful world that existed here and mere moments away from his old home. It's not that he felt that he lost any kind of appreciation for nature: it was more like he forgot how wonderful it could be.

"It's nice out here," Christopher said, although more to himself than to James. He felt oddly comforted underneath the patchy, dark green ceiling of the forest, almost as though the trees were there to catch him if he fell off the world and up into the endless sky.

"It's not bad," James said. "You remember that time when we all went down to Virginia, at that one forest park?"

"Yeah, wasn't it Shennen…Shannon-doe-ha, or something like that?" Christopher stopped for a moment to let the dog sniff around at the base of a tree. It was probably interested in some kind of animal's scent or droppings. Dogs love those kinds of things.

"Yeah," James said, as though the name sounded right to him as well. "This place reminds me of that park. Remember Mom spotted the baby bear there, along the trail?"

"Oh yeah," Christopher said, "everyone was so excited, and after a while a crowd had gathered around to watch it. Everyone there was so happy to see it, for some reason."

"Ha, yeah," James said, "until someone pointed out that when there's a baby bear out it's usually common for the mom to be around as well, and then everyone was all freaked-out 'cause they thought we'd all get eaten or something."

Christopher laughed a bit, remembering the moment. "I was even scared. I wonder if there are any bears out here. I hope not. Well…I guess if Poppy were there, she would've scared them off."

"Yeah, right before the bear ate her," James said, chuckling. "That dog would be a small snack for a bear, and then we'd be the main course. Besides, I'm pretty sure that's Kate."

"Right…," Christopher muttered, slightly uncomfortable with the thought of being eaten, and a little annoyed because he was pretty sure that this was Poppy after all.

"Oh…" James pointed up ahead. "We're here."

Alena's Cave was nestled into the face of an exposed bluff. Roots and toppled trees dangled precariously over the entrance of cave, almost completely obscuring it from view. The small yet swift creek seemed to fork off there, with the smaller rivulet flowing directly inside the cave. Indeed, the distant sound of rushing water could be heard beyond the entrance, perhaps telling of a waterfall inside the cave itself. The two brothers stood at the entrance for a moment, gazing into the opening. A soft, cool breeze caressed their faces, and the wind through the cave made an odd humming noise similar to the sound of electricity, or the low whine of a toy motor.

Flashlight in hand, James carefully pushed back some of the branches and made his way into the cave. The entrance chamber was lit fairly well, and seemed to be large enough to hold a group of about ten or so people. The walls and floor of the cave circled around a large pool, offering space spanning the circumference of the water's edge where one could either sit or walk around the pool. Christopher slowly shuffled behind James, though he needed had to stop for a moment, as Poppy appeared very hesitant about entering the cave.

"Look at this." James shone his flashlight on the cave wall. "There are some drawings here."

Christopher brought his own flashlight's beam over to join James'. On the wall there were some crude, child-like drawings of a house and what looked like some animals. "I don't think these are Indian cave drawings."

"Alena's then?" James whispered, shuddering for a moment. "These are definitely not Indian drawings, though."

"She must have played here." Christopher scanned through all the pictures with his light. A lot of the work was faded, or at some spots smudged so badly that it was nearly impossible to tell what a lot of the works were originally intended to be.

Christopher brought his flashlight's beam around to focus on the large pond in the center of the entrance chamber. The water was crystal-clear and he could even make out some tiny fish in the slowly rippling water. "I could see why this was a holy place," he said. "It's very peaceful-feeling in here. It's very nice."

"Yeah...." James probed through the rest chamber with his flashlight. "I wonder if Alena came here to get away."

"Get away from what?" Christopher asked.

"I don't know. Just the world, I guess."

Christopher sat down upon the ground for a moment. For being inside a cave it was surprisingly dry and level enough to be comfortable. Pulling the dog closer, he carefully removed his backpack and picked through it, looking for something to eat. He pulled out a sandwich made with some kind of meat. Christopher wasn't sure, but he really hoped it wasn't related to the scary meat had fished out of the refrigerator earlier. He fumbled around for a bit and finally managed to remove the sandwich's plastic wrapping.

"Hungry already?" James was still running his flashlight beam across the drawings on the wall, as though he was searching for something in particular, something he expected should be there.

"Nah, Poppy looks like she needs a snack." Christopher tore off a bit of the sandwich and put it down on the ground next to the dog.

Poppy cautiously sniffed at the food for a moment, and immediately after seeing this Christopher was almost assured that this was the scary meat. Poppy quickly cleared his suspicions, though, and handily gobbled down the snack, devouring it in a few bites.

"She likes it," Christopher said. "You're a good cook."

James chuckled. "Nice…."

Christopher wrapped up the portion that was left and placed it back into his pack. Rising back to his feet, he continued the search for whatever it was exactly that they were searching for. He noticed a larger run-off of water from the pool that led into a smaller tunnel. Pointing to the back of the cave, he said, "You think back there is where they found her?"

"Probably…." James swung his flashlight around to join Christopher's beam. "You ready to go further in?"

Christopher gulped. "I guess so," he muttered, though he didn't feel ready at all. He gripped Poppy's leash more tightly, and that made him feel a bit safer. "We should have invited Kylie to come along; she wanted to come too."

"That would have been romantic for you two, wouldn't it? Here in the dark, looking for the scary ghost girl," James teased as he made his way to the back tunnel. "She would have probably have run away already anyhow."

"I don't think so. She seems really cool," Christopher said, and he really did wish, in a way, that she was here. Maybe, if she was scared, she could hold on to Christopher's hand. He was pretty sure he wouldn't have minded. "Maybe next time we can…"

"Shh…," James hissed, holding his finger to his mouth and then whispering, "What the hell is that?"

Christopher slowly—very slowly—tip-toed over to James, hoping to see what he was so fixated upon. He inched toward James' back, cautious and silent with his movements until he could feel James' hand against his chest, stopping his advance.

"What is it?" Christopher whispered, almost inaudibly. He lightly tugged on Poppy's leash to bring her closer to him.

"Glowing eyes…," James said, his voice faint and wavering. "Glowing eyes in the dark ahead."

Christopher continued to inch Poppy closer and closer, terrified by the thought of something horrible out there in the darkness of the tunnel. What could it possibly be? Some bear, or some other beast? Something evil, ready to tear them to pieces at any moment? His head was full of so many unpleasant things that he thought his racing heart was going to wear itself out, and then Poppy started barking furiously, terrifying both Christopher and James. The dog's already loud cries were made deafening by the echoes produced from the cave walls.

Both of the brothers' flashlight beams fixed on the owner of the eyes as it approached them from the dark. James clutched his chest as if he was having a heart attack, and let out a sigh followed by a bit of a laugh when the creature stepped from the shadows. "It's a damn cat," he said.

"It's Stinky!" Christopher exclaimed, happy that he was not going to be eaten after all. "I think that's Stinky—Bones' cat."

"Jesus…," James muttered as the yellow-eyed, gray-white feline ran past the three. "A cat…."

Poppy whined, as though she had wanted to go off bounding after the cat, nervously pacing around when the cat was well out of view. Christopher brought her close and gently petted her on the head. "Good girl."

"At least we know there's nothing bad in here after all; otherwise, it would have got the cat." James said, forcing his laughter as he continued down the tunnel.

Christopher ran his hand down the side of the tunnel as they walked down further inside. The walls felt wet and slimy against his skin, and it reminded Christopher of something of a frog's skin. The light from the entrance was all but gone at that point; the only light in the cave emitted from the flashlights he and James had with them. The trickle of the larger rivulet from the pond flowed dully beneath their feet, making the tunnel a little slick and dangerous to walk on. Christopher hoped that Poppy wouldn't get nervous and try to take off or anything. She'd fall for sure.

"It splits up here," James said, illuminating the intersecting passage ahead of him.

Ahead of them there were three two other directions, the straighter one leading to a huge drop-off into a black abyss. The water was flowing in from outside, and possibly gushing up from the seemingly bottomless pool in the entrance chamber, and it branched as a result of natural, deep grooves in the floor that created a series of miniature waterfalls that fell down a long way and crashed into jutting rocks below, the sound of it all being audible even from outside the cave's entrance.

James walked to the edge of the falls and shone his flashlight down into the darkness. He could barely see the bottom—it more resembled a misty gray smudge from this height and, for a second, he could have sworn he saw something glimmer. "I don't think we'll be going this way," he said, stepping backward. "That's a hell of a long way down."

"We'll have to go this way, then?" Christopher asked, pointing his beam away and to the right. Curving counterclockwise just before the drop-off was a smaller tunnel that was much dryer (though small trickles of water still ran down it) and far easier to traverse, as it only sloped down at a slight angle. It was spacious, and from a cursory glance it looked like Christopher and James could walk shoulder-to-shoulder through it, at least a good ways from where it began. Christopher was a little scared about going down this tunnel, though—in fact, he was more in the mood to turn back already. He imagined that he'd feel better if the sunlight was still shining in from outside, so at least he wouldn't feel so far away from the outside world.

"Yeah," James said, "let's see what's down here."

"Hopefully nothing," Christopher muttered as he reluctantly followed James, keeping Poppy close behind him. "You know, if there are any kid-killing clowns down here or anything like that, I'm going to blame you."

"It'll be fine," James said. "I just want to see what's down here. Besides, you've been reading too many horror stories."

Christopher, James, and Poppy circled farther down into the darkness of the tunnel. The passageway seemed to go on forever, gradually winding down and to the left and repeatedly circling around and behind the falls as it descended to the bottom. The air around them grew cooler and cooler, yet the walls became narrower as they went down further and further.

As a result, Christopher grew more and more nervous with each descending step. He wondered if they would be going downward forever and what would be at the end—if they ever arrived. There were so many thoughts going through his head, so many ideas. He felt as though he would never be out of there. The only comforting thing was the cool wind that occasionally blew around him, tossing his hair about and refreshing his lungs and skin. In a strange way, it felt as though the wind was attempting to comfort him.

"Finally," James whispered as the tunnel came suddenly ended, opening up into a large chamber where the sound of constantly crashing, echoing water filled the air. "This room here is huge."

Christopher carefully followed James into the large chamber, wildly swinging his flashlight beam about in an attempt to uncover everything there was to see as quickly as possible. Water rushed down into an out-of-the-way corner of the large chamber, collecting in a pool comparable in size to the one at the entrance. There was yet another stream that flowed from this pool, this time disappearing into a nearby wall of rock. Christopher was floored with the beauty of this place, as all around him the walls seemed to shimmer and dance from the beam of both he and his brother's flashlights. Every surface scintillated in beautiful, unusual ways. It didn't appear that the cave went on any farther, though, but for that Christopher was rather thankful that it seemed to be impossible to go any further deeper inside.

"That's up where we were earlier," James said with a sense of accomplishment. He pointed the beam of his light up to the cave's high ceiling, but could only see the mouth of the drop-off, and even then it was only visible when he shined his light on the water pouring out of it. "The tunnel we were at just winded around all the way down here. It's amazing."

Christopher searched around the area, amazed at every sight his light happened upon. Something he found on the cave floor made him stop completely in his tracks.

"This…," Christopher whispered, "…this is what we were looking for."

"What is it?" James asked, walking toward Christopher.

Both beams affixed upon the floor in the center of the cave, where a large white cross was painted on the ground. There were no signs of shoes or a necklace being left behind. Yet this didn't stop the feeling of sadness, eerie strangeness that suddenly washed over both Christopher and James.

"This is it," James whispered, his voice noticeably trembling. "This is where they found her stuff."

"I wonder who painted this cross…." Christopher traced his hand over the paint. "Maybe the parents."

"Probably…," James answered. "It's sad."

"Yeah…," Christopher whispered.

For some time the brothers continued to search the area, to see if they could find anything more. Once they were content that there wasn't another passageway out, or anything else of superstitious interest or unnatural nature, the two sat down against the cold cave floor with Poppy beside them.

Christopher rummaged through his sack and pulled out the remnants of his sandwich, and after sniffing it gingerly, took a healthy bite out of it. "It's not bad."

"Of course it's not!" James retorted. "Bones didn't make it."

Christopher burst out laughing, almost choking on the sandwich. "His cooking…wow, it's really crappy. I mean, I'm happy he tries."

"My stomach is never happy that he tries," James said, laughing as he pretended to throw up, complete with accompanying guttural noises.

"It's not that bad."

"Oh, it is."

Christopher pulled the canteen out of the pack, taking a long drink of water. He tugged on Poppy's leash, bringing her closer to him. Having Poppy near made him feel so much more comfortable about hanging out at the bottom of the cave's falls. Christopher placed his arm around Poppy's shoulders and stretched out his feet alongside her. "So…did you find what you wanted to find…down here?"

"I don't think so," James said, the humor that he had now gone. "Then again, I don't know what I was expecting."

"Do you at least feel better, I mean…about things?" Christopher asked, although really he didn't even know if he himself felt better.

"I don't think so…," James said, hanging his head in his hands. "I don't know exactly what I expected to find down here. Maybe I just wanted to believe in something that wasn't normal, something that wasn't normal everyday reality. It's just seems like every day is full of sad events, and that the world is full of people who have lost people and many other things."

"I know what you mean," Christopher whispered. To have to think about things like this just made him feel sadder, yet it was a truth that he knew. "Even the people we've met here. I mean, look at Bones, he lost Grandma…and Kylie's family, her father's gone…Alena, well, she disappeared from here…then there's us…."

"Then there's us…," James repeated. "I think I just wanted to have something to show me that there was still magic left in the world. That if there were spirits here or that something strange had happened here…then maybe, just maybe, there was something else to this world than just sadness and losing people you care about."

"I'm sorry you didn't find it here," Christopher whispered. "What you were looking for."

James lifted his head from his hands and shook his head roughly, as though he was trying to shake away all of his unhappy feelings. "You remember what dad use to say whenever unfair things would happen?"

"Yeah…," Christopher said, sorting through his thoughts for a moment. Sometimes it was hard to remember things about his father, and it was especially hard to remember much of anything right then, as deep in the cave as he currently was. "That stuff changes, basically because we're not meant to be in control, or something."

"That things change, because we as people don't have the authority to change them," James added. "I don't think I've ever understood that until now…I think it's about feeling helpless.

"I feel helpless a lot," Christopher said, gently rubbing the back of Poppy's ears. "I've felt helpless every day since they've left."

"Yeah…." James rummaged around in his backpack, pulling out his sandwich. He slowly unwrapped the plastic, and when he was finished he tore off half of the sandwich, throwing it to Poppy. "Here you go, Kate," he said, petting the old red dog.

Christopher chuckled a little. "You're going to give her a complex."

James shook his head and cracked a little smile. After taking a bite of the sandwich he looked at it, a bit disappointed. "What do you miss most…about home?"

"Hmm…" Christopher thought for a moment. "Videogames."

"Bones has a TV. This isn't the Stone Age here…you know?" James pulled his canteen from the bag.

"It's black and white. Plus, I don't even think I can hook up the Nintendo to it," Christopher said.

James laughed. “Maybe it *is* the Stone Age here, then.”

“What do you miss most?” Christopher asked.

James glanced at his sandwich once more. “Taco Bell....”

Poppy let out a low whine, followed by a genuine crying noise.

“I think she’s got to pee,” Christopher whispered, looking over toward James.

“Let her go in the corner, it’s no problem,” James said as he packed his lunch items into his backpack and then rose to his feet.

“No way!” Christopher exclaimed. “This is a holy place; if I let her pee in here who knows what bad things will happen to me. I’ll get cursed and I’ll never be able to pee again, and then I’ll explode.”

“That, or maybe Pennywise the clown will come and get you,” James added, laughing at the thought.

“That’s really not funny here!” Christopher protested. “That book gave me nightmares!”

“Let’s get out of here then,” James said as he turned back toward the tunnel they had previously followed.

The brothers made their way back through the winding passageway, and neither really had anything much to say as they continued the journey. Occasionally Poppy would whine, letting the two know that they should pick up the pace a bit, lest they go ahead and test that theory about bad things happening if she marked a bit of the territory as her own. Yet, for obviously being a dog that was not very well trained, she showed an awfully large amount of restraint.

It took Christopher's eyes a great while to adjust to daylight once again when he finally exited the cave. It was a painful process just trying to keep his eyes open enough so that he wouldn't trip over anything or fall into the creek. Once Poppy answered her call of nature, they all walked back home, and on the way Christopher went over every little detail of the adventure he and his brother had had in the cave just moments before. After all, that's what it was to him—an adventure. Like something out of a videogame. Of course, there was no battle against an almighty evil that was to be fought at the end of the "level."

That night, after exchanging stories with Bones about all that they had accomplished that day, they readied themselves for bed. For once in a long time, Christopher actually felt like sleeping. He dragged himself up the stairs to his bedroom with the heavy feeling that often comes after going through an exciting day, and having seen something that not everyone in the world had seen. Maybe he had even gained a better understanding about the feelings that he and James were both apparently going through. It was an amazing feeling, especially since this was only the third day that they were here. It really was starting to feel like a home. Everything really and sincerely was starting to feel good again. Just the thought of it, to Christopher, was simply amazing.

Exhausted, Christopher climbed into bed, Fred the stuffed dog in hand. James wouldn't be sleeping beside him this evening, yet he was all right with that. He was content to be alone, and he felt great. Outside the crickets sang, and this time it seemed as though they had brought a few tree frogs along with them for their performance. It was so easy to let the sleep in that night, almost too easy.

Some time passed as he slept, and Christopher was unaware of exactly how much time had gone by. He felt strange once again, although this time there was no fear. Like his first night here, he was awake without any good reason or cause to be.

"Am I even awake?" He could feel his lips move as he spoke. Perhaps, he thought, this must be a dream. A dream would make sense at the moment, yet he felt awake. Perhaps he was having a dream about feeling awake?

"That doesn't make much sense." He could feel vibrations in his head as mumbled in the darkness. "If I'm awake, I can open my eyes." He grasped for control over his body. He tried to open his eyelids, paused, and attempted it once more. Slowly the room filled into view, and it was only a touch brighter than the darkness that existed when his eyes were closed.

"This doesn't make much sense." He could hear himself talking now. Christopher was startled when he realized he could *see* himself speaking, too, and he watched as those exact five words puffed out of his mouth—in English—as tiny billowing white puffs that danced and flowed until they disappeared into the ceiling, dispersing like smoke.

"What is this?" Christopher asked in a panic, and then the question—*What is this?*—seeped out between his lips. Christopher stayed panicked. His breath felt hot and short. He struggled to lift his arms, finding he could not move them; he struggled with his legs, and found they were equally paralyzed. If he was dreaming he desperately wanted it to end; if he was awake he sincerely wanted to be sleeping. "Help me…," he pleaded.

Help me—the words danced off of his lips and into the air, this time twirling around and around as though a wind had caught a hold of them.

Wind, Christopher thought to himself. There was a wind in here. Not just any wind either; this was a familiar wind. It filled his lungs and cooled his throat, which surprisingly no longer burned or felt constrained. The feelings also drifted away, and Christopher was now sure that this was not, after all, a dream. "Not a dream…."

Not a dream…. The words drifted from his mouth and danced across the room, twirling about in the wind before disappearing into the far wall.

Christopher found it very strange that he should feel so relaxed, especially with everything that was going on. As far as he remembered (his mind was rather cloudy, after all) words just don't go around visibly materializing and blowing around like that. The more that he thought about it, the more amused he became.

"Weeeeeeeee!" Christopher said, and smiled as he watched it—*Weeeeeeeee!*—billow out of his lips, catching the wind in the room and tumbling end over end into the wall. "I shouldn't be okay with this," Christopher thought to himself, growing more and more aware of how weird the situation was. "I really shouldn't be okay with this."

"Four score and seven years ago…the forefathers of this great nation ate some eggs and bacon." Christopher declared, and then, to his great amusement, watched as the long train of smoky white words emanated from his mouth. Just as before, once the long sentence caught in the familiar wind—the wind of the cave—the words went tumbling around like fallen leaves in autumn. I've *lost it,* Christopher thought. *It's not James who went crazy…it's me.*

Strange, though, that he should feel so content. "I shouldn't feel happy about this."

Just when things couldn't possibly get much stranger, Christopher could feel something soft squirming about underneath his left arm. "Fred?" Christopher said, and the words came out and danced about the room. *That's Fred again,* Christopher thought.

Fred the white stuffed dog, a little worse for wear from the tear of time and attention, climbed up to his feet and made his way up to Christopher's face. He plopped down lightly on his neck, since he was full of fluff, and embraced the side of Christopher's face, giving him a great big (or as big as he could manage) hug.

"Thanks, Fred," Christopher said, and again he produced smoky, magical words from his mouth. "I've really lost it."

"You should be sleeping, Christopher," Fred whispered. His voice was kind and gentle; the voice that Christopher had always thought Fred should sound like, if he had had the ability to talk. "The wind is here now," the stuffed dog finished.

"The wind is here now…," Christopher said, the words visibly eking out of his mouth one final time as his eyes suddenly grew heavy. Before he could think or attempt to move, he was asleep.

Perhaps he and James had really brought something back with them after all.

Chapter 5: The Plan

A spoonful of magic is worth more than an ocean of gold.

Christopher's eyes slowly adjusted to the morning light, noticing they seemed a bit more unwilling to cooperate than usual. He rubbed his eyes violently, hoping that it might possibly speed along the process of restoring his vision. Painfully, he sat up—this was, strangely, also a more difficult feat than usual. He thought long and hard. There had to be some reason that he felt so strange this morning, hadn't there? It pained his mind to think so hard about something that he couldn't quite grasp, and only made him feel that much worse.

The more and more he struggled to think clearly, the more and more he thought about the night before. There had to be something…there was definitely something to remember. A memory, maybe even a dream. Lost, like some elusive butterfly that was so small that even the most tightly-woven net could not catch it. It felt important to remember, anyway. Maybe just the fact that there was something to tell was important enough, something that might just help James.

Once he could see properly, Christopher scanned his current surroundings, finding things not to be quite right at all. Instead of being in his upstairs bedroom where he should have been, he was sleeping on the downstairs couch in the main room of the house. Covering him in lieu of a nice warm blanket or sheet was a pile of old newspapers and a couple of hunting magazines that Bones kept around on the coffee table. Christopher felt a flood of emotions—of confusion and slight embarrassment. He thought back, and knew it had not been but two years ago when he had done a bit of sleepwalking. He didn't remember the exact incident himself, but his parents had told him that on a vacation he had tried to just get up and walk right out of the hotel room. When they asked him where he was headed, he would not reply. He would just keep walking, causing his parents to eventually have to restrain him in the bed for a short time.

Christopher pushed off the surrogate blanket, attempting to refold the newspapers and restack some magazines, so that no one would wake up and see what he had done. As long as no one had already seen him, that is. When Christopher lived in Bloomington, he had a friend whose cat was such a heavy sleeper his friend used to move the cat to other places of the house without it waking up. Christopher realized now how the cat must have felt.

Before Christopher could finish tidying up,

somewhere in the room a telephone started to ring, or rather, blare, sounding mostly muffled and clueing Christopher in that it was definitely not somewhere in plain sight.

"I didn't even know there was a phone in this house…," Christopher muttered as he began searching the room. He rummaged through the mess, pushing boxes aside and picking things up that probably hadn't been touched in years.

The phone continued shrieking, seeming much closer this time.

They're going to hang up before I even get the thing, Christopher thought, lifting up an old dirty shirt that, for some reason, smelled faintly of fish. The phone had been sitting right underneath it. "Hello?" he said into the phone, hoping that whoever was calling had not already hung up.

"This is Doctor Jameston's office. Is Mathias there?" a woman asked.

Christopher was unsure as to who exactly they were asking for. "I'm sorry?" he replied after a short moment of silence, irrationally wondering whether or not she meant him.

"Mathias Janes…," the woman said, her voice becoming fainter and trailing a bit, as though she thought she had called the wrong number and was about to hang up.

"Ooh...," Christopher said, recalling that Mathias was Bones' real name. He had heard it used next to naught and almost forgot that Bones wasn't his given name. "Yeah, he's..."

Before Christopher could finish Bones came quickly through the door of his bedroom, looking as though he had just woke up. He wasn't even dressed.

"I got it," Bones said as he grabbing the phone away from Christopher.

Christopher was surprised to see Bones so active and nervous over something; he always seemed like such an easygoing person. He hoped that this was nothing serious, especially the call being from a doctor.

"Yes?" Bones asked, the phone to his ear.

Christopher sat there on the couch, mostly curious at the situation, since he could no longer hear what was being said on the other end.

"Oh...," Bones said. "Oh, yes, of course...not a problem at all.... I'll be in today."

Bones slowly returned the phone to its carriage, looking somewhat upset, and then let out a protracted sigh.

"Is everything all right?" Christopher asked.

"Yeah...," Bones said, hesitating for just a

moment, as if he had forgotten that Christopher was in the room. "No problems; just missed my damn check-up. Hate those things, you know?

"Oh…," Christopher said, feeling a bit relieved yet just as equally unsure. He knew that sometimes people say things to make others feel better; he hoped that this wasn't the case.

"Oh, come now!" Bones exclaimed, cracking a half smile at Christopher's slight frown. "Don't be like that; it's perfectly fine. I just have a phobia of hospitals, somethin' I've carried with me my whole life. Anyhow, I should be getting into town anyway; we need supplies."

"I'd like to come!" Christopher said, perked up for a moment.

"I'm sorry," Bones said, shaking his head reluctantly. "I'd love for you guys to come with me, but honestly I need the room for stuff this time."

"Oh…," Christopher replied. "It's okay."

"Next time, though, definitely," Bones said. "Besides, you guys wouldn't like hanging 'round the hospital for hours, would yuh?"

James made his way downstairs about a half-hour or so later, making it the first time since the brothers had arrived that Christopher was up before James. This actually made Christopher feel a bit better; it was nice for James to actually be there in the morning. All of the other days, he would already be out of the house by then.

Bones remained surprisingly quiet throughout breakfast that morning, and didn't even volunteer to cook anything. Even James seemed concerned when he was told that Bones would have to see a doctor today. Just as he had with Christopher, Bones quickly dismissed James' concerns and made joking comments about doctors and how "Their day isn't complete until they've had their cold, gloved finger up someone's ass, and today it's my turn."

Picturing such an event disturbed Christopher more than just a little bit.

With nothing really planned today for the Janes brothers, it was decided that they would be dropped off at the Bait 'n' Tackle, and then left from there to do whatever their hearts desired. James had pretty much demanded that they go there today; saying something about there being something important that he "Really had to ask Kylie." Christopher didn't mind this much at all, because if she was there today that would just make him all the happier.

The drive to the shop, just as the breakfast that preceded it, was filled with an uneasy quiet. The sky was dark and threatening of rain, yet the heat remained as relenting as it had the day before. The truck's windows were rolled all the way down; otherwise it would have been like being trapped in an oven. Christopher was happy to finally see the store as they rounded a curve, for being there would end the invisible tension that hung in the air of the truck. He knew how it felt to be afraid of doctors, yet it just seemed to Christopher that Bones shouldn't be so afraid of them. After all, he remembered, Bones fought in a war. He thought that if you can fight in a war, you shouldn't be really afraid of anything at all in the whole wide world. In a way, it made Christopher realize that Bones was a lot more human than he might have initially thought. Despite the tattoos, the hard drinking, constant smoking and gruff exterior, he really was just like Christopher and James inside, where it counted.

Kylie was at the Bait 'n' Tackle, as Christopher pleasantly discovered. She sat there in the exact spot as the time he had first met her, on that dusty brown bench underneath the store's archway, just a few feet from the front door. This time however, she was reading a book. As the truck approached, she slowly lowered the book to her lap. For a moment her piercing blue eyes caught Christopher's as he looked at her through the window. This time, she smiled, and so did he.

"You guys went without me?" Kylie said, frowning and shaking her head once Bones had left. Then she displayed an expression of deep interest, biting her bottom lip as she spoke. "So how was it?"

"It was creepy…," Christopher said, and then backtracked a bit. He didn't want Kylie to think that he was some kind of scared little kid, after all. "But it was amazing in there."

"We found it," James said, "We found where Alena disappeared."

"Seriously?" Kylie asked in awe. "What was there?"

"A white cross!" Christopher exclaimed, as if couldn't keep it inside any longer. "It was crazy…."

"Yeah, the family must have painted a cross on the ground where they found her shoes and necklace," James added, and continued in a serious tone, "Did you know about that?"

"That's so sad…," Kylie said. She placed her hand over her mouth for a moment. "I didn't know; ain't really never been down there. I've been real curious about it, but I never wanted to go down there by myself. Besides, after the story and all that, my mother would kill me."

"I'm glad you're here today," James said. "I really need to ask you…do you know what Alena looked like?"

"Wow…," Kylie said, pausing for a moment. "I don't really know, I heard that she was real pretty though…. I'm sorry, I…"

"Do you know anyone who might know?" James pressed, and there was urgency in his voice.

"Hmm…," Kylie mumbled, biting her lip again in concentration. "My mom, she might know a bit. Why do you want to know so bad?"

"You'll think I'm so crazy," James said quietly,

sighing heavily and then turning to Christopher. "You remember how I told you that I thought I saw a girl crying in my room that one night, but I wasn't sure if it was a dream or not?"

"Yeah…," Christopher said. For a moment he also remembered something else, something important that he wanted to tell James, but before he could put it into words it slipped away again. "I remember, she said she was sorry for what happened to our parents, right?"

"Yeah…," James said. "I saw her again last night, I'm almost certain this time I wasn't dreaming.

"No way…," Christopher whispered. "Why didn't you say so before?"

"A girl in your room?" Kylie said, unconsciously placing her hand right over Christopher's. "Like a ghost girl?"

"I think so…no…I'm certain of it now." James' eyes became distant, as though he was drifting back to some far-off moment. "Sorry I didn't mention it earlier. I was still trying to work it all out in my head. At first I thought I was going crazy, but last night it was like she wanted me to know that she was really there."

"Do you think it's Alena?" Christopher asked. His palms were sweaty and his voice a bit shaky. He could feel the warmth of Kylie's hand against the back of his hand; it tingled in an odd way that felt like pins and needles, like it had fallen asleep.

"I know it's Alena...," James said.

"How do you know?" Kylie asked. She cleared her throat as she moved her hand from Christopher's hand and back to her own lap, looking embarrassed. She glanced over to Christopher, seeing that his cheeks were bright red.

"Something she said to me last night, right before she disappeared," James said. "That there is still some magic left in the world."

Christopher forgot about his feelings of embarrassment for a moment and his jaw fell open. He remembered back to the conversation he and James had when they were in the chamber with the white cross. There was no way that the girl, or ghost girl, could know about that. Not unless she really was Alena. Just the thought gave Christopher a shiver that ran from the bottom of his spine and that burst in a cold surge at the base of his neck. Hearing James talk about seeing Alena made him feel more and more like he was forgetting something important.

"What does that mean?" Kylie asked.

"When we went down the first time," James replied. "Me and Christopher were talking about stuff, and I said that I thought there was no magic left in the world. After everything that has happened, that is. You know, with our parents."

"I'm sorry...," Kylie whispered. The corner of her mouth dipped into a frown on one side, her eyes narrowing. "It must be hard. Bones told us about it…me and my mom, that is, a couple of days 'fore you came."

"It's okay," Christopher said. "Don't worry about it." He remembered that Bones had said something about Kylie's dad no longer being around or something like that. He secretly wanted to hear about it, but really did not feel like asking.

"I was hoping you had heard something about what she looked like, so I'd know for sure," James said. He was nervously rubbing his head, making a small part of his hair stand up on ends. "Even if I don't know what she looks like, though, I'm sure of it now. I'm sure it's her."

"I want to go…," Kylie said with hesitation in her voice, and then, with confidence: "I really want to go."

"You can come with us," Christopher replied. He was trying not make it too obvious that he really just wanted to stay with Kylie. Besides that, having three companions (and one canine) would make him feel just that much better about going back down there, which was something he honestly wasn't sure he really had much a heart to do.

"I feel as though I need to go back," James said. "We could go today…."

"I can't today…," Kylie said, sounding rather disappointed. "I promised Mom I'd stay around and help with the store today."

"Your mom runs this store?" Christopher asked, wondering why he had never heard this before.

"You mean you didn't know?" James said with a chuckle.

"Yep!" Kylie said, swinging her arm around as if she was presenting it as some prize on a game show. "My mother owns the spectacular Bait 'n' Tackle, the jewel of the Ozarks, and one of the many wonders of this tiny—so tiny you can't even call us a town—place called Pine Hallow."

"That's great!" Christopher said, very much amused.

"It's not so great, though," Kylie said. "Business hardly keeps up well enough to even call it a business. Mom sometimes says that's why dad left us, 'cause the store was losing so much money."

"Where did he go?" James asked.

It was a question that Christopher had really wanted ask, but felt too odd asking about.

"Don't really know, not far enough though, wherever he is. My father was a real angry guy," Kylie said, looking down toward the ground. "He didn't even like me calling him dad. I think that he was ashamed of us in a way. He left a lot of his stuff behind, after him and mom got into a huge fight. He left *her* with a black eye. I never want to see him again."

"I'm sorry…," Christopher whispered. He thought back to something James had said the day before, that everyone here has lost someone and that the world was full of pain. For a moment, he really did feel that that was the truth.

"Are you ever afraid he'll come back?" James asked.

"Mom is sometimes—she keeps a gun around at night because of it," Kylie whispered, as if someone might overhear. "I don't really think he'll ever come back here. Towards the end, he was just acting so strange all the time. Like he was sick, and didn't care about anything anymore."

'That's horrible…," Christopher said, shaking his head.

"Yeah, well…," Kylie said as she finally shifted her gaze from the ground to Christopher, "…we don't need him. He's a dumbass anyway."

The three of them had a good laugh. Christopher felt a new sense of respect for Kylie since he knew a bit more about what she had gone through. In a way he felt a bit closer to her just knowing that she had been through something similar. It may not seem as though it was something as bad as Christopher and James losing their parents, yet it was definitely painful and real enough for her. Christopher wondered if this meant something. This couldn't just be random, could it?

It just made him feel better to think that he was supposed to meet Kylie. Better in the same way that James was searching for a world where everything wasn't all pain and loss. A world where there might be more than that. A world where there just might be a touch, and just a touch...maybe not enough for everyone to know about it, see it, and get used to it, and then find it commonplace and boring. Just a spoonful of this special something, in the ocean of everyday reality. If that could exist, then Christopher and Kylie truly were meant to meet each other. These thoughts filled Christopher with such a sense of hope that he believed if the possibilities were really realities, the three of them could grow wings at that very moment and they would fly away.

The three talked for a bit longer, and, as the clouds slowly gave way to the sun, the heat grew close to unbearable, yet they took little notice as they had such wonderful ideas and plans to discuss. The three agreed that the next morning Kylie's mother would drop her off at the Janes' house, and from there they would go off in search of something they all really wanted to find—a bit of magic in the world.

"Tomorrow then...," Kylie said, raising a hand to shield her eyes from the midday sun. "We'll all go together."

Chapter 6: Bones' Celebration

A dream may sometimes be just a dream, no matter how many mountains you move, giants you slay or miles you walk in order to reach it.

It was well after dark when Christopher and James finally heard Bones' truck rolling its way up the rock-covered driveway. It was a good thing, too; the brothers were growing more and more concerned with each passing moment Bones did not return. They had managed to fend for themselves regarding dinner, having found a few old boxes of macaroni and cheese stored underneath a cabinet sink. They wondered how many decades the boxes of mac-'n'-cheese might have been in there, but eventually hunger and a slight case of desperation quelled any further debates on whether or not they should partake of the ancient food. Besides, they mused, pasta lasts forever, doesn't it? They wondered about how they would care for themselves in the absence of Bones never returning, but they also worried much about him. Had the visit to the doctor gone well? Was coming home so late a sign of bad things to come? The two secretly hoped it was not the case, but neither would speak to the other about it. Instead, the two would pretend as though they were fine, not wanting to make the other worry. They had worried about so much lately, anyway; more worrying wouldn't make it any better.

The front door suddenly flew open from a kick on the opposite side, startling Christopher and James. Bones stood in the doorway with a big grin on his face as the door swung on its hinges, bouncing off the wall next to it. He was quite a sight: he managed to balance an upward-tilted cigarette in his mouth that seemed as if it would burn his eye if he made one wrong move, and in his long arms he held several swelled bags and boxes, in the end somewhat resembling a much skinnier, chain-smoking, creepy version of Santa Claus himself.

"Got more in the truck." Bones strained a bit, placing everything he was carrying on the living room floor. "Would you guys mind?"

"What's all this?" James asked, surveying with wide eyes the large pile before him. "Did you go out and buy a whole store?"

"There's more, too?" Christopher asked.

"It's time to celebrate!" Bones stretched his arms out widely. "Let's go get the rest!"

"To celebrate what?" Christopher asked. He and

James were both trying to keep up with Bones' energy as they headed out to the truck.

"Well…," Bones said as he stepped outside with them. There was pep in his step and happiness flowing through his voice. "How about you guys being here for five days and everything going so well? Or maybe just…maybe just celebrating life. Or…how about birthdays? When are your birthdays anyway?"

"September twenty-ninth…," Christopher said, amused and confused at both the same time. Quite an odd combination, he thought.

"August fifth…," James said.

"Okay…," Bones said, still with an upbeat tone. "Well, so it's not your birthdays, but it's close enough, isn't it?"

The back of the white (well, originally and partially white anyway) rusty old truck was completely full of boxes and bulging plastic bags. It reminded Christopher of Christmas back in the older days, when things were normal. It reminded him of waking up on Christmas morning and stepping down the stairs to a tree surrounded by presents. He and James would have so much fun tearing through them, comparing what they each had gotten, and then spending the rest of the day playing. He was already very grateful for everything that Bones was doing, and for Bones to go and do this for them as well…it was just simply amazing!

It took them quite a few trips to finally unload

all the contents of the truck. Some of the items were from a grocery store, and they were real groceries for once, too. Their meals would no longer consist of mystery food, faux-sausages, or boxes of pasta from the Paleolithic Era. Instead they would have real, legitimate brand-name canned foods, and frozen pizzas, hamburgers, hot dogs, and ice cream. Nothing really healthy, save for a few cans of fruit cocktail. However, this was very impressive, given Bones' track record.

After unpacking the food, Bones excitedly led the children back into the living room to start going through the boxes. It really was just like Christmas. Bones had gotten them a few things that they needed: some packaged T-shirts and socks, extra toothpaste and things that you don't really care about too much when you're at the age the brothers were. However, they were things you'd miss when you didn't have them. The rest of the stuff, in contrast to the things had gotten them that they needed, were fun things. Things like games, a copy of Scrabble, a portable CD player and a sampling of random CDs. It was questionable whether these were actually bands that Bones listened to, or whether he had just grabbed a few things that he thought they might like, or looked popular. There were some magazines, as well as a couple of videogame magazines for Christopher, which he became very excited about. Inside the mound of magazines was a copy of *Playboy*, which Bones quickly grabbed out of James' hand, much to his dismay. Bones had meant to remove that earlier, yet had forgotten in his excitement.

A big whiskey drink in hand (another thing he had purchased in large supply), Bones sat back against the couch, a great big smile on his face as he watched the brothers sort through all their new stuff. As they got to the last box, Bones got to his feet as though this last box was extra special. Pulling the box open himself, Bones paused for dramatic effect.

"For all your further explorations...," Bones announced, carefully pulling out of the box the mother of all flashlights. It was one of those large deals with the high-powered beam on the front and a room-illuminating lantern attached to the back. The battery was so large it looked as though it could power an entire car on its own. "No more cheap-ass, crappy plastic Wal-Mart flashlights here...."

"Amazing...," Christopher said in awe of the super flashlight.

"That's great!" James exclaimed, taking the flashlight from Bones and immediately starting to play with all of the features, momentarily blinding himself in the process. "This is perfect," he said, trying to blink away the big purplish blob that was now swimming before his eyes. "We're going back down tomorrow...this is wonderful."

"That's not all!" Bones said with the gusto of a salesman proudly showing off his various wares. "I saw your shoes the last time you guys went out there...not very pretty."

Bones pulled out two pairs of black, ankle-high rubber boots, the perfect kind for going through water or trudging through mud. After handing a pair to both

Christopher and James, he continued sifting through the big box of cool cave junk. He paused with each item, just as before, until he revealed a length of rope, a few chemiluminescent glow sticks, and a single head-mounted flashlight for hands-free cave exploring. Then, the final topping on the proverbial cake: a pair of walkie-talkies.

"Now you guys are real explorers." Bones started cleaning up a few of the boxes, pausing for a moment to take another drink of whiskey.

"This is all just so amazing…." Christopher toyed around with the head-mounted light. "So much great stuff; thank you so much."

"Yeah…," James said. He was still trying to figure out all the bells and whistles on the large flashlight/lantern. "This is awesome. Thanks…."

"Hey, no problem." Bones pushed a few more boxes up into a growing pile. "Just consider these all early birthday presents, as I've already well-forgotten when your birthdays are."

Christopher laughed hard at the reply. "Still, this is great. Thanks."

"So, going back in there as soon as tomorrow then?" Bones sat back and relaxed on the couch, content with what he had done, and mostly just happy to be back home. This was where he was when he seemed most comfortable.

"Yeah…," James said as he laced up his brand-new boots. "I think there is something down there after all."

"Really?" Bones said. "The other day you said you didn't really believe there was anything strange down there."

"Well…," James said, sliding a foot into his boot. "I think I may have been wrong about that."

"We think Alena's spirit is still hanging around here," Christopher said, unearthing his buried nose from one of his new videogame magazines.

James quickly shot a glance over to Christopher, as though he had said something he shouldn't have. Then James continued, "We're not really sure about that, but we have reason to think that something strange could be going on down there."

"Hmm..." Bones took another drink from the glass. "Well then, you be sure to be extra careful."

"Kylie's coming, too," Christopher said, looking up from the magazine once again. He was really excited about that part.

"Then you guys will be extra, extra careful…," Bones said as he rested his head back against the head of the couch. "Anything happens to her, or if she gets hurt out there, then Ms. Leiter will have me for lunch."

"Ms. Leiter…" Christopher placed the

magazine down for a moment, remembering something he had wanted to ask. "Kylie's mom—do you know what happened with her?"

"Her dad was a jerk and took off," James said. He wondered why Christopher was asking questions to which he already knew the answer. "Just like Kylie said, remember?"

"I mean, do you know why he left?" Christopher reiterated.

"Hmm…" Bones emptied the rest of his glass down his throat. "That was a few years back…let's see…I remember that it had somethin' to do with the store not doing as well as Mr. Leiter either thought or was told that it would. Really though, out in this place you got to not expect too much. It's not like we're on the side of a busy highway or Disneyland or anything like that."

"Kylie mentioned something about that, and that he hit her mom…," Christopher said.

"Yeah…that did happen," Bones said. "From what I got out of it, things got to the point where he was always gone. Ms. Leiter—Janice—suspected that he was having an affair with some other woman. One night before he was about to leave she confronted him about it, and he got real angry and just snapped on her."

"Why, though?" Christopher asked.

"Probably 'cause it was true…," James said.

"Don't rightly know," Bones said. "Next thing I hear happened was that he just hauled right back and punched her right in the face. She was on the ground, crying, and when Kylie came into the room to see what was going on and all, she saw what had happened and just grabbed her mother's hand and started to pull her away toward the front door."

"Damn...," James said. "Kylie had said that he gave her a black eye but I didn't know it was like that."

"Well, what happened next is the worse part...," Bones said as he sat upright, setting down his empty whiskey glass so that he could concentrate more on his story. "Her father sees her trying to pull her mother away and gets into the kitchen drawer and pulls out a knife. So Kylie and Janice are just terrified; they don't know what they did to set him off, but he's back there yelling and screaming about how everything is their fault and that he's going to go ahead and just kill them."

"Really?" Christopher interrupted, more out of complete shock than anything. He had thought that it was bad enough before, but Kylie had mentioned nothing of this. The more he thought on it, he could really see why she had not.

"Indeed," Bones said, continuing with the story, "So they set off into the woods, both running as fast as they could. They managed to make it to Jack Olen's, this area's resident guardian angel, apparently, luckily enough for them, he's there. They burst in on him, yelling and screaming. Of course, he's in there in bed with that Bill guy he goes with. Well, anyway, Jack manages to get enough information out of Janice and Kylie to realize that he needs to get his shotgun, and fast. So he and Bill go out and convince Mr. Leiter that he needs to go back, unless he'd rather be filled up with buckshot."

Christopher remembered the conversation. He had asked Kylie if she was ever afraid if her father would come back. He didn't realize at the time how that question must have affected her. It was strange that she was able to laugh about it though. "So they never saw him after that?"

"I hope he never comes back here," James said.

"Well…" Bones rose creakily to his feet, stretching for a moment and then sitting back down. "Janice and Kylie stayed up there at Jack's cabin until the authorities arrived in town, had to come all the way down from Springfield. They searched through the house and the whole area, but found no sign of him. He didn't take any of his stuff or anything, just up and disappeared. The police hung around for a few days and took turns camping out in their cars front of the house. He didn't ever show back up then, so everyone figured that the trouble had gone and past."

"Kylie is so brave…," Christopher whispered as he thought of the ordeal Kylie had been through. It only seemed to make him feel more toward her. She really was an amazing person.

"Yeah," Bones agreed. "Janice, she's brave too.

Just an amazing woman, just went and took over the store and managed to do okay on her own. One time, though, when I was up at the store, she let it slip to me that she still saw him hanging around sometimes."

"You're kidding," James said, dropping the boot that he was lacing to the ground.

"No, it's true," Bones said. "Although it was never for very long, and always just in the strangest places. She'd see 'im in the rearview mirror of her car at times, or in the corner of a window at the store. Things that never really made much sense yet were just enough to make her jump a bit. She never really took it too seriously, though; just figured that what happened to her and Kylie scared her so much that seeing him around sometimes was just the 'after-effects.'"

"It's good that he's not really there, though," Christopher said. "I couldn't imagine how terrifying that would be if he ever came back for them."

"If I were Ms. Leiter, I would have wanted Jack to just go ahead and shoot him," James said, shaking his head. "At least they'd know for sure."

"Well…," Bones said, pausing for a moment. "No one knew exactly why he acted out like that; it was just theories. You can't just go shooting people based on theories."

"I have to agree, though." Christopher pushed aside the magazine he had been reading and reaching for his boots. "I couldn't imagine living with that, knowing that at some time someone could be out to kill you. Especially after seeing them every now and then and not knowing whether or not it was real. That's just scary."

"Well, the world can be a scary place." Bones let out a long, deep sigh. "Besides…James?"

"Yeah?"

"Are you prepared for the possibility that there really is nothing at all magical in Alena's Cave?" Bones said in an unusually serious tone, his eyes fixed on James. "That what you might have seen is just an after-effect of a traumatic event?"

"I really don't think it is," James said, trying to sound assured. "Why would I see someone else's 'after-effect' anyhow…?"

"I believe in it, too," Christopher said, backing up his brother.

"I'm not saying…" Bones smiled for a moment, as though had said something he really didn't mean, or at least didn't completely believe. "I just want you to be happy with whatever happens. Don't listen to me; I'm just growing bitter. Too many bad things happen in the world. Just be careful, so this won't be one of 'em."

"I don't think it is," James said. "I don't feel like it's bad. If it is Alena, then I don't think she means to hurt me in any way. Even if she is just a girl in my head, then still I don't feel like it's a bad thing to believe that she'd want us to know about her either…

"Very true…," Bones said. "I think it would make her happy that someone cared about her after all these years. Sometimes I think that's just about the best thing that people can hope for is that when they're gone someone remembers them…."

"Yeah…," Christopher said. The thought made him feel very empty and sad inside. He had never really thought about himself dying. He did have to agree, though, that if he ever had to leave, he'd want to be remembered. After all, he still remembered his parents. He liked the idea of them maybe feeling better because of that.

"Don't mind me anyway," Bones said, chuckling for a moment. The laugh sounded more empty and false than jovial. "I get so serious when I've been drinking, anyway. It's a big day tomorrow, then, and you guys should get some sleep."

"We should," James agreed. It was rather late, after all.

Christopher and James made their way up the stairs, a few of their new gifts in hand.

"I'm really glad that you're both here," Bones said as he rested his head on the back of the couch. "If I haven't said so before."

Before either Christopher or James could reply, Bones snored very loudly. It was obvious that he was already out like a light. They shared a quiet laugh between themselves before walking the rest of the way up the staircase.

That night James proposed that they should sleep in the same room, just in case they had any mysterious visitors. If one should happen to wake and see the girl, he could wake the other and a small part of the mystery may finally be solved at last. It seemed like a great idea, after all.

The two of them lay together in bed and talked about rather unimportant things. Outside the window, the wind would occasionally press and blow against the house, causing a howling sound. The haunting noise, followed later by the sound of rain tapping gently against the ceiling, left the brothers sleepless for but a few moments more than they would have. It was Christopher who fell asleep first, yet, unfortunately, it did not stay that way.

Christopher's eyes slowly adjusted to the darkness as he opened them. He knew that he had been asleep for some time. A lot of things were running through his mind, like why he was awake again.

I feel pretty normal, Christopher thought to himself. Then again, why should he have any reason to not feel normal? As far as he could remember, he had had quite a few nights where he had woken up like this. Perhaps this was just something that was becoming the usual, something that he would have to get used to. However, in the back of his mind, there was something that he just couldn't quite shake: an idea, or maybe just a feeling. He experienced some strange sense of déjà vu, like when he lay awake and unmoving the other nights before.

There was a difference this time. He didn't feel any different. He couldn't remember much about what had happened the last couple of times he woke up like this. One thing he did remember, however, was that the other times just felt so different. Odd, even, and possibly too strange to even remember.

Christopher quickly shrugged off these feelings and rolled over on his side. He could see James next to him, sleeping, and breathing rather heavily in the process. With each passing moment he shook a little, as though he was either really cold or really scared. *He's having a nightmare,* Christopher thought to himself.

"James…," Christopher whispered, attempting to calm his brother. "James…it's just a dream."

This reassurance appeared to have no effect on James at all. He continued to lie shivering, as a naked child out in a snowstorm, as if the wind was bearing down on him and ice was crawling up his legs. Every now and then, amidst the intense shaking, he seemed to mumble something, something that was barely audible and a little creepy-sounding to him.

"James…," Christopher said a touch louder this time. He cautiously placed a hand on James' shoulder. He did not want to scare him any further. "It's just a nightmare."

James pushed Christopher's hand away in a

swift, violent motion. "Who are you?" he asked, still very much asleep.

"It's Christopher. You're having a nightmare…."

"Alena?" James rolled over on his other side, facing away from Christopher. "Are you Alena? I've been looking for you. What are you doing in here?"

James suddenly stopped shaking, and then in an instant started breathing normally.

"Why…are you…crying?" James asked, sounding half-asleep.

"It was just a dream…," Christopher whispered to himself. The thought of it troubled him more than he could ever possibly realize. If this was a dream, did it mean that all the other times James saw the girl…was that just a dream too? Just the idea made Christopher's stomach sink, and a strange feeling like motion sickness washed over his entire body. "It was just a dream?"

Chapter 7: Alena's Cave Revisited

We're on the edge of the cliff, one last step before the fall. Or will we fly, with the wind in our hair and the stars in our eyes?

Christopher stayed quiet that morning, feeling that, on the one hand, he should let James know about his nightmare the night before. On the other hand, he didn't want to disappoint James, or have him lose out hope on his dream of finding something magical. He had wanted to let what he had seen slip a few times, yet kept the fact so tightly locked away that the chance of it actually slipping out was next to impossible.

"What's with you this morning?" James asked as he helped Christopher into his new caving boots.

"Nothing…," Christopher said. "I'm just still a little sleepy."

"You slept in today a lot longer than I did," James said, sarcastically laughing for a moment. "Besides, Kylie's here: that should make you happy enough."

Kylie had walked over early in the morning, while Christopher was still asleep. It seemed that she was just as interested as James was in going to the cave. She was in the upstairs bathroom getting into more suitable clothes for their adventure. And, in a way, James was right; just the thought of her being there, in Christopher's new home, made him feel really happy in an excited way he couldn't quite explain. Christopher only wished that James had woken up last night to hear what he had. The singular nature of that knowledge cast a shadow over any sort of joy Christopher might hold within. He did not like to keep secrets.

"I'm happy," Christopher said, not really sounding happy in the least.

"Right…," James said, chuckling and playfully pushing Christopher's head away. "You'd better cheer up a bit; this is an adventure after all. You don't want Kylie to think you're a bore, do you?"

"Do you think she does?" Christopher asked. The feelings of sadness shrank away, only to have them replaced with burgeoning concern. He definitely didn't want her thinking he was boring; after all, he definitely didn't find her even the least bit boring.

"Oh, come on!" James said, playfully shoving Christopher once again. "I'm just messing with you."

"Did you see anything last night?" Christopher asked, casting James' hands away.

"Hmm…" James paused for thought. "Don't think so. Why, did you? That why you're so quiet today?"

"No…," Christopher said. He really wanted to tell James of how he talked about seeing a girl in his sleep, but, just as before, he kept it inside. It puzzled him quite a bit as to why James didn't remember the dream himself. "I was just thinking about what Bones said. Like, what if there's nothing really down there?"

"Well…," James began, seeming serious for a moment. "I guess we won't know until we know. Besides, Bones was so drunk last night after he said that he passed right out. He was still there on the couch when I woke up this morning!"

"Yeah…," Christopher said, shaking his head. "That's true."

"Who's ready to go?" Kylie exclaimed as she poked her head around the entryway to the kitchen. She had come down the stairs quietly and they had not heard her.

Christopher whirled around to greet her, happy to hear her voice. As soon as she filled his view, his heart immediately reacted to her presence, making frantic leaps in his chest and spreading intoxicating warmth which traveled from his head to his toes. There she was, as beautiful as every other moment that Christopher had seen her, her black hair contrasting wonderfully with the morning sun as it bathed her body in bright light that formed a white nimbus around her, and all the while her blue eyes shimmered—or maybe they weren't really shimmering, but it seemed to Christopher that they were, or should be. All the thinking he had done before, all the worrying about whether or not Alena was real, everything else seemed to fade away in Christopher's mind. Kylie had dressed for the adventure in somewhat distressed blue jeans, a pair of work boots, and a long-sleeved shirt that clung to her slender figure, yet looked a bit uncomfortable for the hot weather. However, to Christopher it looked as if she was wearing the most elegant, beautiful dress ever conceived. To him, nothing else mattered, and he just couldn't stop staring at her.

"Hey…," Kylie said, well-knowing that she had Christopher's undivided attention, and appearing a bit embarrassed about this fact. "Christopher…good to see you."

"Yeah," Christopher said. He was slowly growing more and more aware that he was doing it again, that he was being weird. "Good to see you too."

Turning to a different subject, Kylie continued: "You know Bones; he's in there on the couch. I asked him how he was doing and he just waved me off and told me he had an awful headache."

"Yeah," James said. "He'll be there most of the day; he had a few drinks last night.

"Oh…," Kylie said, giggling.

The three of them walked around to the back of the house, where the dogs were kept. They had decided that, just as when Christopher and James had gone alone, they would take one of the two dogs along for safety reasons. After a short debate on whether the dog with the black collar was Poppy, or the one with the red collar was Kate, they leashed up the dog with the red collar, as it was her turn this time. Decided by a vote of two to one (Christopher and Kylie both voted against James), the dog was definitively called "Kate."

Christopher, James, Kylie and Kate made their way throughout the woods with flashlights, gear and other supplies in hand, ready for their new adventure together. They spent the short walk together talking about things that wouldn't really seem important to anyone else but them. Things about what TV shows they liked to watch, or what kind of activities James and Christopher participated in back in Bloomington. Christopher and James learned that Kylie was actually a fairly accomplished guitar player and that she had practiced since the age of six or seven. It was strange to Christopher, to so obviously like someone so much and not really know that much about them at all. It didn't seem to matter much to him, though; the more he found out about her the more there was to like about her.

"So that's it then?" Kylie asked. She kneeled down against the grass alongside the creek that led to the cave entrance. "That's the cave?"

"Yep," James said. He pointed out the cave opening, which was slightly obscured amidst the branches and roots along the bluff wall.

"It's in such a pretty area," Kylie whispered as she gazed up at the bluffs. "It's very quiet…calming here."

"Just wait until you see the pool and stuff inside there," Christopher said.

The three of them, dog in tow, cautiously made their way past the roots of the great trees and into the darkness of the cave entrance. It took their eyes a few moments to adjust to the low levels of light inside, and James got into his backpack to retrieve the large flashlight/lantern he had received from Bones.

"These drawings…are they Alena's?" Kylie asked, lightly tracing her fingertips over the pictures on the cave wall.

"We think so…," Christopher said as he stood beside her, admiring her just as much as she was admiring the works on the wall.

"This is where she must have hung out," James said. With a huge flashlight in one hand and Kate's collar in the other, he brought the dog over to the pond so that she could have a good long drink, since the walk and the blazing sun had noticeably tired her a bit.

"Back farther…," Christopher said as he brought out his flashlight, pointing the beam to the very back of the circular pond room. "That's where there's a drop-off and then a long winding tunnel that leads to where we found her cross."

"I wonder what drove her to go back there…," Kylie said, bringing up something that neither Christopher nor James had even thought about. "I wonder if something forced her to go that far in."

"I'd hope not. That drop-off is one nasty fall," James said, shaking his head.

"If she had fallen, though, they would have found something more than her shoes and necklace…," Christopher said, growing concerned at the thought.

Christopher and James sat for a moment to catch their breath as Kylie explored the main chamber. The cave felt much cooler this time, much to their delight, as the weather outside was very unforgiving. The sound of wind in the cave also seemed a bit louder this time. Christopher didn't know whether this was true or just something in his head. Every now and then the wind would flare up, coming across as a faint howl like that of coyotes at night. Coyotes in the cave: something Christopher didn't want to think about too much.

Content that the first room had been explored thoroughly enough, the four gingerly made their way down the tunnel that wound around the falls in the adjoining chamber, their small steps more like splashes in the small trickles of water that ran down the tunnel floor. Once they were further inside the cave, the group turned on all their flashlights, as the sunlight from the entrance was growing dimmer and dimmer until it wasn't visible.

This was the part that Christopher hated most: leaving the comfort of the light from the entrance. Although they all had new flashlights and gear, it just worried him that if the lights were to go out, or be dropped and broken, they would not be able to see at all. This was especially worrying given that there was a huge drop-off into the blackness, one that they would not be able to see if they hadn't any light. He figured that the sound of the running water near the drop-off would be warning enough, but the thought of just going on sound alone in this place terrified him.

The extra light sources on this trip afforded a much greater view of the cave than what Christopher and James had previously had before. As they stood at the drop-off, careful to keep a safe enough distance from the edge, James pointed the beam of light downward.

"That's where the main chamber is." James attempted to shine some light on the bottom without very much success.

"That's such a long way down…," Kylie said, instinctively taking a step backward and bringing her body against Christopher's.

Christopher felt both comforted and strange at this. Perhaps she was just scared of the fall, or maybe she had wanted to be closer to him. She slowly brought her hand back to hold his, squeezing it, as if to comfort herself further.

"It's okay," Christopher whispered, although he wasn't quite sure why he had said it.

"I just…," Kylie whispered, "…I just don't like high places, sorry…."

"I don't mind," Christopher said, tenderly squeezing her hand back. He was actually surprised with himself for a moment; usually he wouldn't know how to reply to a girl. Yet this felt like the right thing to say. Deep down inside, he just wanted to go ahead and tell her that he liked her. He wondered how she would react to that.

As they made their way down the winding tunnel in silence, there was a heavy, ominous feeling in the air. The wind, which had seemed a bit more pronounced before, was now intermittently gusting much more strongly against them.

"Is this normal?" Kylie asked, shielding her face from a great burst of the cool cave air.

"There was some wind last time…," James said, shaking his head, "…but nothing like this. It should be all right. It's calm at the bottom. I know it."

They pushed on ahead. At some points the wind was cold and bitter and seemed to be trying to turn them back. Other times the wind was a comforting sort of cool, and calm, ushering them to tread further inside. It was a strange feeling, and Christopher recalled something like it happening a few nights ago. It was even stranger to him that he should be remembering it now. Something about a wind in his room…was it this same wind maybe? Once again just thinking about it confused him deeply. It was like a trying to remember dream he had forgotten, and maybe it was. It made him think of James tossing and turning as he dreamt last night, and Christopher quickly forced the thought away.

Just as James had promised, the wind at the cave bottom was practically non-existent. With Kate's leash in hand he led the small group into the bottom of the chamber. The light from the large lantern illuminated the entire place, causing the subterranean walls to sparkle like gems with a million facets of light. It was a sight that could easily steal one's breath away and threaten to never return it.

"Beautiful…," Kylie said, gasping. She circled around the main chamber, looking up to the vast expanse of the cave ceiling above. She couldn't see it; it was so dark farther up.

"It didn't look like this…," Christopher said, amazed at the sights around him. Everywhere the light from the lantern danced and played, as though they were in a room surrounded by millions of fireflies. Fireflies that, instead of being pale green, were hot, brilliant white and their light never extinguished.

"It's the light," James said. "The lantern's so bright it reflects off the water everywhere…."

"This is the cross," Kylie whispered as she turned her attention to the floor beneath her.

"Yeah," Christopher said. "This is where they must have found her stuff."

"It's so strange…," Kylie said as she gently took Christopher's hand once again, "…to disappear from somewhere so beautiful. It's so strange to think that something bad might have happened here. Any other part of the cave I could imagine it, but not this part. It's too wonderful here."

"Bad things happen almost everywhere…." James joined the two, giving a little tug on Kate's leash, and, in turn, she let out a little grunt and plopped down on the ground right next to them, resting her muzzle on her paws.

"So what do we do?" Christopher asked. He was looking around the cave for some sort of sign that really wasn't there, or at least not readily apparent. "What are we looking for?"

"I don't know…," James said as he sat down next to Kate on the cold cave floor. "I guess I didn't have that part planned out."

"Still, it's so nice here," Kylie said, gently pulling on Christopher's hand so he would sit down with her. "This was worth it alone."

"Are you here, Alena?" James asked, his voice echoing throughout the cave walls. He paused, his hand to his ear as though waiting for a reply. As moments passed and nothing came but small murmurs of wind amongst the rushing falls, he let out a bit of a chuckle. "Of course not…."

"That's a kind of creepy thing to do," Christopher said.

"Well, she was here…," Kylie said. She squeezed Christopher's hand as she spoke, more for his comfort this time, since it was obvious that he was a bit nervous. "Can't expect her to just hang around forever, right?"

The three of them unpacked their lunches and extinguished all the lights save for the large lantern. It did such a good job of illuminating the area that it seemed like a waste to have the others on. Besides, conserving battery power was in their best interest, as Bones hadn't really thought to buy any extras.

Christopher rummaged through a sack that was packed up for him in his bag. It contained some sausages and cheeses, and was quite a step up from the sandwich he had enjoyed on the first trip into the cave. *I'm really moving up in the world,* he thought sarcastically as he tore a large piece of summer sausage in half, throwing it over to Kate.

Kate, excited at receiving such a luxurious snack, leaped at the piece of meat, knocking over the lantern in the process.

"Shit!" James said as the lantern fell over, shutting off and leaving them in darkness.

"Sorry!" Christopher nervously lunged forward, fumbling around for the lantern in the dark.

"Wait…," Kylie whispered to the two, "…there's some light in here…."

"What?" James glanced around in the darkness.

"I think I see it…," Christopher whispered. "At the wall. Over there."

"You see it?" Kylie asked as she reached for Christopher's hand in the darkness, gripping it tightly.

"Yes…." Christopher pulled Kylie by the hand and brought her closer to him. "It's very faint."

"I still don't see it," James said. He scanned the room once more, and finally caught a glimpse of something in the far corner of the pitch-black chamber. It was a faint, dirty brown light. "What is that?"

"I don't know…." Kylie slowly crawled over to the light, pulling Christopher along with her. "It's definitely there, though."

James fumbled around with the lantern, hitting the button and illuminating the room once more in its bright light. He saw Kylie and Christopher, standing hand-in-hand up against the far wall where the light had previously been.

"Turn it off," Kylie whispered, waving her hand in frustration at James. "It's just a solid wall when the light is on."

James crawled on all fours, Kate doing the same behind him, to the section of cave wall where Christopher and Kylie were, whereupon he extinguished the lantern. "It's still there…."

"What is this?" Kylie asked, placing her right hand flat against the slightly lit-up, dirty brown area.

"Don't touch it!" Christopher said.

"It's fine," Kylie said. "It's cold…and smooth."

Christopher placed his left hand on the brown area, right next to Kylie's hand. It did feel familiar, and complexly flat, almost as if it was an unnaturally smooth surface covered with a small layer of what felt like dirt or mud. There was obviously some sort of light behind it. Instinctively, Christopher brought his other hand up to join the other and pushed hard against the surface, curling the fingers of both his hands and scraping downward in the process. A brilliant beam of white light shone through the now-crumbling wall as his hands continued to slide down, removing much of the layers of dirt and mud from the surface, which was becoming as smooth as it was flat. "What is this…?"

"Oh my god…," Kylie whispered. She slowly wiped her hand down the section her hand was on, uncovering more of the same bright white light which shone from beyond it. "It's a window…."

"What the hell is this?" James asked, bringing

his head close to the light. "This is impossible…."

Christopher brought his face as close as possible to the grimy section that he had wiped off; the light hurt his eyes and seemed to almost be pure, white light. As his eyes slowly adjusted, however, everything eventually came into focus. It wasn't just light he was seeing, but a window, and, beyond that window, a room. "This can't be real…."

Kylie, who had her face pressed right against Christopher's, saw the same strange sight. A complete white-walled room, a regular every day room that you'd find in your own house. "This is impossible."

James, not wanting to be left out, yanked his shirt off and started furiously rubbing it against the dirty surface. The more and more crud he cleaned off the window, the more and more astounded he became at the view beyond. His jaw slackened and fell open as he fell back against the ground. "What is this doing here?"

Christopher slowly sat back on his haunches, gently pulling Kylie back to sit in awe with him. The view, now completely clear, was definitely that of some kind of room, and at the bottom of a cave, no less, built right into the stone and earth of the cave wall. Through the distortion of the glass he could vaguely make out what looked like a bed, covered in white sheets with light blue pillows on top, and some kind of dresser—definitely a dresser or chest of drawers. There was some kind of stuffed animal on the bed as well, although it was too distorted to make out completely.

"I don't believe what I'm seeing...," Christopher whispered, unable to look at anything other than the room before him.

"I don't believe what you're seeing either...," James said, sitting and looking forward in complete shock.

"I think I'm dreaming, or I've hit my head," Kylie said, her hand still rather roughly gripping Christopher's. "Because what I am seeing could not possibly ever exist."

"I can't be seeing this," Christopher said. "Right?"

"We're all seeing this...," James said, attempting to retrieve some sense of composure. "We're all not dreaming either."

What followed was a series of more moments spent in shock and awe, and many more moments of questioning and discoursing what they were seeing. This included Kate, who, with her head cocked to one side and her ears perked straight up, stared quizzically at the sight. It seemed as though the canine was just as confused as the humans. They finally came to the agreement that this was real, and you can only imagine the feeling of pure, unfiltered strangeness that they were all filled with. A feeling like that of being the first person to shake hands with an alien as you climbed aboard its ship, or having tea with a ghost; a feeling of final acceptance of the sheer impossibility of that which you beheld, that you were living in an impossible moment.

James returned to his backpack and put his flashlight back; there was no longer any need of light, as the light from the window illuminated the entire cave in soft whiteness. He frantically tore through his belongings, tossing things aside into a mounting pile if they weren't what he was looking for.

"What are you doing?" Christopher asked. He was still too shocked to properly react to anything, and was slowly realizing that his hand, which Kylie was gripping so tightly, was becoming sore.

"Getting my screwdriver out," James said.

"What for?" Kylie asked.

"For opening the window; I'm going to pry it open," James said as he had one of those "*Aha!*" moments, and held his screwdriver out in his hand for everyone to see.

"You can't be seriously thinking about opening that up…," Christopher said, dread creeping into his voice.

"We can't turn back now!" James ran over to the window, quickly getting to work on scraping out the debris from within the window frame itself.

"He's right…," Kylie said. She let go of Christopher's hand, pausing to nod at him reassuringly.

"Okay…," Christopher whispered. Although he really didn't feel okay, just having Kylie looking at him like that did make it feel like it could really be all right. "Okay."

James worked hard and swiftly, running the tip his screwdriver over every part of the window that wasn't glass, as Kylie used James' shirt to brush away the dirt and debris from the work area. It was but a few moments, and then, finally, their work was finished, revealing the square wooden frame of the window before them.

"Okay…," James whispered, nodding in agreement with himself.

"Okay…," Kylie agreed.

Christopher took a deep breath, holding it for a moment before letting it back out into the world. His head felt heavy and hot, as his heart was full of both caution and wonder. "Okay…."

James jammed the screwdriver into the bottom portion of the window, using the windowsill as a fulcrum and pulling down on the butt of the screwdriver. As he did the window creaked open a bit, and then it immediately launched upward with a resounding thud, causing the glass in the frame to waver. Cold air poured out of the open room and a faint roaring sound filled their ears. The air was so cold it was painful on the eyes and took many blinks to get used to; the sound was like the roar of an approaching windstorm or snowstorm. However, just as quickly as the fierce current had begun to blow, it died down. The rushing cold air slowed down to a short breeze, and soon the sound was barely audible.

"Okay…," James said once more, and then continued, "…I didn't do that. I'm not *that* strong."

"What do we do now?" Kylie asked. Her gaze was fixed on the room before her.

"I don't want to go in…," Christopher said, even though no one had even proposed the possibility yet.

"You don't have to," James said. He returned to his backpack, searching through the pile that he had made next to it when was trying to locate the screwdriver, and pulled out the long length of rope that Bones had gotten for them. He made his way back to the window, rope in hand; ignoring the wide-eyed look that Christopher gave him as he tied the rope around his waist.

"You aren't going to…"

"I can't *not* go…," James said, cutting Christopher off as he threw the other end of the rope to him. "You and Kylie…you guys don't let go of that rope, okay?"

Christopher and Kylie looked at each other in sheer amazement. James was actually going to through with this?

"Just don't let go of that rope. I'm going to go

in…," James said, sensing that the two of them were too shocked to answer. "*Okay?*"

"Okay…," Christopher said, more out of reflex than anything else.

Kylie nodded.

Christopher gripped the rope tightly, having already securely wrapped Kate's leash around his wrist. Kylie gripped a section of the rope right behind Christopher's. James nodded at the two and closed his eyes for a moment, as though he was doing some kind of silent prayer for protection or something like that. After he opened his eyes, he offered everyone one more nod of his head, and then he cautiously placed his right foot through the open window.

"It's cold!" James exclaimed as his foot passed through the opening. Where he and the window met the very air seemed to ripple, almost as if he was stepping into water. He slowly allowed more and more of his body to pass through, inching his way further and further inside. "It's okay…."

"Turn back if it gets bad," Christopher said, still shocked that James was really doing this.

James edged more and more into the window, until only his head was left. He took a deep, long breath, as though readying himself for the plunge. He hesitated once, twice, and then released his breath. "I can do this…," he repeated to himself, taking one more huge breath before letting go of the window and dropping into the room.

Christopher and Kylie watched in terror as James' head and hands disappeared from the opening and a strange sound like paper being torn came from the opening as the last bit of James passed through. For a moment James was completely out of view as he dropped down to the ground below the window.

"Is he okay?" Kylie asked.

"There he is," Christopher said as James appeared before them, although he no longer looked quite right. It was as though he was moving underwater or in really, really slow motion. Each movement that James made seemed either deliberate or ponderous. It reminded Christopher of all those old black-and-white movies where the action either seemed too fast or too slow to match up to how things should realistically move.

"I think he's trying to talk to us," Kylie whispered, watching James intently. "It looks so strange in there…."

Christopher watched as James continued to move strangely. Every now and then he even looked as though he was part of some weird movie that was missing frames. One moment James would be trying to wave and the next he would be attempting to mouth some words only to be cut off again by some sporadic flashes of brightly-colored light. "You don't think he's in trouble do you? Should we pull him out?"

"I don't know," Kylie said, sounding very

concerned.

The next flash they caught of James was him giving them a thumbs-up. He must have realized that Christopher and Kylie could not hear him. Christopher nodded at his brother, relieved; however, the action inside was so inconsistent that he did not know if James actually noticed him or not. Christopher continued to watch, unable to do anything else or even think clearly about anything else. It seemed as though every other moment James simply floated around the room, sometimes there would be more than one of him. At one time Christopher counted at least six James' in the room. Christopher couldn't quite make out exactly what James was trying to do. Sometimes James would look back to them, other times he would be interested in something in the room, or he would simply not be there at all, replaced instead by strange twinkling lights and small glimpses of his body.

"Why is it like that?" Kylie whispered over to Christopher, unable to keep her eyes away from what was going on inside.

"I have no idea," Christopher whispered. "It's insane."

When James finally appeared before them in a coherent fashion, he was in the center of the room and looking directly beneath him. Christopher could hardly make out what his brother was regarding so intently through the strange, shifting light. It was a book.

"I think he's found something," Kylie whispered,

tightening her grip on the rope.

They watched in silence as James slowly and, mostly in a logical sequence this time, kneeled to the ground to pick up the book. Christopher held his breath as he watched James' hand inch closer and closer, each frame of movement bringing him nearer the object of interest at his feet. As James' hands slowly closed around the book, something terrifying happened.

The light coming from the room went out completely, blanketing the room in utter blackness.

Christopher panicked, gripping the rope as tightly as he possibly could. "Pull him out!"

"What happened?" Kylie exclaimed, heaving back on her end of the rope with all of her strength.

A huge crash came from the dark aperture, loud and deafening like thunder, or a gun going off next to your head. Following this was a deafening whine of something that sounded like rusty metal scraping along metal. The window shook violently and slammed down on the rope.

"No!" Christopher screamed as he and Kylie fell backward.

Christopher scrambled to his feet and ran over to the window, forcing the window open and off of the rope. He then picked the rope back up and clenched his hands around it as tightly as he possibly could. Kylie quickly followed his lead. They gave one giant tug on the rope, putting all their weight behind them as they did, and, without warning, James shot out of the window as if propelled from a cannon, barely missing Christopher and Kylie and crashing to the ground next to them in a sobbing heap, embracing the book he had found.

"James!" Christopher said.

"Are you okay?" Kylie cried as both she and Christopher rushed over to his side.

"Mom and dad…," James said, between tears and sobbing. "I saw mom and dad…."

"What?" Christopher asked as he stumbled back in shock. This was impossible. His parents were dead. There was no seeing them again, not anymore. It just wasn't possible.

It took James a few more moments to get himself gathered up and back in shape. He slowly rose to his feet, his arms still wrapped around his shirtless body and clutching the book. He did not speak further, and would not do so until he properly calmed himself down. When he was ready, he finally spoke to a shocked Christopher and Kylie, who were both hanging on his every word.

"It was back when we were all on vacation…," James said uneasily. "You remember that time we went down to Yellowstone?"

"Yeah…," Christopher said.

"It wasn't anything important, or any important moment or anything. It was just a happy moment. I was sitting there with you. I think you were sleeping. I was sitting there in the back seat of the car and mom and dad were just talking to me."

"Did you ask them what was going on?" Kylie asked, confused at the situation.

"No, I just…," James said, struggling with what had happened. "I just sat there and listened to them talk. I didn't feel like I do now. I felt like I did at the time, just happy and content. I just kind of sat there and listened to them talk for what seemed like hours. They didn't even talk about anything important. They were just talking…."

"Are you okay?" Christopher asked, still in a state of disbelief. He had been watching James through the window; when had this happened?

"Yeah…," James said, scratching the back of his head, but it didn't really itch. "I can't explain it, but I feel better now. I don't know what happened. I was just reaching down for this book…."

Christopher watched in horror as James eased his grip on the book, revealing the cover. Christopher recognized the book instantly. It was a copy of *Watership Down*. The book was worn in the corner and had a small tear at the top, just like the copy he had owned. If this wasn't his book, then it certainly was in the same condition. "Is that…?"

"Yeah…," James said. "It's yours."

"That was in the car…," Christopher whispered, and he felt his eyes burning, and soon a tear came streaming down from his eye.

"Yeah…," James said, placing a hand on Christopher's shoulder.

Kylie watched in shock as James handed the book over to Christopher. "How is that possible?"

Christopher ran a hand over the book's cover; he had never expected to see it again. He eased his thumb underneath the cover and lifted it up, revealing the first page. There, just as it should have been, was Christopher's name, written by his mother: *Christopher Jacob Janes*. Christopher almost dropped the book in shock. "It's my book…."

"They were so happy…," James said as he turned back toward the window. The light in the room had returned while they were talking, and everything looked peaceful once more. "I'm happy I could see them again…."

"Amazing…," Kylie whispered. She placed an arm around Christopher and stared off into the open window.

Christopher bit his lip as he tossed the idea around in his head for a moment. Could this be real? Could this really be possible? He looked back down at the book that James had brought back with him, and then stared back to the window ahead of him. Here was his proof. He took a deep breath before he said, "I want to go in…."

Chapter 8: Christopher's Discovery

Dreams at sunset, remembering loved ones passed.

"I want to go…," Christopher repeated as he gazed off into the window. His hands were balled into fists at his side, his determination growing inside of him.

"Are you sure?" James asked, placing a hand on Christopher's shoulder. "I'm not going to stop you, but it's really intense. I mean, I don't even know what to tell you to prepare for what you're going to see in there."

Christopher nodded as continued to stare at the window.

"Are you really going to go in?" Kylie asked as she reached for Christopher's hand.

Christopher kept his hands firmly balled up,

unwilling to take Kylie's, as though the resulting comfort might weaken his resolve to go inside the window. He merely nodded, although he could feel himself weaken a bit. Was he really going to do this?

James picked up the book that Christopher had left upon the cave floor and thumbed through it to the first page, seeing Christopher's name, just as he had suspected all along. "This book is why you're going, isn't it?"

Christopher nodded once again; he had so many feelings pent up inside of him he didn't know any other way at the moment to respond. It was like seeing that book again brought on fresh feelings of pain and loss regarding his parents, feelings he had not even discovered yet. If everything that James said wasn't real enough, then it was the book, which was proof beyond any possible doubt that all this was real and was something he had to do. Christopher could feel the fear inside of him, deep down in the pit of his stomach, ready at any moment to overtake him and keep him from moving. He fought with every fiber of his being to keep that from happening.

"Please…," Kylie whispered, upset that Christopher was not responding to their questions.

Seeing her upset broke Christopher's deep concentration for a moment. He just hoped this wouldn't make him not want to go. His apprehension was growing and growing. *Don't give in to it,* he thought to himself, over and over again. He turned to Kylie, taking his eyes off the window for the first time since he had seen his name in the book. His eyes began to burn again as his feelings welled up and were caught in a knot in his throat. Tears came. "I'm sorry…."

"It's okay…," Kylie whispered. She was glad to see that he was at least responding. She knew that this was important to him; she knew how bad it must feel for him. After all, she had been through this kind of grief before. "It's okay. If you have to go, then do it. Just please…be careful…."

"I will…," Christopher said, very much shaken. He wanted—so much—to tell her now how much he liked her, how much he really cared for her. If only he could assemble the correct words and just let them pour out, everything he'd felt, everything he'd thought about. Instead he just smiled and looked into her eyes, and, somehow, that was good enough. That was all he needed. He took one step forward and picked up the rope that had been fastened around James' waist and then proceeded to tie it around his own.

"All right," James said as he helped his brother tie the rope into a good strong knot. "Don't trust what you see in there, it can be real confusing. Just keep thinking about where you are, and you should be okay…."

"Okay…," Christopher said. He searched down deep within himself for any kind of courage that he could rally up and take with him.

"When you first step all the way in, it'll be real hard to breathe…," James said. "You'll feel real dizzy, but just concentrate on something else and it will pass."

"Okay," Christopher said. He took a few more steps toward the window and prepared to step into it.

Kylie reached out to Christopher, embracing him tightly. The moment, to Christopher, seemed to last almost forever and he treasured every second that passed in her warmth.

"You'll be okay," she whispered in his ear, "You'll do great."

"Thank you…," Christopher whispered back, wanting to say more. He always wanted to say more to her.

"Don't be afraid," James said. He gripped the other end of the rope firmly in his hands, handing some of the length over to Kylie. "It can be real easy to freak out in there and want to run back in, so if you need to come back just pull on the rope."

"All right, I'll try my best," Christopher said as he raised his right foot up and over into the open window. It felt as cold as ice and made him want to withdraw from it almost immediately. It was a strange kind of feeling; it burned and chilled him at the same time. It made him feel as if his body was full of pins and needles.

"It's really cold, but it gets better," James encouraged.

Christopher placed both of his hands upon the window pane and eased both of his legs the rest of the way into the window. The burning sensation in his lower body was almost overwhelming, and he thought he might cry again. He was worried that he might even pass out from the pain. James was right, however; the more time he spent on the other side, the less it pained him. It was kind of like stepping into a cold pool on a hot summer day; although being unbearably cold at first, he slowly got used to it. Christopher was now through the window all the way up to his chest. He sat there, shaking, not quite ready to slide the rest of the way off of the windowsill just yet.

"You can do it…," Kylie whispered, gripping her section of the rope more tightly.

Kate barked twice in succession, as though giving Christopher her support as well.

Christopher mustered up as much courage as he possibly could, and then simply pushed off of the windowsill. Then there was nothing around him but darkness.

Where am I? Christopher thought. He could feel his body falling out beneath him, or was he floating? It felt as though he might be soaring, soaring through the darkness. But where was he heading, and, if he was indeed falling, what about the rope?

Christopher panicked at the thought, and felt around his waist for the rope. Thankfully, it was still tied to him. It didn't make much sense, though, because he felt as though he was moving. Then, before he could give it anymore thought, the world came into focus.

Christopher's heart was pounding in his chest; he could feel each and every beat echoing throughout his entire body. He felt like every part of him was simultaneously throbbing as his heartbeat became more pronounced, and he could feel the warm, rushing weight of his blood coursing through him. He tried to draw in a long breath, so he could calm down, yet felt so much pressure on his lungs that he might as well have taken in a huge breath of water. In a state of panic he thought about giving the rope a quick pull. What if he died in here? How would they know? He remembered what James said and tried to calm down. *This too will pass.*

He turned toward the window; there he could see Kylie and James lying at the opening, with Kate sitting behind and above them in the background. It looked as though they were completely frozen in time.

"I'm okay," he said, although he found the words difficult to say, and when they finally did come out they sounded garbled and delayed. It was as if his voice was being played on an audio recording device at a really slow speed. He tried to wave, but found that too was a really difficult thing to accomplish.

Christopher thought back to when he was sitting on the other side, and James had tried to let them know that he was all right. He signaled a thumbs-up, remembering that would probably be the only way he could let them know how he was doing.

He attempted to make his way about the room, his steps seeming so slow and laborious that he had to concentrate on where he wanted to place each foot. He scanned around the room, trying to pick something of interest to investigate. The room looked as it had from the outside: the walls were distorted and shone like wet snow, as if someone had painted them with a coat of glitter and sunshine. Even the floor glittered and glistened. It was almost enough to make him motion sick. Christopher slowly pivoted his head toward the bed; it looked like a fairly ordinary bed, with sheets straightened and made up for daytime. On the bed he spied the animal that he had seen before; it appeared to be some kind of stuffed bear. It danced and shimmered the same way the rest of the room did, forcing Christopher to look elsewhere, lest he get sick.

Christopher slowly hopped toward the door. He imagined that this was how astronauts on the moon must have had to walk. He paused for a moment, wondering if James had tried to open the door or not. He carefully placed a hand on the doorknob. Did he really want to do this? What was on the other side? These thoughts terrified him but he thought better of it.

"What am I looking for…?" Christopher said, or rather, garbled out. He bounced his way over the dresser in the corner. On top of the dresser was something he could barely make out, something that didn't seem to have the same shiny quality as the rest of the room. Christopher wondered if that's why James had been attracted to the book—perhaps it hadn't been shimmering either.

"A photograph…." Christopher's voice sounded garbled. He struggled closer and closer, utilizing all of his energy to get a better look at it. He reached a hand out to grab the photo when it was at arm's length, yet hesitated for a moment. The room had grown black when James had reached for the book, would the same thing happen to him?

Christopher paused for a moment, unable to decide on whether or not he should try and touch the photo. Then again, perhaps this was what he had to do in order to see his parents, as James did. That was the real reason why he was here, wasn't it? Christopher once again searched inside himself and pulled up whatever courage he could find. As delicately as he could, he let his finger brush across the photo, and, just as he had feared, everything went black.

Christopher sat at his old kitchen table, light pouring in from outside and bathing the room in a soft orange light. It must have been almost evening. He looked down at his hands, although he wasn't exactly sure why he wanted to. Fork in one hand, and napkin in the other, he eyed the salad on the table before him. The salad had ranch dressing smothering it, just as he always liked it, and then there was cheese, and lots of it, to easily defeat the healthy purpose that the salad may serve otherwise.

"Don't poke at your salad Christopher," Christopher's mother said as she shook her head and continued to eat her own meal. "Eat it instead; it's good for you."

For a moment Christopher forgot that she was sitting there, although he couldn't remember exactly why. He stared long and intently at his mother's face, framed by the window, sunlight streaming into her long brown hair, her kind brown eyes smiling back at him.

"What's wrong, honey?" she asked, tilting her head to the side and frowning for a moment.

Christopher didn't like the frown; he wanted her to be happy. "Oh nothing. I'm just not feeling hungry all of a sudden…."

"You should eat up. Tomorrow is a big new day, you know?" she said, smiling and then turning her attention back to her meal.

"Yeah…," Christopher said, straining for a moment to remember why tomorrow was a big day. "Oh—graduation."

"Like you forgot…," she said, laughing under her breath. "And once summer's over you'll get to go to high school…are you excited?"

"More worried…," Christopher answered, picking out a carrot from his salad and sticking it in his mouth. It tasted like a carrot when he chewed, and, when he swallowed, he felt it go down his throat.

"Worried? Why honey?" she asked, bringing a hand up to her face.

"Just about kids…," Christopher said. "You

know, there are a lot of people in Bloomington I don't know and they'll all be at that school."

"You'll be fine...." She reached across the table to place her hand over Christopher's. "How could the other kids not like you? You're a great kid. And I should know; I raised you!"

Christopher smiled. She always did have a nice way of making him feel better about things; even if he knew that they weren't exactly the truth. He didn't feel very great anyway; he was barely graduating, thanks to his grades.

He slowly rose from the table, feeling dizzy for a moment. Perhaps he was just tired. He tossed the remains of his salad in the trash and put the plate in the sink, rinsed it off, and then made his way out of the room. He was a bit hesitant at first, as though part of him wanted to remain there with his mother. He turned to look at her.

"Not too much time tonight with your games," she said as she smiled at him. "You've got to be up early tomorrow."

"Okay...," Christopher said, giving her one last smile in return.

As Christopher began to make his way upstairs to his room, James and his father came in through the front door.

"Son," his father said coldly, nodding to

Christopher.

"Hey…," Christopher quietly replied. He and his father were not getting along, mostly due to his bad grades. He had been grounded for the better part of the semester and had just had his beloved videogame system privileges returned.

"How was soccer practice?" Christopher asked, turning to James. For some reason it was strange to see James, although it didn't make much sense as to why, since he always came home around this time after soccer practice.

"Eh…" James bounced his soccer ball once off of his knee and then missed it, the ball bouncing to the floor. "Not bad."

"Hey, not in the house…," their father said as he removed his work jacket and placed it on the hanger by the door.

"Sorry…," James said as he retrieved his ball. He looked up at Christopher from the bottom of the staircase. "Going up to play games?"

"Yeah, I think so," Christopher said. He wasn't sure as to why he added the "think" part; of course he was going up to play some games!

"Cool," James said, nodding. "I'll be up later to kick your ass in some *Street Fighter*."

Christopher shook his head and continued his

way up to his room. He paused in front of the door to his room. Why did he feel so strange today? Maybe he was getting sick. He hoped not, not with graduation tomorrow. He had big plans. His parents were going to take him out to dinner, and then to the mall. Hopefully he could weasel a videogame or two out of his parents. Well, as long as his dad still wasn't pissed at him about his grades. At least he was graduating, though; what was the big deal?

Christopher shook off the strange feelings and placed his hand on the doorknob. A sense of fear overcame him, something about fear of what was on the other side. He quickly flung the door open, closing his eyes. To his complete lack of surprise, he was in his bedroom. He cautiously stepped in, curious as to why he was being so cautious. He had watched a scary movie a few days before, *Poltergeist*; maybe that was what was making him so jumpy.

Christopher had to laugh at himself for a moment; he was acting so silly and irrational. He fingered through his game collection looking for something to keep him amused for the few spare hours he had before he had to sleep. He finally decided that it would be the *Goonies 2* game that he had just picked up at a used game store before being grounded. The game wasn't all that great, and the graphics were rather dated, yet he loved that movie so much. He thought about how much fun it would be to go on an adventure just like that one, to go exploring some hidden cave full of pirate treasure while on the run from the Fratellis and befriending Sloth, the gentle giant.

James came bursting into the room a few hours later. “Mom says we got an hour,” he said as he sat down next to Christopher on the carpeted floor, regarding the television with slight disgust. “Not this game again.”

“We don’t have to play, just let me save,” Christopher said as he readied to turn the power off.

“I want to play *Street Fighter*. That game at least has some good graphics. I don’t know why you still play this old Nintendo when you’ve got the new Genesis. The graphics are so much better,” James said, shaking his head as he helped Christopher hook up the other system. “Besides, by the time we get this all hooked back up we’ll have to go to bed.”

Christopher and James sat in silence, playing games together for a while. For Christopher it was such a happy, treasured moment. He wasn’t exactly sure why he felt that way. Besides, they had played games together just the other day. Why was he feeling so strangely lately?

“Bedtime, boys…,” their mother announced, popping her head in the door, a great big smile on her face. “Christopher, I don’t need to remind you about tomorrow.”

“All right, all right!” Christopher said, casually tossing his controller down to the ground. “James beats me every fight anyhow.”

James laughed hard as he wrapped the cord

around his controller, and then got to his feet. "You just need to practice on your reflexes like I do."

"Yeah, you practice your lightning-fast handwork in the bathroom everyday with dad's bikini girl magazines…," Christopher said as he playfully pushed James out of his bedroom.

"Boys!" their mother exclaimed. "Watch that language, Christopher."

"What? I didn't say any bad words," Christopher said, well-knowing what he had implied was bad enough.

James laughed hard as he made his way back to his own bedroom. "Night, Christopher!"

"Night, James!" Christopher said as he got undressed and ready for bed.

Christopher lay snugly tucked into his sheets, his head full of excited thoughts of everything that was possible the next day. He hoped that he wouldn't do anything to embarrass himself on his graduation day. He had once heard that a girl the year before had not worn anything underneath her robe for some reason, and when a good strong wind came blowing through she accidentally exposed herself to the entire student body and their respective parents. He wondered if that story was true. A lot of his friends had believed it, but something about it though didn't sit right with him.

Christopher drifted over to the thought of

starting at a new school. That seemed like such a scary thing to him. Of course James would be there, that was something of a comfort. James had a lot of friends at school; hopefully they would be his friends as well. Hopefully no one would decide to pick on him and make him do anything embarrassing like push a penny across the floor with his nose, or sing the school's anthem as loud as he could at lunch. Those were other things his friends had warned him about, but unlike the story of the naked graduation girl, however, he believed in these.

The door to Christopher's room cracked open a bit, letting some of the hallway light into the room. Confused and startled, Christopher sat straight up.

"Christopher…," his father said quietly, as though he was testing to see if he was sleeping or not.

"Yeah…," Christopher replied. He hoped that this wasn't going to be one of those lectures about how he needed to better in school, or that he should take up more important things like James. His father was always comparing him to James; it made him sad a lot of the time.

"Ah…," Christopher's father said, pausing for a moment, as though he was unsure of what he was trying to say. "I just wanted to say goodnight."

"Oh…," Christopher said, a little unsure of what to exactly say himself. "Goodnight dad."

"Yeah…," his father said, and then continued: "I just wanted to say that I am proud of you…."

"Oh, thanks," Christopher said, coming off rather surprised. After all, his dad had been riding him about his grades all school year.

"I am very proud of you for graduating. You've done well."

"Thanks," Christopher said, attempting to peek through the door. It looked as though his father was actually hiding behind the door. It didn't surprise him that much; his mother told him once before that his father had some trouble showing his emotions and did not do it very often.

"Right…," his father whispered. "Good night then, son."

"Goodnight, dad."

Christopher lay back down in bed as his father shut the door, darkening the room once more. He thought about what had just happened. His dad had told him that he was proud of him. Just hearing the words made him feel so much better. He let his mind drift off as his eyes grew heavier and heavier. Just as he felt sleep begin to greet him, something suddenly felt completely wrong and out of place, and he thought he was going to be sick. There was something wrapped around him, something squeezing him around his waist and tugging him out of bed.

Christopher panicked as he felt something yanking him back with great force. He could feel his body literally pass right through his bed, and then through the floor. He thought that maybe there was a tornado or something and the house was collapsing around him. When he finally opened his eyes he could see himself flying away from his house, the tiny lights of his front porch swiftly disappearing as it melded with the lights of the rest of the neighborhood. He was able to make out the tiny network of lights of the entire city below him, and then the lights of all the cities around Bloomington.

He could feel the air rushing around him and soon found himself among the clouds. If he wasn't so terrified at the thought of what was going on, he would have been vastly impressed with the view before him. As the clouds that surrounded him slowly broke off and passed beneath him, he wondered exactly how far up he was going. And then he saw it: the Earth. Not the if-you-looked-down-right-now-you'd-see-floor-and-that-would-technically-be-considered-seeing the-Earth kind of Earth; he was seeing it in a completely different manner, the same manner that astronauts and aliens see it, shining like a round blue gem and rotating ever so slowly miles beneath him.

Christopher was so confused he felt as though his mind would explode under the stress, and then there was one more violent pull from whatever it was that had latched onto him in his bedroom. Then there was a sound, something like that of thunder. It sounded so alien, yet so strangely familiar.

Christopher opened his eyes; the strange feelings were slowly washing away. He was on his back again;

however, he was not in any kind of bed. It was cold, smooth, and a bit uncomfortable really. In the dim light he could barely make out James, a girl, and a dog.

"Are you okay?" the girl asked, bending down over Christopher's face.

"Kylie...," Christopher said, although it came out more like a sob or a cry. He found his whole body shaking as his mind finally caught back up with him. He was back, back in Alena's Cave. He had been with his parents; he had seen his parents again. It was so amazing, yet so upsetting. He just couldn't seem to stop crying about it.

Christopher slowly got up to his knees, embracing Kylie as tightly as he could. His tears streamed down onto her shoulders. "I love you...," he blurted out through the tears.

"He's real emotional; you remember how I was when I got out," James quickly added as he placed a hand on Christopher's shoulder and brought his brother's head next to his. "It's all coming back, right?"

"Yeah...," Christopher whispered as he wiped his face with the sleeve of his shirt. "I'm sorry...."

"No, it's fine...," Kylie whispered. She was just happy that Christopher was back, and also very eager to learn as much as possible about what had happened.

I just blurted out that I love her, Christopher thought to himself, feeling rather embarrassed and strange. She might not have noticed. He had been in such a shape that maybe she just passed it off as crying. After all, he had been sobbing rather loudly.

"So what happened in there?" James asked.

Christopher spent a few moments explaining everything about how he was having dinner with mom, how he and James had played games, and how later on in the evening his father had come in to tell him that he was proud of him. It was all so amazing, as though he had gotten to completely relive a memory that he had all but forgotten. A day that didn't seem any more important to him than any other yet was so much more important since he had gotten to spend that time over again.

"Amazing…," Kylie whispered as she gave Christopher another warm embrace.

"I'm so happy that you got to share that time with them…," James said with a smile on his face. He turned his attention to the photograph that was clenched in Christopher's hand. "What did you bring back with you?"

"Oh!" Christopher exclaimed. He had completely forgotten about the photograph. "I have no idea."

"Let's see it," Kylie said excitedly.

James and Kylie crowded around Christopher as he brought the photograph up into the light so that they all could see it. Christopher stared at it blankly; confused for there was no one in it that he readily recognized. In the photograph was a man dressed up in a military style uniform, dancing with a rather attractive young woman. People were similarly dressed up all around them and it appeared that everyone was having a great time. It was some kind of dance or ball, definitely some kind of celebration.

"What is this?" Kylie asked, being the first to give voice to their collective confusion.

"Hmm…" James scratched his head. The book at least made sense; it was Christopher's. This photograph didn't seem to belong to Kylie, James, or Christopher.

Christopher jokingly showed the picture to Kate, whose ears perked up at the picture but really showed no notable response. In doing so, however, Christopher noticed that there was some writing on the back of the photograph. "Something's here…," he said, and began to read the small print on the back. "Mathias Janes and Catharine Shultz…May tenth…nineteen fifty-four."

"Bones!" James exclaimed.

"That must be your grandparents…," Kylie said, snatching the photograph away from Christopher.

"Does that mean we should bring him here?" Christopher asked, attempting to put together something that might be a piece to a puzzle. "I mean, James went in, and found my book."

"So then you went in, and found Bones' photograph," Kylie finished as she sat there, staring into the picture.

"Don't you want to go in next?" James asked, looking over to Kylie.

"Me?" Kylie asked, shaking her head. "I don't think so…at least not yet anyway. I mean I wouldn't know what to expect in there. I haven't really lost anyone. I mean my father is gone, but I definitely don't want to see him in there."

"Right…," James said as he nodded. "Sorry."

"Doesn't mean I won't want to see it for myself at some point," Kylie said.

"So, Bones then…," Christopher said. "We have to show Bones this."

Chapter 9: The Photograph

Memories are only lost until we remember them. The one's that have passed only stay gone as long as they are forgotten.

It took quite a bit of convincing for Christopher, James and Kylie to get Bones to listen to what they were they were trying to tell him. Bones sat there on the couch nursing a glass of orange juice and rubbing his forehead. It appeared as though he was still suffering from his hangover, even though it was by then late afternoon. The three has rushed back from the cave as fast as their feet could possibly carry them, excited to let Bones in on everything that had happened.

"One at a time!" Bones exclaimed, shaking his head as if it would relieve his headache. "Sorry…I just have a horrible, horrible headache."

"We found something…," James said, quieting

Christopher and Kylie in the process. "We found something down in the cave."

"Really?" Bones asked, sounding more skeptical than anything. "What did you find down there?"

"A window…," Christopher said. There was really no other way to put it. As nonsensical as it was, they had found some kind of window, a window to another world.

"A window?" Bones asked, confused. "Like, broken glass?"

"No…," James said. "A window in the cave wall…a window that led into a room."

Bones scratched his head as he continued rubbing his aching forehead. "Are you being serious with me, or is this like a joke? 'Cause if it's a joke, I'm not in that much of a mood…."

"Here…," Kylie said, reaching down into her pocket and pulling out the photograph that Christopher had found.

"This is our proof," Christopher said. If there was anything that was going to convince Bones that there weren't messing with him, then this would be it. Then again, he could understand why Bones didn't believe them. Christopher almost didn't believe it himself, and he had been there!

"What's this now?" Bones asked as he reached

for the photograph. “This…this is…”

“We found this in the room,” James said, “The room in the cave wall.”

“This is impossible….” Bones’ voice was heavy and wavering as he brought a shaky hand up to his mouth in disbelief. He pulled the photograph closer and closer to his face, as though studying every point and part of it. It seemed like he expected it to disappear at any moment. “This photograph, it’s not possible….”

“It is you, right?” Christopher asked, sitting down on the couch next to Bones.

“Well…,” Bones whispered, his gaze squarely fixed on the picture. “Yeah…. How did you…?”

“Christopher found it when he went into the room in the cave,” James said as he kneeled down next to Bones to get a better look at the picture. “There’s more—turn it over.”

Bones carefully flipped the picture over, his hands now trembling. He scanned the words on the back over and over again before dropping the picture to the ground in complete and utter shock. “It’s…it’s Cat’s handwriting….”

“Is that the two of you, back then?” Kylie quietly asked as she bent down to the ground to retrieve the photograph for Bones, gently handing it over to his still-trembling hands.

"This is..." Bones stared off into the picture of himself and Catharine. "This was the night that I met Cat.... I'd come back from the Korean War about six months prior to this, and the war was well over at this point."

"So this was how you met?" James asked.

"Yeah, this was the night," Bones said, appearing deep in thought and saddened. "This really was the first real social thing I attended after the war was over. When I got back I would just sit in my house and think about everything that I had been through, all the people that I had lost. In a way I felt as though all the memories were eating me from the inside out.... Anyway, this was back in Saint Louis; the area I was living in at the time was having some kind of ball for all of us soldiers that had made it back. A few of my friends finally got me out of the house, although honestly I didn't want to go. I didn't feel like being out in the world again yet."

"You look happy...," Kylie said as she sat down next to Christopher.

"Yeah...," Bones said. "I was happy after I met her there.... It seemed as though she could take all those unhappy thoughts away, and she did. However...this picture shouldn't exist anymore."

"Why?" James asked.

"Well...," Bones said quietly as he turned the photograph over, looking again at the date written on the back: May 10th, 1954. "Well…after we were married in nineteen fifty-six, we got our first apartment, and pretty much most of our belongings at the time burned right down to the ground with the building. This is a photograph that should have been destroyed nearly forty years ago, yet…here it is."

"So you believe us then?" Christopher asked, drawing closer the Bones.

"Yeah…," Bones said, shaking his head in disbelief. "I mean…how can I not?"

Christopher and James, with Kylie's help, continued to tell Bones about everything they had seen and been through down in the cave. Bones listened intently, now believing every word that he was hearing was the definitive truth. James talked about the room, how strange it was, and about the book he found, about how he was able to relive his memory with his parents. Then Christopher explained how he had found the photograph, and how he had also apparently gone back in time.

"That's a lot to digest…," Bones whispered, covering his eyes with his hands. "I mean, you live your whole life thinking that it's one way…."

"So…," Kylie whispered, "…are you going to go in?"

"We think there's a reason," James said, "A reason that we found this picture."

"I don't know...," Bones whispered, taking in a deep breath. "I just don't know...I mean, how am I supposed to prepare for something like this? If this is real—I mean, I know it's real...if she's down there...Cat...."

"You can see her again," Christopher whispered, placing a hand on Bones' shoulder. "You can be with her again."

"Even if only for a moment," James added.

"Yeah...," Bones agreed, shaking his head once more before continuing. "I hate to be the one to say it, though. We don't know what we're dealing with here. It's a great thing, obviously, but—and this is a big but—we have no idea what force is at work with this kind of thing."

"We don't think it's bad," James said. "If it wanted to hurt us, it had plenty of opportunities."

"Yeah," Kylie agreed. "Christopher and James both went in, and other than being shaken up quite a bit...they were fine."

"Not that it's not scary though," Christopher added as he remembered all the uncomfortable things he had to go through to actually get to the picture. "But it's worth it, it really is."

"I know...," Bones whispered, appearing very strained and conflicted. "It just has been so long since I've seen her, you know? I've been through the loss once, and I don't know if I'm ready to deal with those kinds of feelings all over again."

"You won't remember...," Christopher said, recalling his own experience. "When you're with her, you won't remember that she's gone."

"I didn't remember either...," James said. "You'll mostly feel just as you had at the time."

"Still...," Bones said. "I'd remember when I got back, and I don't know if I could deal with that. I'm not saying no, however. Just...just give me some time to think about it. I'll decide tonight."

"Okay," Christopher said, speaking on everyone's behalf.

A loud knock came from the front door, startling everyone in the room.

"That'd be your mother, Kylie," Bones said as he painfully rose from the couch. "She said she'd be by to pick you up on her way back from the shop."

"Crap!" Kylie exclaimed as she jumped to her feet. "Stall her and well...tell her I'm in the bathroom. If she finds out I've been playin' in the cave I'll never hear the end of it!"

Bones slowly made his way to answer the door as Kylie ran off to the bathroom to get herself cleaned up. He paused for a moment at the door, buying her a bit of extra time before he opened the door to let Janice in.

“Evening, Janice,” Bones said, nodding his head in acknowledgement.

“Bones…,” Janice said, nodding back.

“Kylie’s in the bathroom. They did some fishin‘ earlier and she’s cleaning up,” Bones said, sounding a little fake in the process.

“No problem,” Janice said quickly, as though she had something on her mind that was more important than what Kylie had done for the day. “Can I talk to you?”

“Yeah…,” Bones said, sounding concerned. “I’ll step out.”

Bones slowly shut the door behind him, much to the disappointment of Christopher and James. Christopher wondered if something was wrong. He hoped not, yet feared for the worst. What could they be talking about out there? He really wished that he could turn himself into an insect and fly out there and hang on the wall and listen to them talk.

“What’s that all about?” James asked, folding his arms across his chest.

“Don’t know…,” Christopher said, doing the same. “Nothing bad, I hope.”

“I’m sure it’s fine….”

"Where's mom?" Kylie asked as she emerged from the bathroom, all cleaned up and ready to head home. "Is she here?"

Christopher let his eyes follow Kylie as she walked up to meet them. *God, she looks so beautiful,* he thought as he watched her. She had changed into a short shirt that clung to her body, and her face was clean and clear of the dirt from the cave.

James gave him a quick nudge to his side, noticing that he was acting a bit off.

"Can we see you tomorrow…?" Christopher asked, or rather, blurted out. "I mean…to figure out what's going on with the cave…and well…everything."

Kylie cracked a half-smile, as though she knew why Christopher was acting so uncomfortable when talking to her. "Sorry…Fridays I have to spend the day with Mom in the shop and help her with errands…."

"That's okay…," Christopher said, very disappointed.

"Next time, though," James said, playfully pushing Christopher once more.

The front door slowly opened, and Bones stepped back into the house, looking a bit troubled. He paused for one more moment, and then forced out a feeble attempt at a smile. "Kylie, your mother's ready."

"Okay," Kylie said quietly as she waved to

James. "See you next time."

"Next time," James said, waving back.

"Christopher…" Kylie reached her arms around him, giving him a big hug.

"Oh, and Saturday…," Bones said, holding the door open for Kylie. "We're all going fishing up at the lake. So you all will see each other on Saturday."

"Great!" Kylie waved to the brothers one last time. "See you then, then!"

Bones closed the door behind Kylie, waving one last time to her and Janice. Then he let out a long sigh as he painfully inched his way back to the couch, sitting down as though he was pulling the weight of the entire world behind him. He reached into his pants pocket, pulled out some sort of pill and quickly swallowed it without any water at all.

"What's wrong?" Christopher asked, very concerned. He didn't know if something that Janice had said was troubling him, or whether the whole entire matter of the cave was troubling him. The only thing that he was exactly sure of was that something was definitely troubling him.

"Janice has decided that her and Kylie will be moving out of Pine Hallow," Bones said quietly, knowing it would upset Christopher.

Christopher felt as though his knees would give

out, and he slowly came to sit next to Bones. It seemed as though the weight of the world was now on him instead. "Why?"

"Are they in trouble?" James asked.

"Well…," Bones said, shaking his head as though this was just another problem weighing down about him. "Turns out Bill—you know, Jack Olen's Bill—he was in Springfield the other day and he swears that he saw Kylie's father hanging around there, and that he was in real bad shape."

Christopher shook his head in disbelief. "They think he'll come after them?"

"They're not sure…. This is something a long time coming, though; Janice has never really felt safe here, so they'll be leaving in a week. Moving somewhere out west…Nevada I think. Janice has some family out there and she's going to try starting over."

"One week…," James quietly repeated, putting a hand on Christopher's shoulder.

"That's so short…," Christopher said. "Was he sure that it was him?"

"Sure enough that he went to the police and filed a report…," Bones replied, rubbing his painful forehead. "And from the way he spoke about him, he looked terrible; covered in dirt, unshaven…looked as though he had gone completely mad."

"I hope they catch him…," James said, sounding very frustrated.

"I'm sure they will," Bones said reassuringly.

"Won't change anything though," Christopher said as he folded his arms across his chest, a great big frown on his face. "They'll still leave…."

"Yeah…," Bones said as he placed an arm around Christopher, although he looked very uncomfortable doing so. Bones seemed like the type of person who was very reserved with his feelings. "Don't think that this isn't hard on Janice, and don't think that she hasn't noticed that Kylie is fond of you. I know it's not fair, but you'll just have to make the best of the time that you do have."

"I know…," Christopher said quietly, nodding in agreement, although the frustration he was feeling inside did not make him feel the slightest bit fond of agreeing.

"Things that change change because we are people who have no authority to change them," James said with a frustrated sigh.

"This wasn't an easy choice for her to make," Bones said. "Life is full of hard choices, and loss. There is hope, though—just look at everything you've accomplished, everything you've found in that cave of yours. If that's not enough to give you hope and make you believe in all the good possibilities that are out there, then nothing will."

"Nevada...," Christopher whispered, like he was speaking of some far-off land that might as well exist on another planet. "It's too far away."

"And your feelings can't reach that far?" Bones asked.

"It's not that...," Christopher replied, still pouting and holding his arms crossed.

"Look at me, for example. It's been four years; do you think I love Cat any less?"

"No...."

"She's not even on this earth anymore...at least as far as I know. But that doesn't mean that I love her any less than I did the first day that we met. I knew from that first day that we would be together, and you know what? We were...," Bones continued, as if he were saying such things as an attempt to convince himself just as well as Christopher. "There are a lot of tragedies in life, that's true. There are a lot of possibilities and love in the world as well, though."

"Like the cave...," James whispered, as though he had figured a small part of what the cave was really about.

"Yeah...," Bones said uncomfortably. "Like the cave...."

That night Christopher was quiet all throughout dinner. It seemed as though there was something weighing heavily on everyone's mind in the house that night. Christopher thought again about the distance that would soon separate him and Kylie, and it just seemed so unfair to him. How come everyone that he cared about had to eventually leave him? Why couldn't God or whoever was in charge of this spinning blue mess just let him be happy for once? After all, that's all he wanted was to be happy and stable with this new, albeit different, family.

Christopher would write to her though, he decided that much for sure. Every day, if she wanted that. Maybe he could even visit her sometimes in the summer or on vacation days from school. No matter how much he tried to reason with himself, though, it seemed like Pine Hallow would never be the same without her. For a brief moment, Christopher could understand exactly what Bones had meant earlier.

With dinner now over, and the view from the large picture window in the living room growing dark and darker, Christopher stood alone; James and Bones were still in the kitchen talking about unimportant things. He stared off through the window into the night. Off in the distance he could see a bright flash of lightning through the thick trees. As he stood there looking into the night, windows took on a completely new meaning to him. No longer would a window just be something that he would look through; from that day on they would be something completely different, almost magical.

"A storm is coming," Bones said as he walked into the living room, concerned that Christopher was standing alone at the window in the dark. "Are you all right?"

"Yeah," Christopher said. "I was just thinking about things, too many things."

"Yeah…." Bones placed a hand on Christopher's back. "A lot is going on."

Outside the wind picked up, causing the window to shudder violently as the flashes of lightning grew closer with each passing moment. Strong winds pushed against the swaying trees so roughly that the noise could be heard from inside the house. It was a rough sound like that of the ocean breaking on rock, or the roar of a jet engine high up in the sky.

Christopher placed a hand against the window, relating it to the moment he had done so at the window in the cave. It felt cold to the touch in the same way the other window had, yet the world on the outside looked as it should. He could feel the strong vibrations of the wind against his hand and the rattling of the thunder.

"Hope the dogs are inside…," Christopher said quietly, his eyes still fixed on the coming storm.

"I'm sure they are…," Bones answered, sounding as though he was doing just as much thinking as Christopher. It appeared that he had quite a few things to work out himself. "They're smart dogs, after all."

"Hey!" James exclaimed, startling both Christopher and Bones as he burst into the room.

"Radio says we're under a tornado watch."

"Best to get away from the window then, Christopher," Bones said as he gently led Christopher away.

"What are you guys doing here in the dark anyway?" James asked, shaking his head and sounding more like a parent than he probably should. "You're both going to get hit by lightning if you hang out at the window."

It was then that the wind picked up so strongly that it sounded as if a violent train was ripping through the area. The dogs outdoors were barking loudly, and the shaking window began to creak and squeal as though it would burst at the just the slightest addition of stress. There was a noisy sound of tree branches striking the house, and hard rain angrily pummeled the rooftop.

"This doesn't sound good!" Bones strained, trying to elevate his voice over the sound of the oncoming storm. He wrapped an arm around Christopher's waist, pulling him as he made his way as far as possible from the window.

"Basement!" James exclaimed as he ran toward the door. He held it open for Bones, who was literally carrying Christopher with him.

The wind pummeled the house violently and the very walls themselves seemed to shake and shudder with each thunderclap and violent surge of wind. The whole house cried and creaked in agony as though the storm was trying to tear it apart around them. The three quickly ran down the stairs, fearing that there was no time to spare.

"What about the dogs?" Christopher exclaimed as he was pulled down farther into the basement.

"They'll be fine!" Bones yelled, sustaining his grip on Christopher. "They're smart dogs! They'll stay hidden."

The three of them huddled down in the cobwebs and dirt of the basement floor. Upstairs they could hear the storm rage on and on. All around them dust blew down from the ceiling, and the basement light, already dim, flickered as it rocked back and forth on its chain. Several successive crashes of thunder could be heard upstairs, followed by the distinct sound of breaking glass. It sounded as though a war was being waged up in the house.

"I hope Kylie's all right…," Christopher whispered, as though if he were quiet enough the storm might not notice them.

"I hope we'll be all right," James added, sounding deeply troubled and concerned.

Then, without any warning, the basement door flew open. Wind rushed and tore its way down the stairs, filling the entire basement with a cloud of dust and cold damp air. The sound of the wind was now deafening, and nothing else of the storm outside could even remotely be heard. Bones wrapped his arms tightly around both Christopher and James, mostly convinced that this was to be the end.

However, it wasn't. As quick as the wind had come, it was mysteriously gone. All around them the house was silent, and the walls no longer shook. The basement light that had been rocking before was completely still, as if it had never moved in the first place.

Bones slowly released his grip around the two and cautiously rose to his feet. "What was that…? What in the hell was that all about?"

"It's over?" Christopher said, still shaky from fear of the storm. "Just like that?"

"I wonder if everything is all right upstairs," James said as he shakily got to his feet, standing next to Bones. "I mean, something happened right? Something bad?"

"I heard breaking glass…," Christopher said, standing next to them. "I hope it's not bad."

"Follow behind me," Bones whispered as he carefully inched his way back up to the stairs. With each step Bones would pause and strain as though he were desperately trying to hear something, trying to gauge some idea of what had just happened.

As the three reached the top they could barely make out the sound of dogs barking.

"At least Poppy and Kate are all right," Christopher thought to himself as he followed behind Bones, slightly troubled by their slow and arduous pace.

Bones stood at the top step, peeking rather comically around the corner and darting his head back and forth as if he expected someone or something to be there to attack him. Seemingly content that he would not be assaulted, he slowly led Christopher and James into the living room. The room was completely dark, and only a faint light could be seen, emitted from somewhere outside. The power must have gone out during the storm.

Christopher remembered the small head-mounted light in his pocket and pulled it out and turned it on, illuminating the room. To their surprise there appeared to be no damage at all.

James flipped the light switch located behind him by the basement door, and, also to everyone's surprise, the light immediately came on. Verifying their first impression as correct, everything in the house was completely untouched and undamaged. It was though the storm had never even happened in the first place.

"What's going on?" James asked as he scanned the room for any sign of the storm that had so obviously blown through.

"Nothing's wrong?" Bones asked, just as confused.

"Wait…," Christopher said as he eyed

something curiously. "Something's there…."

"Where?" Bones whispered, scanning the area that Christopher was fixed upon.

On the coffee table before them was Christopher's copy of *Watership Down*, the one that James had rescued from the cave. That, however, wasn't the strange part. The strange part was that standing on both sides of the book were two shimmering, smoky blue rabbits. The two strange creatures perked their ears up, noticing that they were being watched.

"What in the world?" Bones' jaw was slack with shock. "What the hell?"

The rabbits quickly darted off and made their way about the room, knocking glasses and papers over in the process. The rabbits, which seemed as though they were made entirely of blue smoke and dust, were panicked and searching for any form of place to hide from the newly arrived onlookers.

"Rabbits?" Christopher asked as he slowly made his way toward the coffee table, careful not to frighten them any further.

"From the book?" James asked, confused as well. "How?"

Christopher reached down for the book, shaking his head in disbelief. "I don't know." The moment his fingers came in contact with the novel the rabbits made some strange kind of puffing sound and floated up into the air, dispersing as a cloud of smoke against the ceiling. They left behind only a small spot of dust and a strange, bluish stain on the dirty white ceiling.

The strange way that the rabbits were made of smoke made Christopher remember back to a night that he had been unable to sleep; there was something about smoke then, too, something about words being formed out of smoke. He was confused as to why he was remembering this now. Before he could think on it any further, he was interrupted by the ringing of the phone.

Bones jumped at the eerie silence having been broken so suddenly by the ringing phone buried beside him. He pushed through a stack of papers, revealing the receiver. Picking up the phone, hand trembling, he asked, "Hello?"

"Who is it?" Christopher whispered, scared that on the other end was a voice of some scary apparition.

Bones waved Christopher off, as though everything appeared to be normal. "Ah, Janice…no…no…everything is fine here…. No, it just passed through. Yes.... No damage, not that I can tell at all."

"So the storm must have really happened then," James whispered to Christopher, who nodded in agreement.

"No damage there either, eh?" Bones continued. "Good…good…no, thanks for calling."

Bones slowly put the receiver down on the phone carriage, bringing his free hand up to massage the temples of his head with his thumb and middle finger. Apparently his headache had returned. "That was Janice," he said, sure that both Christopher and James had already heard. "A pretty bad storm blew through the area, possibly even a tornado. No damage over there though. They were worried that it had hit us…."

"It did," Christopher said as he stared down at the book he was holding. "Maybe something stopped it."

"Do you think…?" Bones was cut off by loud music coming from the kitchen.

Off in the other room, in the darkness, the radio was playing a catchy, upbeat song. It sounded like a much older song, one of those big band numbers from quite a long time back.

"I know this song…," Bones whispered, a serious look upon his face. "I know this song!"

"It was on the weather alert station," James said as he stared into the dark kitchen.

"Dean Martin…," Bones said as he began to recite the lyrics of the song being played. "'Memories Are Made of This'…."

"What does it mean?" Christopher asked, wondering if this was just another part of all the strange things that were happening.

“It was our song…,” Bones said as he plopped back down on the couch with a heavy sigh. “Me and Cat’s…I think it was one of the songs we danced to….”

“Do you think that something stopped that storm from hitting us?” James asked, still staring into the kitchen as the music hauntingly played out of the darkness.

“I do…,” Bones whispered as he placed his hands over his head. Above him the photograph of himself and Catharine floated down from the ceiling, as though it had been blowing around the room like a leaf in the wind. “I think I will be going down into that cave after all….”

Chapter 10: The Forty-Year Dance

Feet together, arms apart, dancing together and joined at the heart—with music in their ears and silence at their lips, beauty beheld in their eyes and rhythm in their hips, they waltz underneath the stars, underneath the world, where everything is beautiful, and everything full.

Christopher could no longer sleep that morning; the sounds all around him were simply too loud and equally too annoying to do so. Grumpy, he forced his eyes open to accept the new day sun. Stretching and forcibly making his way up to his feet, he looked at the commotion going on around him. Bones and James were already up cooking some kind of breakfast together. The three had decided to all sleep down in the living room camp-out style, complete with sleeping bags and a lantern in lieu of a campfire. After the events of the night before, everyone in the house was just a bit shaken up. Even Kate and Poppy were brought in to sleep with them, and Bones had said that was a special treat which had never occurred before.

Christopher, now mostly awake, made his way to the large window in the living room, the same one that he was sure had been completely blown out the night before. The view outside was a rather unique one. Across the property a large majority of the trees had either toppled over or been severely damaged. It looked as though a twister had actually come blowing through after all. Then it was true; something had saved them and the house as well. Surveying the damage outside, it was nothing short of a miracle that the house was not in a similar state of ill repair as the newly distressed trees.

"Did we wake you?" Bones asked, poking his head through the large kitchen doorway.

Did we wake you? Christopher thought sarcastically to himself. "How could you possibly not wake me…?" After all, they were carrying on like a pair of wild dogs in there; in fact, Poppy and Kate were better behaved and silent than Bones and James were. He finally said: "Yeah, I just got up…."

"Oh good!" Bones exclaimed, his head disappearing back into the kitchen. "It's almost breakfast time!"

James and Bones rushed through their breakfast that morning; it was like the two had a competition to see who could pile down the most food without choking. It was unclear as to who exactly was winning either; however, they were each making an impressive mess of themselves. Christopher poked around at his breakfast.

The eggs were a lot better this time; it looked as though Bones was actually improving his cooking skills. However, he did not feel like eating as much as the other two. He never did well with having to eat in a hurry and was always curious about people who could, like the kind of kids at school who would just cram everything that they had at lunch down their throats in less than five minutes so that they could have the rest of the period to play outside. Christopher was always a more patient and slow eater. Besides, what was the point of hurrying when you could end up choking!

"Eat up!" James encouraged, his mouth full of a meaty substance that was either bacon or sausage. "We're going back today. Bones is going in."

"Yep…," Bones confirmed with a great big smile on his face. It was as though he was going on some kind of vacation, or pleasure trip.

"You're feeling awfully up about going in today…," Christopher said, looking over to Bones, who was cheerfully eating away like there was no stopping, not ever.

"Well…" Bones paused for a moment to swallow down more food. "Why not! Life is too short, and good days are too far and few between."

"So you're not worried anymore?" Christopher asked.

"Have you looked outside lately?" James answered for Bones.

"Yeah," Bones said. "Have you? It looks like an A-bomb hit those trees over there. That could have been us, but something stopped that from happening. The same thing that gave me my picture back—hell, the same thing that got you your book back to you."

"Yeah…." Christopher slowly took a bite of food. Bones did have a good point, and he really did feel so much better after going in and seeing his parents again. It almost gave him a sense of closure that he couldn't have gotten any other way. Still, was this the right thing to do? Even if it was helpful, was it really harmless? "I guess that is true…."

"You've got to live!" Bones announced, holding his fork high in the air, a skewered piece of bacon stuck to the tines. "Live for the moment, live for the adventure."

"Adventure!" James parroted, holding up his fork as well.

"You guys are crazy…," Christopher said, shaking his head as he got up from the table. "I'm going to go get dressed."

Christopher made his way up to his bedroom, pulling out one of his suitcases from under his bed. One of these days he would actually have to spend some time unpacking. He did, after all, have a dresser in his room. Still, there had been so much going on that it just wasn't at the top of his to-do list. Christopher looked out of the bedroom window; a lot of the trees were down around the house on that side as well. It was as though every tree surrounding the house had either been blown down or damaged.

"Amazing…," Christopher whispered to himself as he started to lace up his boots.

James knocked once, letting Christopher know that he was coming in, and then quickly flung the door open. "Hey when you're done, come downstairs. You've got to see this."

"What is it?" Christopher asked, wondering if something *else* had happened.

"Just come down!" James said, slamming the door shut behind him and laughing hysterically.

Christopher shook his head once more. Everyone was losing it around here. He went through a short mental checklist to make sure that he had everything ready to go back down in the cave. Content that he had everything he needed, he continued through the door, making his way back downstairs to the living room.

Once there Christopher looked over and saw Bones, although not how he was used to seeing him. There in his dark blue military uniform was Bones, dressed up as though he was ready to hit the town on a hot date. His tattoos were covered, his face (for the first time) was cleanly shaven, and his salt-and-pepper gray hair was slicked back with gel. He looked rather impressive, albeit very overdressed for cave exploring.

"You know you don't have to dress up...," Christopher said, looking at Bones as though he really had lost his mind completely. "I think the memories...they give you clothes to wear while you're there."

"You're going to get so dirty...," James said, laughing hard at the sight of Bones.

"You may laugh all you want," Bones said in a very stern and dignified manner, "but I know I look good right now."

Christopher shook his head and laughed. The more he thought about it, he was happy to see everyone in such a good mood. Bones looked wonderful and acted like he felt like a million dollars. James was talkative, in good spirits, and just as crazy and adventurous as Bones. Christopher wished that he could share in their happiness; however, the truth was that he was still worried about quite a few things. He couldn't help but worry about Kylie. After all, what would happen between them after she left? Did he have enough time to let her know that he liked her?

"Right...," James said as he pulled his backpack up to his shoulders and started to brief Bones about what would happen. "When you get through the window, it'll feel cold. Like really cold, but it will pass after a while, so don't get scared."

"Yes, sir!" Bones quickly barked back, mock-military style.

Christopher chuckled as he got his gear ready. "Don't go messing your shirt up either, soldier!"

"If everything goes as before," James continued, "you should see something. It will look a lot different from the rest of the room, but it won't look as strange."

"Or as shiny—it won't shine," Christopher quickly added, remembering that the whole room in the cave seemed to glisten like wet snow, everything except for the photograph. "You might even feel like you're drawn to it."

"Right, sir!" Bones said, nodding and still playing his soldier routine. "Don't worry about me; I've been through a hell of a lot. I won't piss my pants and run when it comes to game time!"

James laughed as he continued on with his advice. "You probably won't remember anything when the memory starts, but when you get out you'll be real emotional."

"You'll probably want to cry," Christopher said. "A lot…."

"Me, cry?" Bones said with a big smile on his face. "Sorry, soldier, not happening today."

The three of them walked—or marched, as Bones had liked to put it—to the cave along the creek. The day was much cooler than any that had come before. Christopher figured that the storm must have cooled down the air quite a bit. The area of downed trees only extended a small distance away from the house, and luckily the way to the cave was not blocked. Other than the ground moisture, it was quite a beautiful Ozark day. The sun was shining and the sky was perfectly blue. It reminded Christopher of the first day that he had spent there, that first morning where he looked out his bedroom window, amazed at the landscape around him. The hills, the trees…it was amazing for him to think about everything that had happened, and in such a short time!

The three cautiously made their way into the cave; the pool had overflowed a bit, making it a bit more difficult to navigate around it and head through the main chamber. Stopping for a moment to show Bones the artwork on the cave walls, Christopher and James then got into their packs and pulled out their flashlights.

In silence, the three slowly made their way down the back chamber of the cave. This time they all had to hold hands, as the water rushing from the pond was a lot swifter and came almost up to the tops of their ankles. James was careful as he lead them on; he didn't want anyone to fall and get swept away and carried over the falls, which would certainly lead to disaster. Bones complained that his nicely ironed slacks were getting wet.

As they made it to the winding tunnel, Bones had to stop for a moment. He wasn't out of breath: he simply needed a smoke.

"You know, second-hand smoke is supposedly

bad for us," James announced as he led them farther down the winding cave to the main chamber.

"It's a good thing you're upwind then!" Bones said.

"It's a good thing I'm behind you then, too," Christopher said objectively, his eyes squinting against the haze. "Thanks, thanks a lot."

"Eh," Bones said as he put out his cigarette against the cave wall. "Sorry."

"Well," James said as he led Bones into chamber at the bottom of the falls, "this is it."

Bones looked up in amazement at the height of the chamber ceiling. "So that's where we were then?"

"Yeah," Christopher replied as he brought his flashlight beam up to the opening near the ceiling. Much more water rushed in from the drop-off above, and he thought back to when the run-off was little but a small series of rushing streams.

"That's a hell of a long way up," Bones said.

"Imagine falling down that," James said as he pulled out the length of rope from this backpack.

"Where's the window?" Bones asked as he scanned the area. All he saw around him were shimmering cave walls.

"We've got to put out the lights…," Christopher said, extinguishing his flashlight.

James quickly followed suit, extinguishing the large lantern. He quietly stepped over to Bones, rope in hand.

"Amazing…," Bones whispered as his eyes adjusted to the dim light coming from the room. "There wasn't anything there before…."

"We figured it has to be dark," James said as he handed one end of the rope to Bones. "That's why we didn't find anything the first time we were here."

"Right," Bones said as he took the rope from James. "Is this necessary? I'd hate to wrinkle my uniform."

"I'd have to insist," James said as he held the other end, handing a length of it over to Christopher.

"Besides, if anything weird happens in there," Christopher said, "just tug on it and we'll pull you out."

"Can't argue with safety," Bones added with a chuckle as he tied a tight knot around his waist. "Well, here goes."

"Good luck!" James encouraged.

"Be careful…," Christopher said.

Bones carefully placed his left foot into the open

window of the room. A pained expression showed up on his face for a moment, but quickly passed. "Damn…that *is* cold."

"Remember, give a tug if you need us," James said, nodding.

"Oh!" Christopher exclaimed, remembering something from before. "When you're able to, give us a thumbs-up so we know you're okay. You can't talk to us any other way."

"Right," Bones said, wincing from the cold. He slowly inched his leg in more and more, until finally he could take no more of it. "To hell with it," he said, and leapt through the window completely.

Christopher and James watched as Bones disappeared momentarily, a loud tearing noise following his entry as he ripped through the portal and into a new reality. They watched as Bones' head slowly rose up to the window, the vision of his face very distorted and shaky.

"Well…," Christopher whispered as he gripped his end of the rope tightly. "He's in."

"I wonder what he'll find."

The two watched in silence as Bones stepped forward, or rather, floated forward, as it looked so awkward and out of sequence that it was hard to tell exactly what he was doing. Then, Bones quickly appeared back at the window, almost as though he had forgotten something. A quick frame of Bones appeared giving Christopher and James the thumbs up signal that Christopher had asked for.

"Good; he's okay," Christopher whispered.

Bones made his way all about the room, sometimes disappearing for seconds, other times turning into a ball of light. He sat at the bed for several frames, and then appeared before the door with a sudden flash.

"About the door…," Christopher whispered over to James. "Did you try it?"

"Yeah…," James said, his eyes glued to the window. "It didn't turn. I tried to pull it but it didn't even feel as though it would budge."

"Oh…I didn't try it. I wonder what's behind it."

"I'd love to know. Oh…I think he's found something."

Christopher and James watched as Bones carefully inspected something on the floor, although Christopher could not make out anything at all. Perhaps it was too small to be seen from the window. Frame by frame, Bones got closer and closer to whatever it was that he was interested in.

"It's going to get dark," James whispered. "Don't freak out."

"I won't." Christopher gripped his end of rope

as tight as he possibly could, ready for anything that could happen.

As Bones' fingers touched the ground, the room went completely black. A huge explosion of thunder and wind shot from the window as it slammed down firmly upon the rope.

"We knew this would happen...," James reassured, looking over to a panicking Christopher.

"We've got to get the window open...," Christopher said in a troubled voice. "Right?"

"Give it some time; we didn't even have to pull you out. It shot you out all by itself," James answered reassuringly. "We were going to give you two more minutes, but you beat the clock by a minute and a half."

"I was only in for that short a time?" Christopher asked, remembering back to his special memory, how it seemed to take place over hours of his life.

"That's right," James said. "You remember I was only in for a few minutes. Bones should be out any moment now."

As the last word had left James' lips the window suddenly flew back open, expelling a huge, cold gust of air that flung Bones out backward and onto his back against the cold hard floor of the cave.

Christopher and James rushed over to Bones' side. They knew that it was going to be difficult for him, especially the first few moments.

Bones slowly moved, curling himself up into a ball upon the floor. A tear could be seen running from his closed eyes. He was clutching something in his hand, and trembling in confusion and from coldness.

“Are you okay?” Christopher asked.

“Give him a moment,” James said as he placed a hand on Bones’ shoulder. “He’s still confused.”

Bones, still trembling, gradually rose to a sitting position. He gave both Christopher and James bewildered looks, as though he did not recognize them. “Catharine…,” he whispered, tears streaming from his eyes.

“Did you see her?” Christopher asked. “What happened?”

“Cat…,” Bones said as he stared down at his hands, “…they’re wrinkled….”

“Bones?” James asked, concerned.

“Are you okay?” Christopher asked, placing a hand on Bones’ other shoulder. It had not taken James this long to recover.

“Damn these hands…,” Bones said between sobs as he stared down at his hands. “These old wrinkled hands, this old painful body. What is it any good for? What am I any good for, anymore?”

"You're okay...," Christopher said, placing his arms around Bones, "...and you're good for *us*, don't you know that?"

"Sorry...," Bones whispered, as though things were slowly coming back to him. "I'm just tired of feeling old. I'm tired of being old, too."

"Well," James said, "at least you get to watch adult movies."

Bones chuckled as he cried, and then looked back down at the backs of his hands. "I had forgotten, you know? They're my own hands and I had forgotten how they looked."

"Did you get to see her?" James asked.

"Yeah...," Bones said, finally letting a smile out. "I did see her."

"What happened?" Christopher asked, happy to see a smile return to Bones' face. He didn't want Bones to be sad; he was important. After all he had done for he and his brother, Christopher believed that he deserved only happiness.

"It was the dance. It...it was wonderful," Bones said with a faraway look in his eyes. "Seeing her again, for the first time. It felt just like the first time too, and so much better than I had ever imagined it. Even the best dreams I had of that moment, they could never come close to that experience...."

"I'm glad that she was there…," Christopher whispered. Hearing Bones talk about Catharine made him miss Kylie.

"She was so beautiful that night," Bones said, his eyes twinkling. "We danced and danced, we talked and we joked. All of my old friends were there, and everyone was so incredibly happy…. Then, at the end of the night we shared one last dance, to Dean Martin's 'Memories Are Made of This'…. As it ended we kissed, and for the first time, too. It was just amazing, so beautiful and wonderful. It was every good word in the dictionary that means something is amazing, and every good feeling that one can experience in life wrapped up into one nice little moment."

"Is that where it ended?" James asked in amazement at all that Bones had gotten to experience.

"It actually ended right before I went to sleep that night," Bones said, nodding his head happily. "I was lying in bed, thinking about all the possibilities. Thinking about Cat and how we could start a whole new life together, about how she would be a new chapter in my life."

"Then you were pulled right out of bed, right?" Christopher asked, remembering the strange experience of exiting his memory.

"Yeah," Bones said, "One hell of a ride, too."

"I bet we could charge money for that ride,"

James said, “We could charge money for all of this!”

“No…,” Bones quietly replied, shaking his head. “This is something special, something small in the world that should remain small.”

“Other people should know…,” Christopher said, a little confused as to why Bones did not wish to share this.

“Well…,” Bones began as he presented a folded-up envelope that he had gripped in his hand. “I think this place is invitation only.”

“What is it?” Christopher asked, staring down at the envelope.

Bones slowly unfolded the thick paper, exposing the writing on the front of the envelope. “To: Kylie” was written in fancy cursive writing. “It looks like it has chosen its next visitor…,” he said.

“What’s inside of it? Should we open it?” Christopher asked, eager to learn more about the strange things going on down there, in the Earth.

“I think we should let her do that,” Bones said as he folded the envelope back up into its original shape. “It’s her part of the story now.”

“She didn’t want to go…,” James said, “I hoped she’d change her mind.”

“I guess we’ll find out tomorrow, at the lake,”

Christopher whispered. He was a bit worried about Kylie going in. What if she had some kind of bad memory involving her father? The room wouldn't do that to her, though, would it? The thought of it left Christopher very uneasy. After all, the cave had done some scary things. Had it meant to scare them, though, or was it just doing things that it had to do? There were still way too many questions left to answer.

"I'm ready to go back home…," Bones said as he slowly got to his feet, dusting the dirt off of the sides of his uniform. He untied the rope from his waist and handed it to James.

"Okay," James said as he packed up the rope.

"Do you think the room has anything to do with Alena?" Christopher asked as he sat on the ground, staring into the open window.

"I don't know…," James quietly replied, looking down at Christopher and then over into the window in the earth.

"If that's where she disappeared to, I can see why she never came back," Bones said as he also turned to the window. "I don't know what kind of forces are at work down here, or who is responsible for them. Then again, maybe I don't want to know."

"I want to know," Christopher whispered, "I just want to understand it."

"If it wants us to know…," James said, "…I'm

sure it will let us, when the time is right."

"Right," Christopher said, rising to his feet. "When the time is right, then."

"Let's head back." James turned on his large lantern and made his way back to the winding tunnel. "Besides, I'm hungry again."

Christopher chuckled for a moment and followed behind James, pausing for a moment to look back at Bones, who was still standing near where the window used to be.

"Thank you…," Bones whispered as he kneeled down onto his knees, his eyes firmly shut. "I don't presume to know who you are, or why you have done this for me. All I know is what I've felt…all I know is what I've experienced. And for what I've felt and experienced, I thank you for that. With every part of everything that I am…I thank you for my life…and thank you for my memories."

Christopher continued on, pretending as though he had not heard what Bones had said, although feeling deeply moved by the statement. Bones didn't seem like the type to be so emotional, but he had thought about this before. Christopher knew now that Bones was a lot like him and James: just another person on this earth, happy to be alive and happy with what they have. Sure there was some tragedy there, but everyone has some sort of tragedy in their life. It was what they make out of it that defines who they really are. To Christopher, this was Bones' defining moment, a small glimpse at the true character inside the person that called himself Bones, originally known as Mathias Janes.

“Thank you…,” Christopher whispered off into the darkness.

Chapter 11: A Day in the Sun

Feet in the water and hearts in the clouds as sunlight gleamed in our eyes. We felt as birds, or at least as free, as our memories soared on giant white wings.

As Christopher awoke to the familiar surroundings of his bedroom, there was a slight early morning chill in the air as red sunlight filtered in through the bedroom window. Arms outstretched, Christopher slowly got to his feet. For the first time since he had arrived at Pine Hallow he felt as if he had finally gotten enough sleep the night before. For that, he was very thankful.

The previous night, after the three had returned from Bones' venture into the window in the earth, nothing of real importance or strangeness had actually occurred. For that, Christopher was also very thankful. It was nice to have a quiet evening for once and talk about things that weren't sad or strange. There were some threads of discussion regarding different memories and moments, things that they might want to relive someday. They also spent a few moments on things that they would never hope to relieve, embarrassing moments, or boring ones involving tests at school or doctor's appointments. At one point Bones had noted that if the cave really was evil, it would just make us relive all of the long boring days of school over and over, without any weekend in sight. They had all gotten a good laugh at that.

Pulling a bulging suitcases full of clothes out from underneath the bed, Christopher carefully selected what he should wear on his trip to the lake today. Any other day Christopher might have just thrown on any old thing that he could find, or anything that was packed on top and easy to access. However, today he would be seeing Kylie again, and that called for a special caliber of clothing.

Finally, after settling on a nice pair of striped shorts, and his shirt that comically read: "I'm not here today, leave a message" (well, Christopher found it comical anyway), he made his way down to the living room with an excited spring in his step. As expected, since he always seemed to be the last one to wake up, Bones and James were already dressed and ready. Both sat on the couch watching the black-and-white television set.

"Morning," Christopher whispered, not wanting to interrupt their television-watching as he made his way into the kitchen, intent on locating himself some cereal.

"Hey!" Bones happily greeted, holding a hand up in the air.

"Morning…," James said, sounding a touch tired from the night before.

"Weather says it's going to be a nice day today," Bones quickly added.

"Sounds good," Christopher replied from the kitchen. He poured himself a bowl of some form of raisin bran flakes. Not really much of a favorite of his, but it was his only choice since someone had already finished all the other brands.

"It just says we can't expect much more nice weather…," James said. "They say Saint Louis is flooding."

"They're saying this year could be the worst flood season ever for the central U.S…," Bones said.

"I hope it doesn't flood around here…," Christopher replied as he walked back into the living room to join Bones and James on the living room couch. "At least I hope the cave doesn't flood. The water was already up a lot higher than before from the storm that passed through."

"Yeah…," James agreed. "I hope the rain holds off until we can figure out what is going on down there."

Christopher and James helped Bones pack up the

fishing gear and supplies that they would be bringing with them, and, in a way, Christopher was very pleased that they were gearing up for a different kind of trip today than the other adventures they had gone on. After all the weird stuff going on, a nice normal trip to the lake would seem like a luxury vacation.

The three crammed into the old white truck, which, just as before, took quite a while to get started and even seemed to cry out in anguish. As they jolted and bounced down the road that morning, Christopher was ever more thankful that the lake was only a few miles away. He wondered how Bones was able to take this rusted piece of junk all the way out to Springfield. It must have been one painfully jarring experience on his body.

“Have you ever thought of getting a new truck?” James asked, trying not to sound offensive.

“And get rid of this beauty?” Bones replied sarcastically. “Nah, I could never get rid of this truck, not after all we’ve been through.”

Now at the lake, and no less sooner than the brothers could have hoped for, the three carefully unloaded the gear from the truck, making their way to a clear grassy area on the lakeside that seemed like a perfect picnicking/fishing spot.

Christopher took a deep breath of the damp, crisp morning air; the day was really shaping up to be an incredible one. He scanned the area all around him, eyes full of the spectacular view of the lake. It seemed as though they could not have chosen a more perfect day to be there. The sky was a light-powered blue as little contrails of clouds spread through the air like tendrils of white charcoal lines. The lake before them glimmered and rippled in the warm sunlight and spread out as far as the eye could see, disappearing off into the horizon and seeming to melt right into a large rolling hill of pine trees and oak.

James and Christopher readied their fishing lines, setting two poles aside for Kylie and Janice. Meanwhile Bones rolled out a large mat that smelled of sandalwood, carrying over the coolers and lunch supplies that he had brought with him.

About half an hour after everything was set up, Kylie and Janice arrived, pulling up in their large black SUV. Christopher dashed up the hill and to the road to greet them. His bare feet were hot with pain, and he gritted his teeth as he ran to them on the gravel road. Once he got close enough, he decided to hobble the rest of the way. As the back door to the SUV opened up, Christopher looked upon Kylie in a childlike state of shock. She was wearing a black one-piece bathing suit with a skirt bottom, the black of the clothes lightening her hair in the sunlight and contrasting with her light blue eyes, making them appear to glow and shimmer in the same way that the lake itself did.

Ignoring the fact that Christopher was blatantly staring at her, she quickly made her way to him, giving him a long embrace. "Great to see you again."

"Great to see you too," Christopher whispered, a

deep and profound sense of happiness filling him. It was almost as though he didn't feel complete or whole until now.

"Nice-looking kid," Janice said as she made her way around the vehicle to greet Christopher, extending a hand out to him.

Christopher blushed at the compliment and returned the handshake. "Nice to finally meet you."

"I've heard lots of good things…," Janice said. She gave him a warm smile before making her way down to the lake to join Bones and James.

Christopher and Kylie stared at each other for an awkward, quiet moment.

"So did you hear?" Kylie asked, referring to the fact that her mother was making her move out all the way to Nevada.

"Yeah…," Christopher whispered. He wanted to say more. He wanted to tell her how he really felt about her and how he really wished she didn't have to go, but he was interrupted by James, who came running up to them.

"Did you tell her?" James asked, a little out of breath from running up the hill.

"No…," Christopher whispered, his mind still on Kylie moving away. "I was going to…."

"Tell me what?" Kylie asked.

"Bones went down the other day…," James said. "It was amazing."

"I wish I could have been there for that," Kylie said with a big smile on her face.

"Yeah, and the night before, before he had decided to go…" Christopher paused, remembering back to the storm that had appeared, and the mysterious music that had played. "We thought we were dead."

"I was really worried about you…." Kylie stopped to correct herself. "I was worried about all of you guys. My mom got a call from Jack Olen, and he told her that a horrible storm was blowing through and that he thought he had even spotted a tornado down by your house…"

"That tornado hit…," Christopher said, still attempting to make sense of that strange moment. "Although something stopped it from hitting us, or at least hurting us."

"Yeah," James agreed. "We heard glass breaking; it sounded like the walls in the house were being knocked down. We had to go down into the basement. It was crazy."

"But when we came back up…," Christopher continued on James' behalf, "…there was nothing, no damage at all."

"That's amazing…," Kylie said, shaking her head. "I'm so glad that nothing bad happened to you guys. I don't know what I'd do without you all."

"Christopher was worried about you the whole time," James said, smiling as he nudged Christopher in the ribs.

"Well," Christopher said quickly, "I knew we'd be fine"

"Right," James said, watching Kylie blush.

"So then…," Kylie began, changing the subject for Christopher's sake, "…because of the storm Bones decided that the cave was good and that he had to go down?"

"Yeah…," Christopher said. He pulled the envelope that Bones had discovered out of the pocket of his shorts. "He found this when he was in there…."

"What is it?" Kylie asked, extending her right hand.

"Bones thinks it's your invitation," James said. "We think that the room wants you to come inside next."

"It's just an envelope. How do you know it's for me?" Kylie asked, sounding very hesitant of the idea of going into the cave. Staring intently at the envelope, she slowly unfolded the letter and looked at the writing on the front. "Oh…it's addressed to me…."

"We didn't open it," Christopher said, trying to sound upbeat, so as to not worry Kylie about the contents. "Bones felt that you should open it."

"Okay…." Kylie paused for a moment, uncertain of what do to do next. "All right, well, I guess there's no point in waiting any further."

After another moment's hesitation, Kylie slowly ripped open the envelope. Holding out an open hand, she emptied the contents into it.

"What is it?" Christopher asked as he watched a glowing object fall into Kylie's hand and shimmer brightly in the sunlight.

"It's some kind of necklace…," Kylie whispered, moving her hand back and forth and watching the silver necklace sparkle. Placing the empty envelope into her pocket, she brought her other hand up to unravel the length of silver chain. As she slowly unraveled it between her fingers, a small white charm in the shape of a cross fell out of the palm of her left hand and dangled in the air from the chain.

"Is that…," James began in disbelief, and decided to change the last word of his sentence as he was speaking, "…yours?"

"No," Kylie said nervously, knowing what James was going to originally ask.

"Is that Alena's?" James whispered, finishing his original question.

"Could it be?" Christopher said, wondering aloud, and slightly terrified at the mere thought of it. If that was Alena's, then why did she want Kylie to have it? Then again, wasn't the necklace one of the only remains they had found of Alena—that, and her shoes? What did it mean?

Kylie looked apprehensively at the chain in her hand, almost as though she wished it was not in her possession. "I don't know what this is…."

"It's got a white cross on it," James said. "Just like the one painted on the cave floor."

"Maybe it *is* hers," Christopher said.

"Why should I have this?" Kylie asked, sounding very much confused. "This doesn't have anything to do with me as far I can tell…. The book and the photograph…they both had a point to them, right?"

"They were both things that weren't supposed to be there," Christopher said, attempting to make some kind of sense of the situation. "Maybe this isn't supposed to be here, but now it is."

"But this doesn't belong to me," Kylie said, shaking her head. "I've never seen this before."

"Well…if it's Alena's then there must be some good reason why she wants you to have it," James concluded.

"I suppose so…," Kylie said, staring apprehensively at the necklace. "I guess that means I have to go in next…."

"You don't have to go," Christopher whispered, not knowing exactly what to say and hoping that this wouldn't upset her any. "I mean…if you can't do it, no one will think any less of you."

"Alena might…," Kylie whispered as she took both ends of the chain and brought them around either side of her neck, clasping the ends together. "She gave me this for a reason. If she's the reason that good things are happening here, then I think we owe it to her…."

"Are you all going to stand up there all day long?" Bones shouted, waving to the three from the lakeside. "I thought you came here to have fun?"

"He's got a good point," Kylie said, nodding. With a mischievous grin, she suddenly pushed both James and Christopher, causing them to stagger backward. "Race you down!"

"Hey!" James said as he chased after her. "You cheated!"

Christopher was laughing hard, and found it difficult to keep up. "Nice!" he yelled as he ran down the hill to join the rest of the group.

There, underneath the sun and with the cooling breezes from the lake flowing over them, the three sat, their minds full of happiness and joy, fishing rods in hand and feet dangling from the short wooden dock into the water. They spent more time enjoying each other's company than actually caring about whether or not they were catching any fish. For one thing, Christopher had hoped that he didn't catch anything. He had never liked unhooking the fish, or even hooking one in the first place. To him it seemed a little mean. Fishing, as far as he was concerned, was more of an excuse to be lazy and enjoy the sunlight and nature.

After fishing and talking with Christopher and Kylie for a few hours, James suddenly hopped to his feet, stating that he had wanted to go see what Bones and Janice were up to. Although Christopher secretly suspected—and this was soon confirmed with a wink from James—that he was really leaving Christopher and Kylie alone so that they could talk about a few things.

Watching James head away from the dock and back toward the grassy area that Bones and Janice were, Christopher turned to Kylie, who was seated next to him. Her dark hair glistened with sunlight as it swayed in the soft lake breeze. Christopher watched her intently; she had not noticed his looks yet. Or perhaps she did, and she just simply did not mind. Her eyes were fixed on the water, and its dancing reflections of light lit up her face, accentuating the soft curves of her face and lips.

"Do you…," Kylie whispered, turning to look to Christopher, her expression serious and her eyes somewhat saddened. "Do you like me?"

Christopher was taken aback for a moment. He didn't think that this would come up, or at least come out of her so directly and honestly. He quickly broke their shared gaze and stared down at the lake, unsure as to why he was doing so.

"It's okay…," Kylie whispered back, faking a bit of a smile. "If you don't, I understand. I just thought that maybe…"

"I do," Christopher interrupted, feeling as though his entire body uncomfortably warm. He didn't want her to continue with her last statement, as he knew for a fact that it was definitely not the case at all. "I really do…."

"Even though I'm leaving?" Kylie asked, sounding very saddened.

"Of course," Christopher said. He reached over to gently place his hand over hers. Remembering what Bones had said to him when he found out that Kylie was leaving, he continued: "No matter how far away you are it won't affect how I feel for you…. My feelings can reach that far."

Christopher felt rather embarrassed, being so open was very difficult for him, especially when it came to how he felt about Kylie. He didn't know why it was such a difficult subject for him; he wished he could just say everything and anything that he wanted to. It bothered him a bit that he had to be and feel so reserved all the time in these kinds of situations. *My feelings can reach that far,* Christopher thought to himself. It sounded a little corny when he thought more about it. He had said that part, right? It sounded better when

Bones had said it; he hoped it came out right. Many unpleasant thoughts were racing through Christopher's mind. He was so worried about sounding right and saying the right things that he was completely oblivious to the fact that Kylie's face was hovering toward his own. An expression of complete shock washed over Christopher's face as Kylie brought her lips up to meet his and they touched.

All of the bad thoughts and the feelings of awkwardness were suddenly washed away from Christopher's mind as new emotions flooded through him. The world felt brighter, the sun felt warmer, the wind cooler. His senses seemed heightened to their utmost. The world had changed in an instant, and though the moment was soon over, he could still feel her presence on his lips. Like a painted handprint on the wall of his memories, it would forever be emblazoned in his mind.

"I really like you, too," Kylie whispered as she smiled contentedly, and then started to giggle uncontrollably.

"What's so funny?" Christopher asked, smiling happily.

"You should see your face," Kylie said, as she embraced Christopher once more.

There, on the docks, the moments seemed to melt away like wax from a slowly burning candle. To Christopher, everything seemed so different and almost as though he was seeing the world through new eyes.

He had never felt so good deep inside, even back in the days when his parents were still around and everything seemed so stable and predictable. It was like the world didn't matter anymore. Things could be bad, things could not work out, yet it all just seemed a million miles away. It all just seemed so small and unimportant.

They sat there for a few more hours, just enjoying being in each other's presence beneath the sky and within the universe that surrounded them.

That evening they all barbequed together at the lake, like one big happy family. Christopher couldn't have imagined a more perfect day, no matter how hard he tried. Everyone just seemed so happy, their faces full of smiles and joy in their voices. They played games together along the lake and swam for a short time when they got tired of running and playing.

As the sun slowly faded from the sky, rain clouds slowly approached from the opposite end of the lake. Much to Christopher's dismay, the day would eventually have to come to an end. There was nothing he could do to stop it, no matter how much he wanted the time to just go on forever and ever.

The group packed up their respective gear and made their way back to their respective vehicles. Tossing the gear into the truck, Bones paused for a moment to thank Janice.

"Lovely idea," Bones said, nodding in acknowledgement. "Thanks for having us all come out here."

"No problem," Janice said with a big smile on her face.

Christopher gave Kylie one more long hug. He felt sad that he had to leave her once again; he wished that they could be together all the time. Reluctantly climbing back into the truck behind James, he waved one last time.

"Can I ask you a favor?" Janice asked, cocking her head to the side as though she wanted to talk in private.

"Always happy to oblige," Bones said, nodding.

The two of them walked behind her big black SUV.

For several moments Christopher and James sat in the truck, wondering what was going on. Not more bad news, Christopher hoped with all of his heart. It was already bad enough that Kylie was leaving in just six more days! He didn't feel that he could take it if it were anything worse than that.

Bones carefully climbed back into the rusty old white truck, a confident smile on his face as he waved his hand out the window to the SUV as it rolled past.

"So what's going on?" Christopher exclaimed, sounding as though he was about to simply explode if he didn't find out.

"Janice is going to head out there to Nevada for three days; she's leaving in the morning…," Bones began.

"Oh…," Christopher whispered sadly.

"So she's going drop Kylie off in the morning, and she's going to be staying with us for those three days," Bones quickly added, noticing Christopher's obvious disappointment.

Oh!" Christopher exclaimed. This wasn't the kind of news he was expecting at all. In fact, this was great news! He would get to see her every day for the next three days! This was the best news he had heard in his entire life.

"Just don't get any funny ideas…," Bones said as he put the truck into gear and started to drive away from the lake. "Remember, I was a kid once, too."

"Yeah, like five hundred years ago," James added, smirking.

"Longer than that," Bones said with a big goofy smile on his face.

They continued on into the night as the last light of the sun day drifted down below the horizon. A light rain started, and Bones had to turn on the windshield wipers to see where he was going. Christopher hoped that this wasn't a sign of bad things to come, as they still had a lot of things to do within the cave, a lot of mysteries to solve.

"That girl of yours...," Bones said as he turned to James, and then back to watch the road ahead of him.

"What girl?" James asked, confused for a moment.

"You remember telling me before that you had seen her, right?" Bones said. "The girl from the cave? What did she look like?"

"It's hard to remember now," James said, bringing his hand to his mouth as though in deep thought. "She was real pretty; she was kind of glowing in the moonlight when I saw her. Her hair was light and looked like it was flowing or floating, like it was underwater or something."

"Did she talk to you?"

"She said one thing, I think...about there being magic in the world," James quietly replied, trying to think back to the time. "Why?"

"I think I had a visitor last night," Bones quietly answered back. "I can't remember it clearly, though. I was sleeping in my bed and I felt like someone was just watching me sleep."

"Do you think it was her?" James asked.

"I don't know. She did look very sad though, when she was watching me."

"Did she say anything?" Christopher asked. He had been listening to the entire conversation intently. Perhaps it was another part of the puzzle, if there was one to be solved, that is.

"No," Bones replied. "That's why I asked. She just kind of stood over me, looking very upset. I remember because I woke up feeling really sick, and she kind of made it go away."

"Are you okay now?" Christopher asked, concerned.

"Oh yeah, right as rain," Bones said. "She took my pain away, though, that night. It should have been creepy, yet it felt so calming. Cool and calming, that's it."

"I wonder if that's Alena. I wonder if she's why we're able to see the window…," James said, trying to figure things out as well.

"If it is…," Bones said, "…I wonder what she wants?"

"I guess we'll have to find out," Christopher said, remembering the necklace. "Kylie got a necklace, and it might be from Alena. I guess we'll know more when Kylie goes in."

"You'll have to keep me up to date," Bones said. "This is so crazy, yet I can't help but be obsessed with wanting to know about it."

"We will," Christopher said as he stared blankly out the truck window. He wondered if Alena had given Kylie her cross. Could she possibly want something in return? Was this really a safe thing to do? Christopher didn't know whether or not he was being overly paranoid because Kylie was involved, or whether he should genuinely feel worried. He shrugged off the bad thoughts, reminding himself of all the good things that the cave and the window in the earth had done for them all.

That night, Christopher lay alone in bed and exhausted from everything that happened from the day at the lake. He kept replaying the moment that he and Kylie kissed over and over in his mind, like a television set in his head repeating the same exact events and feelings a million times over. He could feel butterflies in his stomach just thinking about it all. As he lay there, the time seemed to fly by. He had to eventually force himself to fall asleep, just so that it would be morning and he would be able to see her again.

Chapter 12: Kylie's Memory

Young eyes, shining in the darkness. The horrors are all human.

"So...," Christopher said, turning to Kylie as they stood at the entrance to Alena's Cave, "...are you sure you're ready to do this?"

"Yeah," Kylie calmly replied, nodding. "I'm ready."

It was about an hour after noon. Kylie had arrived just hours before and the three of them had already set out for the cave, eager to learn what her place was in all of the big mystery. Christopher was so happy that she was there with him and his brother, and could hardly contain himself as he spent the morning counting down the seconds until she arrived.

They had wanted to leave earlier, but were forced to wait since the rain had been a lot heavier that morning. However lighter the precipitation was now, however, it was still raining, and the three—Christopher, James, and Kylie—were dressed accordingly; all three wore yellow rain jackets that made them group look rather comical, almost as though they were dressed and ready for Halloween as three brightly colored and tacky ghosts.

Cautiously, they made their way into the cave entrance, where, much to their surprise, the rain had had a big effect on the entrance chamber. The central pool was already slightly overflowing the time before, now it filled the entire cave entrance.

"Stay close to the sides," James said as he led the way in, skirting the cave walls. The water at some points was way past their ankles.

"You can't even tell where the center pond is…," Christopher said as he reached backward for Kylie's hand.

"Will we be able to make it all the way down?" Kylie asked, holding on to Christopher with one arm and steadying herself along the cave wall with the other.

"Should be all right. Looks like the flooding is mostly by the entrance," James said, shining his flashlight beam back down the area where a discernable pool used to be. "It'll be a bit slick; we'll just have to take it really slow."

"Right," Christopher said as he gripped Kylie's hand firmly. The thought of getting swept away and being flung over the falls and onto the floor of the cave's largest room seemed like a rather painful journey he did not wish anyone here to make.

The distant static-like sound of the waterfalls at the far end of the tunnel gradually increased to a roar as the three carefully treaded down the passage. The ground beneath them was slick with water that flowed strongly against the backs of their ankles. They all had to hold on to each other and the wall in order to safely get through.

"Let's not look down the drop-off this time," James said as he shined the beam up ahead of them. The water was rushing a lot more violently up ahead. "Unless one of us wants to go over."

"Yeah, then we'll have to come to the cave to relive memories of you," Christopher said, chuckling.

"Right," James said sarcastically as he led them to the right and down into the winding passageway that curved around the waterfall chamber.

Luckily, this area seemed as though no water had affected it yet, which was strange given that the winding passageway headed straight down. Perhaps it was a bit of the cave magic at work, or perhaps the other way was just the path of least resistance.

The wind in the passageway felt light and cool.

As they made their way down, every now and then Christopher would pause to look behind him and make sure that Kylie was still all right. He didn't know why exactly he was being so protective of her. The more he thought of it, it was kind of obvious why, but he realized that he must look rather silly to her regardless. Instead of telling him how silly he was acting, she would just smile and nod each time he glanced back at her, letting him know that everything was fine.

As the three entered the bottom of the waterfall chamber, James hastily extinguished the light of his lantern, revealing the window in the cave wall. Their eyes adjusted as the cave filled with the soft white glow of the magic window.

"The water is getting closer…," Christopher said, pointing up and away to the falls.

"Yeah…," James said, looking over his shoulder. "If it keeps up who knows how long it will be before the water is up to the window."

"I wonder what will happen then," Kylie said. "Will water go into the window?"

"Hard to know," Christopher said, shaking his head as he spoke. "Hopefully the rain will stop soon." It did worry him a bit, however, to think about what might happen to the window if the rain did not stop. Would the magic wash away from the cave? Would the room fill with water and be inaccessible?

"Right," Kylie said as she reached into the

pocket of her rain jack jacket, pulling out the white cross with the silver chain attached to it. She slowly placed it around her neck and clasped the chain together.

"Remember," James said, starting his safety speech, "it'll feel very strange in there, but don't panic and it will go away soon enough."

"And it'll be pretty hard to move around. You really have to concentrate on where you want to get to," Christopher said.

"I watched you two both do it," Kylie said as she tied a knot in the rope around her waist. "So I should be all right."

"Just remember to pull on the rope if you want out," Christopher said as he readied himself, rope in hand, for Kylie's entrance into the window. "For any reason."

"I will," Kylie whispered. "I can do this."

Kylie gave Christopher a quick embrace, kissing him on his cheek. Then she inched her way to the open window, her fists tightly clenched at her sides. Tentatively, she let her foot slide into the opening as she winced from the pain of the coldness.

"It will pass," James said. "Just don't think about it."

Kylie allowed herself to pass further and further into the opening, and soon all that was on this side of reality were her hands and face.

Christopher watched her face slip through the threshold, rippling as though passing through water. As she disappeared into the window's portal a familiar tearing sound was heard as the window gave one final shudder. "She's in," Christopher whispered, seeing the back of Kylie's head slowly fill up the view of the window.

Christopher and James watched as Kylie flickered in and out of their sight, appearing to struggle a bit with the strangeness of the room. She made her way back to the window for a moment and Christopher could have sworn that she was staring at him. Then, both Christopher and James caught a glimpse of her blowing a kiss to Christopher.

"What a show off…," James whispered, shaking his head.

Christopher chuckled. He was glad to see that she was adjusting well and was in such high spirits in there. He remembered his time in the room: he had been way too uncomfortable to even think of something clever, so he had just given a thumbs-up as James had.

Kylie made her way about the room, appearing here or there, shimmering and seemingly fading in and out of existence. Just as Bones had done before her, she paused at the door before continuing onward. Christopher wondered if it was locked for her as well. He was a little embarrassed to admit that he had been too afraid to try the door himself, and wondered if it was locked when he had been in there as well.

"Looks like she's found what she's meant to," James whispered, his hands instinctively tightening on the rope.

Kylie could be seen reaching for something on the shimmering white bed; it was too small to clearly be seen from the window.

"I don't think I'm ever going to get used to the part that happens next…," Christopher whispered as he watched Kylie reached down to pick up the object.

"Well, here it comes anyway," James added.

As Kylie's hand clasped around the item on the bed, a familiar darkness quickly filled the room, and blackening the cave with it. Cold air rushed out and wind howled throughout the cave, a mighty boom echoing throughout the darkness. Then, just as it had happened every time before, the window slammed shut on the rope.

His hands sweaty and anxious, Christopher gripped the rope as tightly as he could. He knew that all of this had become routine, yet he couldn't help but worry with Kylie in there—not that he hadn't worried about James or Bones when they had been in there, but he felt more responsible for Kylie, and if anything happened to her he would never be able to forgive himself.

"She should be out any moment now," James

whispered to Christopher.

Christopher counted down the seconds nervously in his head as he waited and waited. It seemed as though it was taking forever. Before he could worry much longer, the window flew back open, launching Kylie out and onto the cave floor. She lay on her back, and she was moving.

Christopher rushed over to Kylie, quickly wrapping his arms around her. She had tears streaming down both of her eyes and looked as though she had been crying long before she had even returned to the cave. How much time had passed in there? What had happened?

"It'll be all right," James said, placing a hand on Kylie's shoulder. "Just give it a few…"

"It's not going to be all right!" Kylie screamed, pushing both Christopher and James away. Tears streamed from her eyes, her breathing becoming heavy and labored. She continued to vent at the two. "Damn him! Why'd it have to be about him?"

"It will be okay…," Christopher whispered, trying to dodge Kylie's wild swings and calm her down. "It's always bad right when you get out…."

"Him? Was it your father?" James asked, confused.

"Damn him…," Kylie whispered angrily, her hands now covering her face in shame as she continued to cry heavily. "How could I forget about that…?"

Christopher once again brought his arms about her, trying to comfort her in any way he possibly could. "It's okay. Things will be okay now…."

This time Kylie did not push Christopher away; instead she reached down and brought his arms closer around her. It didn't seem as though she was getting any happier, though. He thought that the cave was only supposed to help you relive good memories. What had gone wrong?

"What did you see in there?" James asked, placing a hand on her back.

"I saw my father…," Kylie whispered, still sounding very shaken and upset. "I saw him with my grandfather…."

"Maybe the memory was supposed to be about your grandfather?" James offered, trying to find something uplifting to think about. It sounded as though he was just as concerned with the fact that the cave had given a bad experience.

"My grandfather was not a good man…." Kylie sobbed, shaking her head and attempting to wipe away some of the tears from her face.

Christopher reached down and pulled up the bottom of his shirt, using it to help Kylie clean away her tears. "I can't believe the window would make you see your father…."

"There *is* a reason...," Kylie whispered, her face seeming clear and her emotions gathered. She slowly sunk into a sitting position, her hands tightly gripped around Christopher's. Resting her back against the cave, she looked around as if searching for some kind of relief that she just could not find. Another tear came streaming out of her eye.

"What happened in there?" James asked, very much confused and concerned.

"The memory...," Kylie began, "...I had completely forgotten it...or I don't know if I forced myself to forget it."

"Was it that bad?" Christopher asked, frustrated and angry with both the window and himself for letting her go into it.

"It started off at home, with my father...," Kylie said in a sad hollow voice. "God, I must have been, like, eight.... My grandfather was still alive then and he was running the bait shop, and my mother never wanted to be around him. I would always ask why, and she would always say that he was a horrible, horrible man. Can you imagine being eight years old and being afraid of your grandfather...?"

Christopher quietly shook his head. The thought alone troubled him. He felt so bad for Kylie, imagining how it had to be to first be afraid of your grandfather and then later in life having to fear your father. Family is supposed to be there to make you feel safer, not worse.

Kylie shook her head, wiping away another tear from her eyes. She took a deep breath to steady herself, and then continued, "My grandfather always hated my father for being with mom. He would always make comments about my mother being worthless, and that I was a worthless piece of trash."

"Sounds like a real ass," James said, a big scowl on his face.

"Yeah," Kylie said. "Well, the memory…me and my father were sitting at home, just watching TV. I remember it was storming outside; it had been raining all day long. Then my father got a call from my grandfather, telling him he needed him to come down to the bait shop, that it was some kind of emergency."

Kylie took in another deep breath, trying to shake off her sadness and uncertainty, and then continues, "Mom was at work in Springfield. She worked as a nurse back then…. So me and my father drove out to the shop…. I remember that my grandfather turned to me when I stepped in and said, 'What is that bitch doing here?'"

"He said that to you…?" Christopher whispered, shaking his head, not believing someone could say something so hateful to someone so young.

"Yes…," Kylie whispered, wiping away other tears that were forming at the corners of her eyes. "My father and grandfather went down into the cellar of the store. He said that there was some water flooding in, and that a wall was coming down in the back. I was supposed to wait upstairs, but it was storming so hard and the lightning was so loud…that I didn't."

"You went down?" James asked, very concerned and scared for Kylie. "What happened?"

"Well…," Kylie said. "I followed them down…. I wasn't supposed to be there…. I wasn't supposed to see what I saw."

"What did you see?" Christopher asked, growing more and more concerned with each passing moment.

Kylie quickly wiped at her eyes again and shook her head. She was finding it difficult to continue. "Water from the storm…water had come down and brought down a section of the wall in the basement. My father and grandfather were trying to pile it back up to cover something up…something….that looked like clothes and bones…."

"A body?" Christopher asked in a state of shock.

"I didn't know what it was…," Kylie whispered, sounding angry and frustrated. She covered her eyes with her arm. "I was only eight…. I didn't know what it was."

"It's not your fault," Christopher said, placing his arms around Kylie and gently holding her.

"My grandfather turns around and sees me…," Kylie said, her voice quiet and muffled. "I'm just standing there, crying.... I was so confused. My grandfather tells my dad to 'Take care of it,' and my dad rushes over and drags me back upstairs. He tells me that...all of this isn't real, and that tomorrow he'll be my normal happy dad again. He tries to make me think that I'm crazy, and that whatever I thought I saw, I didn't see."

"So that's why you probably hate him so much...," James said. "Maybe you just forgot exactly why."

"When I got home, he made me drink an entire cup of something.... I didn't know what it was back then, but now I know that it was vodka.... I was sick for hours.... When my mother got back the next morning from work he just told her that I had gotten into it...," Kylie continued, sobbing once again. "That bastard.... If that was a body, then he knew about it all this time.... My grandfather was a monster and my father knew about it and just let him be one."

Christopher could find no words to comfort Kylie; he wrapped his arms around her as tightly as he could as though trying to shield her from all the unhappiness.

"I'm sorry...," James whispered, at a loss for words.

"I need to talk to Bones," Kylie whispered. She gently pushed her way past Christopher and got to her feet. "I need to find out some things about this."

"All right," Christopher whispered, saddened that things had taken such a decidedly horrible turn.

"Do you think that Bones knew your grandfather?" James asked.

"It's possible…," Kylie said in a quiet voice as she made her wait back up the winding passage, not even pausing to wait for James and Christopher to collect their things and follow. "If my memory is right, then who knows what horrible things my grandfather and father have done…."

The three walked back in complete silence, now with Kylie in the lead. She did not pause for breath or stop for the brothers as she marched her way out of Alena's Cave. Christopher was scared; he had never seen this side of Kylie. She was acting so strangely, although he could definitely understand why. Just the thought of someone keeping that kind of secret horrified him.

Outside the cave the rain was coming down much more strongly than before. Kylie, however, did not even pause to raise the hood on her rain jacket. She was drenched and her hair clung to her face. Christopher worried that she would get sick, and he had a hard time even keeping up with her as she walked hurriedly, almost running, all the way back home.

"I was just about to come after you guys, with the rain like…," Bones began as the front door flew open, and he stopped mid-sentence when he saw a very cold and rain-soaked Kylie.

"Bones...," Kylie said with tears and rain soaking her face. "Did you know my grandfather...?"

Bones quickly rose and made his way to the bathroom in great strides, knowing that Kylie was following him. He reached for a towel and started drying her face off. "I only ran into him a few times.... Often he'd be at the store when I first moved here; your dad ran the place then."

"What kind of man did you think he was?" Kylie asked, her voice sounding deeply saddened and hollow.

"I don't know.... I'm sorry...," Bones whispered, knowing how upset Kylie was about this. "He would always eyeball me, but I just figured he hated outsiders.... I wish I knew more.... What is this all about?"

"Her memory...," Christopher said. "Her memory in the cave...."

"My grandfather and father are hiding a body in the cellar of the bait shop...," Kylie whispered, tears coming down again from her eyes as though she had finally let it sink in completely.

"Are you sure?" Bones asked with his mouth open in shock. "I mean, you saw this in the cave?"

"Yeah...," Kylie said. Her feet gave out beneath her and she fell heavily on the cushions of the couch.

Christopher quickly made his way to be at her side, holding her hand tightly. "None of this is your fault Kylie. None of it."

"He's right," James said.

"If they did anything…," Bones said as he sat down next to her, visibly disturbed by the revelation, "…then you should not feel responsible in any way…. If it's true, then people should know about it, and the family of whomever is down there…."

Kylie quickly brought her hand to her mouth as a shocked look washed over her face. "What if…what if Alena's parents didn't just leave after losing her…?"

"We don't know anything," Bones said, trying to reassure her. "Just please, don't think about it. Wait until we know more…."

"It makes sense though…," Kylie said. She had a vacant look on her pale face as she shivered from the cold. "Why else would the cave show me that…unless it had something do with Alena…?"

"If it does, then maybe they just wanted to be found…," Christopher said, squeezing Kylie's hand. He just wanted her to be okay again. He was starting to worry that she would never be all right ever again!

"We have to go…," Kylie whispered. "We have to go see who is down there in the shop's cellar."

"We can go…," Bones said. "We can take the

truck out in there. We'll take some tools and we'll search the cellar."

"Oh—Kylie...," James said, as though he finally remembered something, "...was there anything for any of us in the room?"

"Right," Kylie whispered. She quietly reached down into her pocket. She carefully pulled out what looked like a large white claw or some kind of huge fang. "It's for you...Christopher."

Christopher reached out to accept the item, his fingers trembling. "But should it be my turn again?"

"I thought it would fall back to me if it didn't go to someone else," James said, sounding a little disappointed.

Christopher rolled the large item around in his hand, which he was pretty sure was a claw, and saw that "Christopher" was crudely written upon it in black ink. Staring at the claw, he thought long and hard yet could retrieve no memory of ever seeing it before. "Why...why me? I don't want to go back in...." It was the truth too. He was perfectly happy and content with the memory that he had gotten. Then he paused, thinking that perhaps this wasn't about him anymore.

"So first we check out the shop, and then tomorrow we'll have to check out the cave...," James said, shaking his head. "This has got us running all around."

Kylie looked at the three around her and let out a heavy sigh. It appeared as though she looked better, or at least maybe felt a little better. "I'm sorry…," she finally said as she reached over and gripped Christopher's hand tightly.

"It's not your fault. None of this is," Bones said, placing a hand on her head and playfully tousling her hair. "Don't ever feel that you should have to apologize for it."

"I'm glad that you're all here to help me with this…," Kylie said, nodding to everyone in the room. "I don't think I could go through this without any of you."

"We are glad to be a part of this," James said as he smiled. "Besides, if this has something to do with Alena then we owe it to her to figure it out."

"That's true…," Bones said as he rose to his feet. "Kylie, are you ready?"

"Yeah," Kylie calmly answered. "Let's go to the shop."

Chapter 13: The Body

In silent dreams, alone for years. No one to talk to, no one to care for, and no one to care. A sad place.

The wind howled against the truck as rain came down in torrents against the window. It was raining so hard it was as if they were passing directly underneath a waterfall whose breadth was never-ending. Already tired and worn, the old white Ford truck struggled with each gust of wind. Christopher was worried that they might be blown off of the road at any moment.

"I didn't think it would be this bad out," Bones said, wiping away a bit of sweat from his forehead with the front of his shirt. "I've never seen it come down this bad out here…."

"Are we going to be able to make it all right?" Christopher asked as he jostled around a bit for a better position, as he was squeezed tightly between James and Kylie. The Kylie part he didn't mind that much. However, James' elbow was tunneling a little home in his ribs with every jolt of the truck.

"Yeah…," Bones answered, sounding uncertain. "Probably."

"Probably?" Kylie asked, knitting her eyebrows and frowning.

"Yeah…," Bones said as he strained his eyes to see the road ahead. "I'd give us good odds."

The world outside the window was so obscured from the rain it looked as though it was some kind of abstract painting. The lights of the truck could hardly be seen on the road and there was a thick fog emanating from the earth that hindered things even more. Every now and then lightning would flash, lighting up the air and rain like a giant flash of a camera, further disorienting everyone who tried to gaze outside.

"He's just messing with us," James said, shaking his head. "He enjoys this kind of thing."

"Just can't get away with anything anymore…," Bones muttered under his breath. "Got me all figured out then, eh?"

Kylie let out a little laugh, a bit relieved that they weren't going to fly off the road and die in the trees, burning in a super hot fireball. "How can you joke at a time like this?"

"Does it help at all?" Bones asked.

"It does," Kylie said with a little smile. "Although I'm not sure I should be in a good mood…especially if I'm right about what I saw."

"Don't look at it that way then," Bones said, still concentrating on the road ahead. "If it's true, look at it like this: if it's Alena's mother or father and she is the one in the cave, then maybe this will bring her a sense of peace. Maybe you were shown this so that you might be able to help her back in some small way. Maybe just knowing that the truth is out there…maybe that's what she wants."

"I didn't really think about it that way," Kylie said in a whisper. "I've been feeling a little guilty about it…. Why didn't I tell my mother? Why didn't I ever say anything? For that matter, why didn't I even remember?"

"You were scared," Christopher quickly answered. "You were little, and the whole thing was too big. Besides, if your grandfather was hiding a body, and he knew that you and your mother knew about it…."

"Who knows what he would have done to the both of you," James finished.

"Exactly," Bones said as he shook his head. "You can't blame yourself for something that you couldn't have any control over."

"I guess that's true…," Kylie said quietly. "I didn't really look at it that way before…. For a while there I thought I was being shown that as punishment."

"I don't think the cave ever intended that," Bones said, a serious tone to his voice. "It just wanted you to know the truth."

The truck skidded into the small gravel parking lot of the Bait 'n' Tackle shop, sliding a few odd feet due to the rain. Bones got out and hurried to the back of the truck, gathering together the bundle of tools that he had packed up for the search. Kylie, James, and Christopher quickly ran around to the back of the building, which was where the cellar door was located.

"It's locked!" Kylie yelled over the rainstorm. "I don't have a key to the cellar…."

"Stand back!" Bones declared as he came grunting around the corner. He kneeled down for a moment as he unpacked a large sledgehammer from the black oversized tool bag. Getting back up to his feet, he brought the large hammer over his head, paused for a moment to aim, and then let the hammer come crashing down on the bolt and lock.

The heavy metal cellar door jolted violently and seemed to jump up from its hinges. The lock and bolt, however bent, stayed intact and kept the door secure. A flash of lightning filled the air around them. A branch from above came crashing down, hitting the roof of the store and giving everyone a good healthy scare.

"I'm going to hit it again!" Bones yelled. He brought the heavy hammer back above his head, letting it fly down with tremendous force. This time it seemed to do the trick, and the lock flew in fragments into the rain. Bones quickly reached down, flinging the door open and holding it as Christopher, James, and Kylie ran down.

"That was pretty cool," James said as Bones let the cellar door slam shut behind them.

"I just didn't feel like being out in that rain anymore," Bones said with a funny little smile on his face. "Besides, that hammer needed to be broken in."

Kylie led the way, cautiously making her way down the cellar stairs. The floor below looked as though it was flooding, and there was about an inch of water reflecting back the hanging lights from the ceiling. She slowly led the group down, looking around for something familiar. "Things are a little bit different than I remember," she said.

"How long since you've been down here?" Christopher asked as he followed behind her.

"I don't think I've ever needed to come down here since. Even my mother doesn't really come down here. She hates spiders anyway and I bet this place is crawling with them," Kylie said as she slowly rounded the corner, her feet making splashes with each step she took in the dirty brown water.

"I could see why; this place is a mess," Bones

said as he rounded the corner, taking in all the sights.

Christopher looked at the area around him; it was full of old metal junk and rotted cardboard boxes, and everywhere he looked he just saw more and more crap—rusted broken bicycles, lawnmower parts, old pipes and rotten wooden boards.... It would take forever for someone to go through all the stuff, and maybe that was why it was all placed down here: to hide something much more sinister.

Kylie cautiously paced farther into the cellar. It was almost like walking through a maze. In some places she had to turn sideways to squeeze through, and in others the group had to climb or maneuver over and around things. "The far wall there...."

"Is that where you saw them?" James asked as he pushed a very large box out of his way.

Kylie nodded as she approached the bricked-over wall. She ran her hand over the rough surface of it, as if she was searching for some kind of hidden opening. "I don't think this wall was here...."

It's possible," Bones said as he made his stood next to her. "It's leaking in quite a few areas. There must be something behind it."

"So how do we get through?" Christopher asked, surveying the area. The entire back wall was covered in brick, and there didn't seem to be any other way around it. They would have to go through in order to find out what was behind it.

"You guys move all this stuff from behind us, and let's see if we can make enough room for me to swing this," Bones answered, bringing the sledgehammer to his chest.

"Do you think you'll be able to break through?" Christopher asked as he and James struggled with a large pile of metal that was in the way.

Kylie quickly went to work on the other side of Bones, pushing back more and more boxes. "It'll have to work; otherwise we'll have to wait."

"And no one wants to do that…," Bones said as he nodded, eyeballing the wall as though it was some manner of opponent. Confident that he had a clear path to swing, he slowly brought the hammer behind him, tightening his grip and gritting his teeth.

"Give it hell," James encouraged, covering his ears.

"Cover your face," Christopher said, looking over at James and shaking his head. "You don't want to get hit from flying crap."

"Oh, good point," James said as he removed his hands from his ears and shielded his eyes instead.

Kylie joined the others and crouched down to the ground, covering her face and biting her lip in anticipation of the coming blow. Bones carefully brought the hammer back just an inch more or so, and then let it fly forward with all of his might. The wall cracked and crumbled. Bricks flew in several directions, bouncing off of all the metal junk around it, and a cloud of dust rose up and around Bones.

"Hmm…," he said as he dropped the hammer to the ground, rubbing his hands and wincing. "That was jarring."

"It did make some progress…," Christopher said as he lowered his arm from his face and surveyed the newly formed hole in the wall. It was a pretty good-sized chunk, but it was not big enough to let them through yet. "A few times should do it."

"Great…," Bones said with a sigh. He picked up the hammer and brought it behind his back. He swung the hammer as hard as he could in an overhead arc, and its collision with the wall produced another resounding explosion of brick and dust, this time causing an even bigger piece of the wall to tumble down at Bones' feet. He quickly stepped back as bricks spilled out and splashed into the water where his feet used to be.

"Nice," James whispered as he came over to inspect the now-much-more-impressive hole in the wall. It was almost big enough for him to fit his head into. His hands gripped the sides of it, and he carefully pulled himself up to peer into the hole. "There's a big space here. Can't make it out, though," he said. "Did anyone bring a flashlight?"

Kylie and Christopher shook their heads. Neither of the two had thought to bring a flashlight for the search. Bones had not either. He had remembered all the other necessary tools; however, the flashlight remained back at home.

"We'll just have to make a bigger hole," Bones said, shaking his head and wiping away the sweat from his forehead with the back of his hand. "One big enough to crawl into, and with enough light to see from the cellar…."

"Good luck with that," James said sarcastically as he stepped away from the opening.

Bones took in a deep, heavy breath and brought the hammer behind him once more. With an impressive amount of force he swung the hammer into the brick wall, continuing the trend of loud, crashing explosions of rock and dirt. That time, however, a large chunk of the wall that was still intact from top to bottom came crashing all the way down. Bones had to jump back to avoid the cascade of debris.

"Well, shit…that did it," Bones said, sounding rather shocked and exhausted. "I thought I'd have to hit it a few more times…."

"You did great…," Kylie encouraged as she tried to wave away some of the dust that was all around her, coughing from all the bad air.

"Good thing, too…," Bones said. "Didn't know how many more of those I could have banged out."

James, fancying himself as being the bravest,

made his way to the large opening in the wall. "I see something."

"What's in there?" Kylie asked, sounding scared of the answer.

"There's definitely some kind of long chest back here," James said. "I can reach the handle, maybe we can pull it out."

"Let me get that…," Bones said, noting the freshly painted looks of concern on everyone's faces. "I should be able to pull it out."

Bones gently brushed James out of the way and crammed himself into the small space. A heavy scraping sound followed Bones' shaky retreat as he and the trunk emerged from inside the wall. It was one of those massive steamer trunks, painted black with the word "Fragile" written on all sides of it in white stenciled paint.

"I really hope that's not what we think it is," Christopher said, watching in disbelief as Bones brought the trunk farther out into the open.

"It's why we're here…," Kylie whispered as she took Christopher's hand, gripping it tightly. "It's the truth about my family…."

"Maybe you should look away when I open it," Bones said as he glanced around the room at everyone. "I mean…just in case it isn't pretty."

"I want to know...," James said as he stood next to Christopher.

Kylie shut her eyes, gripping Christopher's hand even tighter, and Christopher did the same. An eerie silence descended into the cellar as everyone seemed to hold their breath at the exact same moment, all of them anxious, for the truth was about to emerge.

As Bones turned the lock on the trunk, it answered with a resounding clank. He slowly opened up the trunk, holding his breath. The only sound in the room was the slow creak of the chest lid opening up, exposing its contents to both James and Bones.

"Oh my...," Bones whispered as he let the lid fall back shut.

James quickly turned away, rubbing his palms together nervously. "So, that's that, then...."

Releasing Christopher's hand, Kylie strode over next to Bones and James. "What was it...what is in there?"

"A body...," Bones whispered, shaking his head, "...or what's left of one anyway."

"Just bones and clothes," James said. He looked away from the chest, as though he might never be able to look back at it.

"Whose body though?" Christopher asked, still standing a good distance away. He felt as though he was too scared to just approach the crude coffin. It was the same sort of uneasiness and fear that he had felt at his parent's funeral. He couldn't bring himself to get near their coffins either, and had, in a way, always felt guilty about that. He felt that he should have at least properly said goodbye.

"Look away…," Bones said, and once everyone had, he laid his hands on the trunk lid and opened it again with a loud creak.

A rustling sound could be heard, as Bones sifted around in the trunk. Christopher had his eyes tightly closed; he wanted no part in seeing what was going on inside the makeshift coffin. He already felt dizzy and sick in such a way that he thought he might pass out at any given moment.

Bones closed the trunk, letting it fall shut with a piercing snap as the latch caught the upper hinge. In the trunk he had found a small brown bag, maybe even an old purse. "I've got something here," he said.

Christopher allowed his eyes to open, since the trunk was closed. "What is it?"

"Some kind of purse," Bones said, devoting all his attention to the mentioned item. He hesitantly reached his hand into the handbag, being careful not to destroy whatever was inside as it must be very old. He felt something, clutched it with his thumb and forefinger, and slowly pulled out an old, ratty leather-bound book. Bones began thumbing through the browned pages, and soon paused. "It's someone's drawings…."

Christopher, Kylie and James rushed over to Bones as he showed them a page from the book. On the page there was a rather skilled drawing of two rabbits—two blue rabbits.

Bones continued to flip through the pages, and there were more pictures, some of them rather crude and others showing more effort and impressive technique. There was a drawing of a blue bear, a stick house and some stick people, and a drawing of a cave entrance everyone knew all too well.

"Is this Alena's?" Kylie asked, her voice trembling.

Bones turned to the very last page, and on it was a handwritten sentence. "Property of Alena Cartwright," he read.

Christopher felt his feet go soft beneath him, and he immediately fell to his knees in the dirty brown water. This was much worse than they had even originally thought. This wasn't the body of one of the parents. This was Alena's body.

"My grandfather…," Kylie said as she let herself fall down to the floor with Christopher, "…was responsible for Alena's disappearance…. It doesn't make any sense. I thought they found her necklace and shoes in the cave? What is she doing here?"

"This doesn't make any sense at all," James whispered, his gaze firm on the book that Bones was holding.

"Regardless…," Bones began as he carefully placed the book down onto the top of the chest, "…she's here…this is what we've been sent to find: not Alena's mother…not Alena's father, but Alena herself. For some reason, she ended up here…her body ended up here."

"I've never felt ashamed about who I am…," Kylie said as tears came streaming down her face. "I've never felt bad about my last name before, but now I wish it was something else…anything else. I hate my last name. I hate my family…."

"It's okay…," Christopher said, placing an arm around Kylie's shoulders. "It's not your fault."

"I know…," Kylie whispered in stern anger. "I will just never acknowledge my last name, not ever again from this day on. I am no longer a Leiter."

"Just marry Christopher…," James said, trying to slightly elevate the mood of the situation, "…then you can be a Janes."

Bones shook his head at James. Now was apparently was not the time for making jokes. "We need to get the police down here," he said.

"What will we tell them, though?" Christopher asked, drawing a complete blank. "Won't they suspect Kylie's mother?"

"Shouldn't," Bones said as he slowly got to his feet. "This was before her time…."

"Not before my grandfather's time, though…," Kylie said.

"Right," Bones said as he started back to the cellar door. "I'm going to go up and make a few phone calls. I'll be right back, and don't worry; I'll take care of everything."

With Bones gone, Christopher turned to Kylie. He could see that she was still very upset at all that had happened. In a way he had wished that she had never gone into the cave, especially with such a horrible result. He wondered how it must feel, to hate your own last name…to hate a part of you and your family so much that you would turn your back on it forever. He could definitely understand why she would choose to do so; however, he could not even begin to fathom the pain it must have brought.

Christopher tightened his embrace on Kylie and looked deep into her eyes. They were red and still damp from all the tears. "I don't care what your last name is…it will never change the way I feel about you."

Kylie returned Christopher's kind words with a genuine smile. She brought her body against his, wrapping her arms around him. She rested her head upon his chest, and just let go completely. Tears streamed down her eyes.

Christopher ran a hand through her hair and just

let her be there, let her release all of the feelings that she was holding inside of her.

James took delayed steps over to the pair, and then hugged the both of them tightly. “We’ve come a long way. I think we’ve really done something good here….”

“Yeah,” Christopher whispered, nodding to James.

“Yeah…,” Kylie said. “Alena won’t just be a story or legend anymore…she’ll be a real person who disappeared…. She’ll be buried, she’ll be remembered….”

Bones came jogging down the stairs, and behind him was a tall lanky man dressed in a large black trench coat. It was someone that Christopher had never seen before. The man marched over to the three, rubbing his scruffy beard nervously.

“Guys,” the man in black said, holding out a hand to Christopher, “I don’t believe we’ve met. I’m Jack Olen.”

Christopher told him his name. “So you’re Jack Olen,” he said. He looked a lot more different than what Christopher had expected. He towered over the three, being much taller than even James, who they considered to be pretty tall. Jack had short-trimmed brown hair and looked as though he belonged in some kind of big city law office, rather than the country.

"Good to know you," Jack said as he extended a hand to James. "Jack Olen."

"James Janes," James replied as he looked up to the tall man.

"Kylie," Jack said as he reached out for her hand as well.

"Jack," Kylie said, "good to see you."

"Definitely could have been under better circumstances, though," Jack said as he nervously eyed the trunk on the ground. "So this is the problem then."

"Yep," Bones said as he came up behind him. "Mr. Leiter and Grandpa Leiter were hiding a pretty big secret down here all these years."

"Yeah, I'd have to say so," Jack said as he kneeled before the trunk and flipped through the small leather-bound sketchbook. "Janice would never be a part of this, though; I'll make sure that they know about that. I know all the cops up in Springfield really well, so don't worry; she or Kylie won't be bothered with this."

"That's why I called you," Bones said with a confident smile. "You have a strange way of being able to take care of just about everything that goes bad around here."

"Yeah, I know," Jack said with a smile and a nod. "I'm working on my guardian angel status. What can I say? I'm just lucky like that."

"So how do we handle this?" Bones asked, folding his arms at his chest.

"Well, the way I've figured it," Jack said, rubbing his beard as he thought out a solution. "We'll run the kids back to your house. The police will be here in about an hour or so. We'll say that you were watching the shop here for Janice and the electrical went out. So, you had to come down here to change the fuse, and noticed the wall here had collapsed due to the storm. Won't be too much of a stretch with all the water here, not to mention the whole lot of it flowing through the wall back there. So you called me for help and we found this down here. That sound good to you?"

"When it comes from your lips," Bones said, "anything sounds good. I bet you could convince horses to eat horseshit."

"Well…," Jack said, thinking it over a moment, "…probably, but that's what I get paid the big bucks for."

"Well, let's get you guys home…," Bones said as he nodded to Christopher, Kylie, and James. "You've done your part; now just let us do ours."

"Yep," Jack said as he clapped his hands and rubbed them together. "Bones, you hold down the fort here. I've seen your truck, and it's an embarrassment operable vehicles—I'll get these guys home."

Christopher, Kylie, and James piled into Jack's truck. This truck, however, was a far cry nicer than

Bones'. The truck, for one thing, was massive. Jack had to help everyone step up into it. Once inside it was like stepping into a nice hotel room, with nice, comfortable seats, immediate heating, and a working radio. Christopher looked around the inside of the truck in amazement. He had almost forgotten what a well-maintained vehicle looked like on the inside.

With one quick turn of the key, Jack started the engine.

"Nice truck," James said as the truck jolted ahead. "You should convince Bones to get one of these...."

"Convince Bones...," Jack repeated with a laugh. He searched for something he found suitable on the radio station, and finally pausing at a familiar rock song. "He's a character. I think he's the only person in the world I couldn't convince something to."

"Have you known him long?" Christopher asked.

"Yeah," Jack said. "We've had run-ins quite a few times. In fact, there was a time when he was probably the only one in this tiny little town that would talk to me, save for Janice, of course. First time I was rightfully asked to dinner was by him and Catharine."

"He thinks pretty highly of you," Christopher said, "especially after you rescued him from the rainstorm and brought his dog back."

"Yeah, I know," Jack said. "I'm 'the nicest ass

bandit he's ever met,' according to him."

Everyone in the car had a nice little laugh at that statement. *That is so like Bones,* Christopher thought. He was nice and caring in a way that was just a little bit off, but never so far off as to be inconsiderate. He did respect how Bones was always so upfront and honest about everything, especially since after his parents died and no one else in the family was so honest or caring.

"Can I ask you a question?" Kylie asked, yet her words were soft and uncertain.

"Kylie, of course you can," Jack said.

"Why are you helping us out? Aren't you weirded out with what we found?" Kylie asked, still sounding rather uncomfortable. It was almost as if she had been through so many bad things that the thought of something good happening just had to be outright questioned.

"Well…," Jack said, tilting his head to the side and then shrugging his shoulders. "Remember when you guys ended up at my house, when your father was chasing you?"

"Yeah…," Kylie answered, nodding in reply. "I never really got to thank you for that. What you did to save us was amazing."

"Well, sometimes in my line of work I do things that I don't feel good about, things I don't like to do even…," Jack said. "Doing things for you and Bones are things that make me feel better about myself. Besides, I trust both of you completely. So, if you weren't involved, I believe it."

"That's an awesome thing to say," James said, smiling.

"I don't know how to ever thank you," Kylie said.

"I do what I can," Jack said as he drove the truck into the rock driveway of the Janes house. "So forget about it."

Christopher waved as he, James, and Kylie reached the front door and the exhausted trio made their way into the house. Jack honked the horn of the big truck twice as he backed out of the driveway, turned around, and the truck's red taillights gradually faded into the night.

Christopher made it to the couch first, plopping down and kicking his feet up on the table. Kylie quickly followed suit, wrapping her arms around Christopher as she sat down. James did as well, and sat on the other side of Christopher. They sat there quietly for many moments. No one was sure what to say, or even where to start.

Finally, it was James who spoke: "Do you think now that we've found her…do you think everything is over?"

"I don't know…," Kylie whispered as she rested

her head on Christopher's shoulder. She was visibly exhausted from the day that they had had. "Either way, I'm thankful for everything that has come out of this…."

"Yeah…," Christopher said, smiling down at Kylie. "In a way, I have the cave to thank for the time I have with you…."

"Not to mention our lives," James added. "Remember the storm…."

"Yeah…," Christopher quietly replied. Then he paused, remembering something that he had forgotten. With his free hand he reached down into his pocket, pulling out the large claw with his name on it. "I don't think the business with the cave is over, even if our business with Alena is…."

"I almost completely forgot about that," James said with a heavy sigh. "And for once I thought everything might be going back to normal around here."

"Around here?" Kylie said sarcastically. "Nothing will ever be normal here. Not ever again…."

"I wonder what the cave is," Christopher said as he fidgeted around with the claw. "I wonder if we'll ever know…."

"Time will tell…," James said as he closed his eyes, leaning his head against the back of the couch. "Only time will tell."

The three slowly nodded off, letting exhaustion

finally get the better of them. Sleeping there, side by side on a couch that almost seemed way too small to ever seat three, there existed a sort of moment of pure contentment. Christopher was so tired, and it was so comforting to have Kylie's head next to his heart that he could think of no other moment that he might have been more relaxed, more fulfilled.

It was a few hours before Bones finally came to the front door, waking James up first, who gave Christopher a good shake, and then Christopher, in turn, woke Kylie. Bones slowly trudged in through the door, tossing his wet coat to the ground and letting out a heavy exhausted sigh.

"Everything's fine," he said as noticed that everyone had woken up.

"Good," James said as he stretched his arms high into the air.

"The police will be around for a while in shifts. Mr. Leiter has got a lot to answer to if they ever find him around here," Bones said as he made his way into the kitchen to pour himself a drink. "So at least we can feel safe about that."

"Thank God," Kylie said as she lay back against Christopher's chest. "And thank you…you were really great today."

"Small thing to do," Bones said with a smile and a chuckle, "for a future granddaughter."

Christopher's face reddened considerably, and Kylie giggled.

"I think you've still got a few years to go...," James said, laughing as well.

"Anyway...," Bones said as he poured himself a big drink. "I'm done...I'm spent...I'm finished for the day. Christopher?"

"Yeah?" Christopher asked, very tired to the point of his eyes being tiny slits.

"Do you mind taking the couch and giving up your room for the night?" Bones asked as he made his way over to his bedroom door.

"No, not at all," Christopher answered.

"Lucky you," James said, chuckling. "Just married and already sleeping on the couch."

"Oh, be quiet already," Christopher said as he gave James a good push, forcing him off of the couch that was now his bed. "No one wants to hear you anymore...."

Kylie laughed as she got to her feet. "Good night, honey," Kylie said with a giggle as she reached down to give Christopher a long embrace.

"Good night...," Christopher whispered with a smile on his face, but then he shook his head. Everyone was picking on him now, it seemed. "If you get lonely, sleep with Fred…he's a good dog."

"Who?" Kylie asked.

"His stuffed dog. He's a grown-ass man sleeping with a stuffed dog," James said.

"Just shut up already, James," Christopher said as he shook his head once more, very annoyed. "Do you ever listen to yourself?"

"Yeah, and I can't get enough of me," James said over his shoulder as he turned to leave.

"I think it's cute," Kylie said. "It'll make me think of you…."

As Kylie and James made their way upstairs to bed, Christopher finally let himself fall back onto the couch. He took in a deep breath of air and released it into the night. His heart was troubled by the discovery of Alena's body, yet, on the other hand, he had so many things to be happy about he didn't know exactly how he should feel. He guessed that was just how life is sometimes, though; good things happen at the same time that bad things do. There's no real set order or alternation involved. Things just come when they want to come. Christopher thought back to what his father had said: "Changes change, because we are people who have no authority to change them." Had he finally gotten it right that time?

He shook his head, hoping all the thoughts and memories could be chased away like butterflies resting upon his mind. He tried to think hard about nothing at all, eventually resting his mind on Kylie, and he eventually fell asleep. He was sure that tonight he was going to stay asleep, too. He was so exhausted. However, someone had other plans.

Christopher woke up to find himself looking at the digital clock across the room. He thought he had heard someone whispering. His eyes were heavy and the red numbers on the digital display were blurry in the darkness of the room. He couldn't remember what had awoken him, or even why he had decided to check the time. He slowly let his eyes focus on the clock, and, to his complete disappointment, it was just flashing *12:00* over and over. The power must have gone out. Perhaps it was storming again.

He slowly got up to a sitting position on the couch, not sure why he did so. It was almost as though something was compelling him to rise, some strange force both unknown and unseen. Whatever reason he was awake, he didn't really want to be. His body still felt the exhaustion that it had earlier.

He scanned around the room, searching for whatever had awoken him. He focused on the picture window, and for a moment thought he had seen a shadow there. He unconsciously let himself fall back against the couch, and panic shot through him as he felt a pain in his back. He quickly reached back, sure that something was either biting him or cutting into him, and then he pulled the large claw that Kylie had gotten in the cave out from under him. He shook his head as he set the claw down on the table. "My fault for leaving it on the couch, I guess…," Christopher whispered to himself as he got ready to lie back down.

However, just as he was about to relax, the same shadow he had seen streaking past the window reappeared, only, this time, it lingered. Christopher, at a snail's pace, got to his feet and made his way to the large picture window. There was definitely something there. Something small.

The shadow turned toward him, exposing a pair of glowing eyes and causing Matthew to fall back in shock. He realized what it was, or rather, who it was—it was Stinky. Matthew placed his hand against the window, careful to not startle the stray cat. "Hey, Stinky…haven't seen you since that first day in the cave…."

The cat curiously placed his paw up to meet Christopher's, and for a moment it was as though they were touching. *That's just cute,* Christopher thought as he watched the small gray-and-white cat. "Was it you, eh? Was it you who woke me up?" he asked.

Very tired, Christopher slowly removed his hand from the window, turning back to the couch. He was convinced that he had found the culprit and was now ready to retire. As he took a few steps forward he felt something rub against the back of his leg. Startled, he whirled around and glanced down. Stinky was there at his feet.

"That's impossible…," Christopher whispered, more to himself than to the cat. "The window…"

Stinky looked up and met Christopher's gaze, the cat's eyes glowing in the dark of the room. It let out a single meow, which came out not only in sound but in complete word form, as though the word had been written down and forced out of the cat's mouth. The word swirled around and danced in the air of the living room, eventually floating up to the ceiling and disappearing in a small puff of hot white smoke.

There's something real familiar about this, Christopher thought. "I should be scared, but, honestly, I have to say that I've come to expect this kind of thing," he said as he reached down and carefully petted Stinky, rubbing behind his ears.

He then shuffled over to the couch, the cat following at his heels. Christopher was a little freaked out. After all, the cat had passed through the window, and then an onomatopoeia—*meow*—had gone up and floated away like smoke from a cigar pipe. Really, though, Christopher was just too exhausted. He half-believed that he was even awake at this point.

Then, as if things could not possibly get any stranger, the cat leapt onto the coffee table in front of the couch and started talking. Not cat-talk either—nothing even sounding remotely like a cat's meow or any other sound one would normally come to expect from a cat. This was regular speech, the usually-reserved-only-for-people kind of talk.

"Are you coming tomorrow?" the cat asked. It sounded more like a woman or girl's voice; it was soft and rather gentle.

Christopher cocked his head, much like he had seen Poppy and Kate do when they were curious about things. "Did you seriously just ask me a question?"

"You must come soon," the cat said. Each of the cat's words followed with a little puff of bluish smoke from its mouth. The smoke would glow for a bit, and then dissipate into the air. "As the water advances, so do the bad things…."

"What bad things?" Christopher asked, more concerned than weirded out by the thought of the talking cat.

"Tomorrow," the cat whispered. It slowly made its way across the living room, leaping up onto the shelf underneath the picture window.

"I…," Christopher said, pausing for a moment as he was very unsure how to answer. Should he go ahead and tell the cat he was uncertain about going back in, and whether it would really make a difference at all? "Yeah…."

Stinky looked to Christopher, his expressionless face offering no reply. Then, as quickly as lightning, the cat jumped right through the window. Not causing any damage, of course, to either itself or the window. However a strange blue layer of glowing smoke was left behind. It rippled and danced like water as it slowly faded, mixing with the regular air.

"Well, I guess I have to go," Christopher said to himself, letting himself relax. Talking to himself helped him relax, too, sometimes. "Unless this is just a dream. It feels kind of like a dream…so, in theory, it could be a dream. Who am I kidding…?" Christopher finally concluded. "This is not a dream…dreams aren't this damn strange."

Chapter 14: A Home in the Earth

Mostly asleep, Christopher attempted to slap at whatever was tickling his nose. He didn't know whether it was some sort of bug, or something much more sinister. After the events of the night before, which, surprisingly enough, he kind of remembered, he came to expect almost anything.

He slowly opened his eyes. It was still very early and the room was filled with the dull gray light of a cloudy summer morning. He slowly got up to a sitting position on the couch, looking around the room for whatever had awakened him. Seeing nothing at all before him, he let out a great big yawn, his arms stretched up and outward, toward to the ceiling.

Just as he was at the highest point of his morning stretch, two arms quickly came at him from behind the couch. He jumped in shock, letting out a strange little squeak. Then, realizing what was going on, he shook his head and let out a little laugh. “Kylie…,” he said.

Kylie bounded over the couch, embracing Christopher in her arms as she giggled deviously. “I couldn’t it help it,” she said. “Besides, I couldn’t wait any longer to see you.”

“I don’t mind,” he smiled, placing his hand on her arm. “What time is it anyway?”

“I don’t know!” she said, sitting down next to him on the couch. “You know, there’s no clock in your room.”

“Yeah I know,” he said, remembering from the night before that the downstairs clock was still flashing *12:00* over and over. “I’m not even sure if there is a correct clock in this entire house.”

“I’d guess it’s seven,” she said, looking out the large picture window. “It looks like about seven or so.”

“It’s not raining today,” he said as he stared out the window as well. “I’m surprised. I figured I’d never see a day without rain again.”

“Day’s just begun,” she whispered, bringing her head to rest against his shoulder. “Can I ask you something?”

“Of course.…” He gently placed his arm around her.

"What do you think will happen to us?" she asked quietly, sounding just a little bit sad. "I mean, when I have to move."

"I don't know," Christopher said. It wasn't as though he hadn't thought about that at all. In fact, it was always in his thoughts ever since he found out, hiding in the far corners of his mind and coming out now and again. If things hadn't been so crazy lately, he figured that he might have thought about it a heck of a lot more. "I hope that we can see each other, even when you're in Nevada."

"Me too," Kylie whispered. "Promise me that you won't forget about me…. Not that I think that you would. It's just that I know it will be hard for me to not get to see you, but I'll feel better inside if I know that you're at least thinking of me."

"I promise," he said, squeezing her closer to him. "I promise I will think about you every day."

Christopher felt a bit sad at the thought, but it was all he really had to offer her. Life had just simply arranged itself in such a way that made things very difficult to think about. The two of them, being so young, had no real control over where their lives would lead them. It was almost as though they were two leaves floating down a stream, and up ahead the stream forked in two directions. The most that they could hope for was that the two separate streams would join once again.

"I hate thinking about leaving," Kylie said, her

voice heavy and sad. "I don't even know what the place I'm moving too will be like; I guess it will be a lot like when you moved here, right?"

"Yeah," Christopher said as he thought back to his first day in Pine Hallow. "I'd imagine so, but eventually I think it will be all right. Besides, at least you are going somewhere where you don't have to worry about your father anymore."

"I know," Kylie said, slowly bringing her face up next to his. "I just wish you could come with me." She quickly leaned in and pressed her lips against Christopher's, kissing him softly. "But in a way…," she whispered as she slowly parted her lips from his, "…you will be."

Christopher blushed at the thought and nodded in agreement. He nodded a lot when he didn't want to talk or was utterly speechless, like now. She seemed to have a talent for making him become completely brainless at times.

The two sat alone upon the couch in silence, their bodies close together as they watched the day outside grow ever brighter. The clouds eventually broke, and a streak of sunlight could be seen shining down into the trees. It seemed as though the morning was putting on a little show just for them as the clouds moved swiftly overhead and beams of sun shone down in streams of beautiful, golden light.

It was Bones who was awake next, coming out of his bedroom fully dressed for a change, and almost immediately making his way to the kitchen.

"Morning," Bones said, smiling at the two before passing through. "Hope you weren't there all night long, Kylie. I'll have quite a bit of explaining to do to your mother."

"She came down to wake me up," Christopher announced, chuckling. "Besides, we have a busy day today."

Bones popped his head back into the living room for a moment. "Going back down to the cave then?"

"Yeah," Christopher said. "Probably for the last time too."

"As long as we've done what we were meant to…," Kylie said.

"Wish I could be there," Bones said as he made his way into the room, a cup of coffee in his hands and an unlit cigarette in his mouth.

"You could come down, too," Christopher said, making a space on the couch for Bones to sit. "I'm sure you'd be welcome."

"Can't today; I've got another damned doctor appointment. Afraid if I miss again they're going to call me up all angry…again," Bones said, clearly annoyed at the thought.

"Are you okay?" Kylie asked. This was, after

all, the first time she had heard about him going to a doctor.

"Yeah…," Bones said. He let out a little smile as he lit his smoke. "Just probably pulled somethin' last night with all that sledgehammer action."

"You really did a number on that wall though," Christopher said, laughing at the memory.

"I know!" Bones replied, alternating between his cigarettes and coffee. "I'm surprised my own house hasn't run away in fear yet." He slowly got to his feet, popping his knuckles as he slipped his shoes on. "You can expect me back later, probably; let me know what happens in the cave, all right?"

"All right," Christopher said with a smile and a nod.

"Right then," Bones said as he opened the front door. "And be careful, too; I don't want to come home to any kind of sad news."

"I'll make sure of it," Kylie answered confidently.

James awoke that morning a few moments after Bones had already left for Springfield. It seemed very unusual to Christopher, seeing that he was actually, for the first time, awake before James was. Christopher didn't think much of it and therefore had forgotten to even ask about what kept him asleep so long.

After a quick lunch, the three went around to the back of the house, leashing up Poppy and then making their way to Alena's Cave. Walking along the stream, Christopher marveled at how wonderful the day was shaping up to be. The sky seemed to grow a more brilliant blue with each passing moment and tiny white clouds blew so swiftly overhead it looked as though they were really ships set to launch on an endless sea.

"I'm hoping since there's no rain today…," James said with Poppy's leash in hand as the four arrived at the entrance of the cave, "…that it won't be that bad in here."

"I hope so, too," Christopher said, pushing away the fallen branches around the entrance.

However, to their deep displeasure, the cave entrance had flooded even further. James took the first step in, handing Poppy's leash over to Christopher before he did. The water came almost all the way up to his knees as he trudged forward, careful to keep to the wall of the cave where the water was its most shallow.

"It's pretty bad," Kylie said as she gripped onto Christopher's hand.

"It's not that bad up here," James announced. He splashed further on into the cave. "It's not nearly as deep."

"I'd hate to see this place if it rains anymore though," Christopher said as he led both Kylie and Poppy on ahead.

The four made their way down the passage, the water's current swift at their feet as they approached the drop-off.

"It sounds like Niagara Falls down there now," James yelled over the sound of cascading water.

The group made their way down the winding passage. It didn't have much water running down it the times they had visited beforehand (it was mostly dampness), but now, however, water trickled down it in a multitude of little streams, and the ground was slick and droplets rained down from the ceiling in a hundred different places. It was almost like being under an indoor rain cloud. As the group reached the bottom of the chamber, things only got worse.

"The water is so close to the window now…," Christopher said, being barely audible over the nearby falls. He noticed that what was once before a small series of streams tumbling from the drop-off was now a roaring deluge, and what was once just a tiny pool in the corner now almost completely filled the bottom of the chamber, covering even the large white cross painted on the cave floor. He made his way through the water and to the only dry area, which was directly in front of the magical window. For a moment he thought back to the strange happenings the night before. Something about the closer the water came to the window, the closer the bad things came. "I don't think we'll have many more trips here…."

"Maybe there won't need to be," Kylie yelled

over the sound of crashing water.

"So I guess you will be the last one to get to go…," James said, sounding a little upset at the notion that he may never get another chance to enter the window.

"Maybe I don't have to go alone…," Christopher said, nodding to James.

"Don't tempt me," James said with a chuckle. "Besides, Kylie and Poppy can't pull the both of us out if we get ourselves in trouble in there."

"Right," Christopher said as James handed him the same length of rope that had been used so many times before. "Well, I guess I'll go check things out."

"Be careful," Kylie said as she wrapped her arms around Christopher, a section of the rope in her left hand. "Come back to me."

"Give us a tug if you need us," James said.

"Will do." Christopher smiled confidently to the two, pausing for a moment to reach down and give Poppy a quick scratching behind her ears.

Christopher took a deep breath, pulling up his courage from within him. Taking a confident step forward, crouched down and let both of his feet enter through the window. The cold came instantly, seizing his legs and burning him as strong currents of air blasted him. Taking a page from Bones' previous actions,

Christopher gripped his hands firmly against the cave floor and in one swift movement launched his entire body through the window, almost accidentally catching his head on the windowsill on the way down.

As it had before, the world around him disappeared completely, replaced by endless black nothingness. There was the familiar sound of something ripping or tearing, although coming much more loudly, since it was now *his* sound to experience. As he fell, or floated, in the darkness he counted down the moments until things would finally be normal, or at least familiar.

The room slowly came into focus around him; it looked pretty much the same as it had the time before. Everything still shone and glittered in the light, everything still felt strange. His heart was pounding in his ears and his lungs struggled as though they were filled with water. Remembering to signal that he was okay, Christopher laboriously made his way to face the window. He stared at James, Kylie and Poppy. They looked strange sitting there at the window, as though they were completely frozen in time. James' mouth was open as if he had been frozen as he was talking. If only he had the ability, Christopher felt as though he would have gotten a good laugh out of it. He'd like James to be frozen mid-sentence more often. Instead gave a little thumbs-up, laboring to get his arms down as he turned back to the room to begin his search.

He wondered what he should be looking for as he bounded about the room. He checked the bed, yet found nothing of interest there. He checked the dresser, and still there was nothing that was in focus.

Christopher turned his head about, scanning the room as best he could. As far as he could tell, there wasn't a single thing in the room that didn't shimmer or seem wavy as if it was underwater.

What am I supposed to find here? Christopher thought as he hopped to an empty corner of the room. He slowly placed a hand against the wall there. Instead of being smooth like a normal wall might, the wall felt as though it was covered in either sand or frost. He ran a hand down the wall, revealing a little five-pointed trail that sparkled and flashed brightly. The trail quickly reformed into, the bright lights slowly disappearing as the whole thing seemed to freeze back over.

Strange, but pointless, Christopher thought. He turned around, bounding his way toward the center of the room. He glanced back to the window. Kylie and James were still frozen in the same exact spot that they had been at before. Christopher wondered if time almost completely stopped for him in the room.

Christopher made his way to the door in the center of the room. It was the last place that he would try, for deep down inside he secretly wanted nothing to do with it at all. He didn't know why he feared it so much. Maybe he just feared the possibilities and the unknown elements that might exist beyond the door.

Ever so cautious, Christopher slowly forced his hand down upon the doorknob. *Be locked,* he wished to himself, closing his eyes and giving the knob a quick turn. Instead of being locked, however, the door suddenly opened, revealing a brilliant golden light behind it. Christopher stepped back in shock as the door opened fully before him. The golden light was so bright it temporary blinded him. He brought his hand up to shield himself from whatever existed inside. Eyes tightly closed, he could feel his body burning. The light was so hot that it literally felt as though it was burning his skin away from his body.

After a few unbearable moments, a cooling air slowly formed around him. Even though his eyes were shut he could feel the brilliant light slowly creep away, and the intense red hue fade from the blackness. He opened his eyes, lowering his arm from his face. To his surprise, he was back at the cave entrance.

However, this was not the same cave entrance that he had entered earlier today. The pool was no longer flooded and the circular walkway around it was completely clear and clean. Sunshine filtered softly through the cave entrance. It was bright and warm, not constricted or blocked by the tree branches, branches that no longer seemed to exist in that version of the entrance. Christopher placed a hand against the wall, wondering if it was all real or not. It felt real enough. The stone was cold and smooth against the palm of his hand. The air felt real enough as well, and it was nice and cool. A breeze drifted into the cave, kicking up a handful of red and brown leaves. The leaves came to rest gently upon the water in the pool, which rippled and sparkled in the sunlight.

Christopher ventured out from the entrance. The woods were in full fall colors; the reds, yellows and oranges contrasting beautifully with the pale blue sky above. The entire ground was covered in the fallen foliage and the stream was but a mere trickle buried underneath it all.

"It's a lovely day," a girl said from behind Christopher.

Startled, Christopher wheeled around, almost falling out of the mouth of the cave completely. There, at the edge of the pond, sat a young woman. The woman had bright, brownish-blond hair that was softly blowing in the breeze. Her skin was pale and her eyes dark, yet they appeared kind. The woman's lips were a dull red as she smiled, slowly nodding in Christopher's direction.

Christopher stared at the woman in complete disbelief. Was this Alena? Even more disturbing was the creature sitting next to her. It appeared to be some kind of bear-shaped animal made completely of bluish smoke—the same kind of smoke that the rabbits in the house and the cat's voice were made out of. The bear sat next to her, motionless and faceless. "Are you…?" he began to ask.

"Alena," the woman whispered as she reached into her purse, pulling out a piece of white charcoal. She then went to work, drawing a picture of a large bird on the cave wall.

"What's that?" he asked, still somewhat frightened at the sight of the blue bear made of smoke.

"He's a friend," Alena whispered as she continued drawing. "He used to be a really bad memory, but he's changed now."

"A bad memory?" he asked, staring at the faceless creature.

"Yep," she said. "I call him Face, mostly because he doesn't have one. He never really had one either."

"What are you doing here?" he asked, finally remembering that he was here with a purpose, after all.

"I pretty much live here," she said, turning to him and smiling. "I pretty much live here and there. Sometimes I live in other places, sometimes in other seasons. Right now I'm feeling like fall.... Tomorrow, though, I might feel like winter. I've wanted it to snow lately."

"So you live here, in the room of the cave?" he asked. He was confused at her answer, which seemed to not really be an answer at all.

"The room," she said as she attended to her drawing. "I go there to sleep sometimes. That's pretty much my room."

"I have to ask...," he started, slowly making his way closer to Alena, and then stopping in his tracks as Face moved in closer as well. "Did you have us come down here...for the memories?"

"I helped," she answered abruptly.

“Is there someone else here?” he asked, even more confused at her answer.

Alena looked toward Christopher and sadly shook her head, looking down to the ground. “No…no one is real.”

“But, you said that you helped?” he asked, still very confused yet not wanting to make Alena any sadder.

“I helped,” she said with a smile creeping back to her face. “I’m not the reason why the window is in the cave after all.”

“What is the reason?” he asked, hoping that maybe he would finally be making a breakthrough.

“The earth,” she whispered, looking around as though someone might be listening. “I think.”

“You don’t really know?” he asked, sounding a little disappointed.

“Sorry,” Alena replied, noting Christopher’s disappointment. “I do know that you helped me in return, if that helps you out any….”

“About the cellar of the store…,” he whispered. It was a subject that he didn’t exactly know how to approach. How exactly do you ask someone why they’re dead? Or how do you tell them that you’ve found their body, especially when said person is sitting right before you, looking as alive as any other person in the world?

"You'd like to know about it, right?" she asked, smiling happily as she fumbled through her purse, searching for something. "I can show you…."

"You can show me?" he asked, slightly concerned.

"I'd like to show you," she said. "I'd like it if someone else out there knew about it. Maybe someday my parents can hear about it, right?"

"I don't know," he said. He thought about it. It had been so long, would her parents even be alive? "I'll watch, though, if you really want me to."

"All right," she said as she got to her feet, dusting off her long powder-blue dress. "Take Face's hand."

"Do what?" he thought as the giant blue bear made its way over to him. He watched as the bear rumbled forward, tiny lines of blue smoke dancing off of its body as the entire surface of the bear's form danced and swirled about. It stopped directly in front of him, extending a large, clawed hand.

Christopher timidly held his hand out, looking at the swirling blue paw of the bear. "All right…," he whispered, trying to convince himself to do so.

"He's quite harmless," Alena said, noticing his concern.

"Right," he whispered as he grasped Face's paw. The moment their hands touched everything turned dark. Distantly, he heard the sound of music.

"These are my memories…. I was fifteen then. I'm still fifteen, though," Alena said, her voice reverberating in Christopher's head. Or could it be the other way around, and he was actually inside of Alena's head?

Christopher felt his eyes being forced open; he could feel his feet moving beneath and his hands swaying beside him. However, he had no direct control over any of these actions at all. It was almost as though he was a passenger in someone else's body. Christopher was filled with fear at the thought; he felt constricted, even a bit claustrophobic.

"Calm down," she said gently. "Just watch…. These are my memories…. Just let go and you will be free."

Doing as Alena said, Christopher relaxed his mind, and he could feel himself rising up out of Alena's body and hanging in the air above her.

"There, that's better, isn't it?" Alena asked, although her voice did not come from the Alena that Christopher could now see below him. It resounded within his mind. "You can talk to me directly."

"I can?" Christopher asked, giving it a try.

"We can talk," she said. "No one else will

respond to you."

Christopher watched as the real Alena walked into the Bait 'n' Tackle shop, and, floating behind her, he followed her inside. She made her way past the display shelves to the back of the store, picking up a bottle of cream soda and picking through a handful of candies. A nice little tune played throughout the store, giving everything a comforting feeling. Alena slowly approached the counter, as if she was searching for someone.

"Mr. Leiter?" Alena asked, placing her items on the counter.

"Oh, sorry…," Mr. Leiter replied, getting up from underneath the counter. "Didn't see you there, dear…was stocking the tobacco…."

Christopher stared at Mr. Leiter. It was strange to see him in person, since he had already figured out what kind of person he was. He had cold dark eyes and a rough face. He looked as though he had been in a few fights, for he had a big scar running down the side of his face. He didn't look as old as Christopher thought he would. This had happened a long time ago after all. He looked as though he was in his early thirties or so, from Christopher's guess.

"It's all right," Alena whispered as she reached into her brown purse, searching for some coins.

Mr. Leiter placed her soda and candy into a brown paper sack, and then quickly waved her away.

"Don't worry about it; pretty girl like you doesn't have to pay me a thing."

"No, please," she protested, bringing out a few coins from her purse. "I don't mind."

"I won't take it," Mr. Leiter replied with a creepy, unsettling smile on his rough face. "Just your company is payment enough."

"Thank you, Mr. Leiter," she said rather uncomfortably, collecting her things and leaving the store. "Have a good day…."

"Oh, I will," he replied confidently.

Christopher followed behind Alena as she walked along the dirt road. He could feel the cool wind around him, and it seemed exactly like late fall. It was a rather amazing feeling, just being able to float along the air. Too bad it had to be under such conditions.

Alena reached an area that Christopher found rather familiar. It seemed as though she was making her way back to the cave.

"Your place is down this way," she said in Christopher's mind. "Bones hasn't lived there yet though."

Christopher stopped following Alena as a car barreled toward her off in the distance, kicking up dirt and dust in swirling clouds behind it. The old black car closed the gap between them in seconds, skidding to a stop next to her. It was Mr. Leiter. What was he doing all the way down here?

"Alena," Mr. Leiter announced as he rolled down the driver's-side window.

Alena nervously turned around, stopping dead in her tracks. "Yes, sir?"

"You need a ride somewhere?" Mr. Leiter asked.

"No, I'm fine," Alena said nervously. "Thank you, of course."

"Suit yourself," Mr. Leiter answered. "You shouldn't be playing down in that cave though; you know it's haunted by them Indian spirits, don't you?"

"I'm on my way home," Alena answered back, trying to change the subject.

"Good," Mr. Leiter replied. He slowly drove off, not taking his eyes off of Alena for even a moment.

Alena made her way into the trees, following the stream and eventually arriving at the cave. Christopher followed behind her, in awe of the area. It was a lot like he remembered it from his time; only, the cave entrance was a lot more clean and clear. She carefully sat down against the cave wall, retrieving her soda from the brown bag and taking a big drink. Letting out a little burp, she set the bottle down as she rummaged through her purse and pulled out a blue piece of charcoal.

Alena whistled a little tune as she drew a picture of a blue house, placing a few stick people around the building. Hearing a strange sound outside, she quickly placed the charcoal piece onto the ground and peered over her shoulder. Shaking her head for a moment, she picked the charcoal up, content that no one was there.

Christopher watched in silence as he saw a looming shadow fall over Alena. The shadow of Mr. Leiter grew taller and taller, enveloping her. He wished in that moment that he could warn her, yet she was unable to hear any of his attempts.

Alena's eyes slowly turned to Mr. Leiter as the piece of chalk dropped from her trembling hand. "Mr. Leiter…"

Mr. Leiter reached down and grabbed a hold of Alena's hand, yanking her up to her feet. "You shouldn't be playing down here. Your parents would be worried about you."

"Yes," Alena whispered, her body shaking. "I'm sorry…I'll head home now."

Mr. Leiter drew her closer, and she could smell the stinking warmth of his breath, could feel his eyes on her.

"Don't worry," he said; "I'm not going to tell on you."

"All right," Alena whispered, trying to free her arm as best she could. "Please…just let go, and I'll head home now. I promise."

Instead of releasing her, Mr. Leiter only gripped her arm tighter. He pulled himself even closer to her. She could feel his other hand running down her back. "Don't worry, I won't tell a soul," he said in a sick, husky voice.

Alena quickly pushed back with all of her strength, and Mr. Leiter stumbled back a few paces, yet she was unable to break free of his hold. "Please! Just let go of me!" she pleaded, flinging her free hand at his face.

Mr. Leiter caught her sailing hand, tossed it aside, and then punched Alena squarely in the jaw, sending her sprawling to the ground. "You little bitch. All you had to do was *listen.* Why can't you even listen?"

"Please…" Alena coughed, holding a hand to her bleeding mouth.

Mr. Leiter shook his head, sweat pouring down his face. He reached down and grabbed a hold of Alena's leg, twisting it until she gasped. "You stupid little bitch. I'm going to have to teach you a few things."

Alena kicked fiercely at him, trying to free her leg. She managed to catch him right in the side of the knee, and he released his grip in surprise and pain and his legs buckled under him slightly. Without hesitating another moment she jumped her feet, crying out and limping a little from the sudden pain that wasn't there before. She ran as fast as she could down the back passage of the cave.

Christopher watched in complete horror as Mr. Leiter calmly regained his composure. His eyes were slated and black like obsidian and resembled the eyes of a snake. His fists clenched and his breathing was heavy and menacing. Christopher had known that this was going to be a bad experience, but had no idea it was going to be this bad. He didn't want to see another moment of it.

"Get back here!" Mr. Leiter said, running down the passage at a lightning-quick pace.

Christopher strained his eyes to see in the dimness passageway. Was he behind her?

"I'm up ahead," Alena's voice said inside his head. "I'm there…."

Christopher could barely make out the Alena's faint form. She was running as fast as she could through the darkness of the passage. As each footfall echoed throughout the cave, he felt his heart grow colder, and soon a moment of realization washed over him. Alena had no light to see by, and there was no trickling stream from the pond to warn her….

With a scream, Alena went forward and down over the edge, as though the ground had simply disappeared beneath her feet. Her scream could be heard for what seemed like an eternity, and then there was a sudden noise that ended the screaming. It was a noise that Christopher would remember for the rest of his life. It was a sound like that of something breaking, something coming apart. It was the sickeningly wet sound of collision.

"I didn't think that I had died," Alena whispered.

"I'm so sorry…," Christopher whispered. He felt so cold, just so cold and so sad. He felt as though he may never be happy again, that every moment would just be this darkness and sadness.

"I was still pretty aware of what was going on," Alena said softly. "I could hear him approaching, and I thought to myself…I thought, 'I'll just lay here and pretend to be dead and he'll just leave me alone. I'll just pretend not to move, and he'll get scared and he'll go away.' I remember it seemed like a long time had passed, and that maybe I should try and get up. My entire body felt like it was on fire, and I couldn't think clearly. Everything just felt like I was drowning. I tried to move, and then I realized that I couldn't."

"I'm so sorry…," Christopher said quietly, not wanting to listen anymore.

"Then I realized," Alena said, and continued, her voice very shaky, "I wasn't pretending. I remember I was laying there just thinking. What was I going to do, what was going to happen to me? I was so scared. I pleaded for someone to help me, though I couldn't talk. I couldn't even move my lips. Then, it happened."

Christopher watched as a light filled the room,

dimly revealing the outline of Alena's broken body against the cave floor. He watched in horror as more and more of her remains were revealed. Her blood stained the floor a bright red, her body twisted in ways that would give Christopher nightmares for many years to come. Then, turning to the source of light, Christopher realized what the light was.

"The window…," Christopher said as he floated next to Alena's body.

He watched in amazement as glowing blue smoke slowly steamed out of her body. First it was just a few trails of the blue swirling smoke, and then more and more came rushing out. They danced and moved in waves as they slowly shifted into a humanlike form.

"Someone must have heard me," Alena whispered. "They made a room for me. First a room, and then a whole world. A whole world where I could live in my memories…."

The new smoky form of Alena unsteadily traveled to the light of the window. It looked back at its former body for a moment, and then disappeared as a puff of smoke against the closed window, causing the window to disappear as well.

"I waited and watched for a long time," Alena said, a sense of sadness and longing in her voice. "He came back later with a lantern, and took my shoes and my cross-shaped necklace and left them here. He cleaned up as much of the mess as he could, and carried my body away. I never saw it again."

"He took you to the store…," Christopher whispered.

"Yes," Alena said. "I remember my parents coming down here with a few people that were helping them. They must have all been looking for me. I waited at the window, watching their every move. I remember banging on the window and yelling to them that I was here, yet no one ever noticed. One day while she was alone my mother painted a cross on the ground, and after that she never came back."

The world around Christopher faded away, engulfed by complete darkness. Then the painful golden light filled his eyes and eventually phased out. He was back at the cave entrance. Alena was still busy drawing on the wall, and Face sat next to her, protecting her.

Christopher fell to his knees, tears streaming from his eyes. "I'm so sorry…." It was all he could say to Alena. He had never seen such sadness, had never seen anything so terrible before.

Alena smiled as she stopped drawing, turning to face Christopher. "Please don't cry."

He rubbed his eyes, trying to hide how upset and despaired he was. "I'm sorry; it's just that I had no idea."

"I know," Alena said. Her eyes were bright and she smiled a little. "I'm glad that you were all here. I got to live in other memories through all of you. For that, I will be forever grateful."

"No…," Christopher said. "It's to you who we are grateful—for saving us, for showing us, and just for…everything."

"It's a good friendship, then," Alena replied, smiling more widely. "I've been alone for so many years…. I just want you to let Kylie know that I will never blame her for anything that her family has done…."

"I will," Christopher whispered as he sat on the ground. "She'll be very happy to hear that."

"Tell her to keep the cross," Alena said. "She deserves it; I never had the time to give her a properly good memory. I do feel bad about that."

"She's happy just to know the truth."

"And Christopher…," Alena said, a serious tone in her voice. "I don't know the future, but I have an idea that bad things can and might happen."

"Bad things?" he asked, remembering the night with the cat. "What are the bad things?"

"I can't say for certain," she said as she continued, her tone still very serious, "but, I know this: As the water grows closer and closer to the window, the closer and closer the bad things are."

"What can I do to stop them?" he asked, very much concerned.

"I don't know…," she said. "You'll just have to make choices—that's all you can do. Some may be right, some may be wrong. Some may bring the bad things closer and some may chase them off."

"So that's all I can do?" Christopher asked, sounding a bit frustrated. If he or anyone he cared about was in trouble he wanted some way to fight this trouble off, or some way to avoid it. How was he supposed to avoid fighting something that he didn't even know of?

"That's all anyone can hope to do," Alena said. "I'm afraid our time is passing."

Christopher glanced out the cave entrance. It was growing darker and the leaves on the trees were falling as heavily as rain. It appeared that the entire season of autumn was taking course in a matter of seconds.

"Can we come back?" he asked, desperately wanting to know more.

"I don't think there will be time," she said with a hint of sadness, shutting her eyes for a moment.

"Never again?" he asked. "There must be some way…."

"There is always a way, but there is never enough time. Sometimes things that are impossible are only impossible because our time is so short," Alena said as she rummaged through her purse, and then produced a large blue feather. Handing it over to Christopher, she continued, “Give this to James. I’d give him more, but he already has my heart.”

Christopher took the large feather, turning it over in his hand. “What’s it for?”

“He comes here in his dreams, you know?” Alena said with a smile.

Before Christopher could ask more questions he felt something tug tightly on his back. “No…,” he said aloud, to nobody in particular. “I’m not ready!” he screamed as a something yanked him violently out of Alena’s Cave and high up into the sky. For a moment he locked eyes with Alena as she ran out of the cave.

“There is always a way!” Alena yelled, her voice fading fast as she became smaller and smaller, and eventually disappeared completely behind some clouds.

Christopher soared backward through the air, and just as before the Earth lay before his eyes, beautiful as it slowly grew dark and stars filled the sky. He stared at the Earth with a newfound appreciation, knowing that he would never see it like this again. A huge tearing sound rippled across his body as he was flung backward through the window and out onto the cold cave floor.

Chapter 15: Journey to a Another World

However dim the light of the world may be, it is hope that brings us back from the edge. However sad the song may get, it is always the dance that makes us happy again.

Once the group was back at home, Christopher sat on the couch and carefully recounted every moment of his experience inside the cave. He left out no detail, going over everything that he had seen, and describing every sound that he had heard. As he finished, he reached down into his pocket, producing the large blue feather.

Kylie and James had listened intently throughout the entire story. When Christopher finished they sat there for many moments, digesting the entire affair. They were both completely speechless.

"So…," Christopher began with a heavy sigh as

he handed the blue feather over to James, "…this is for you."

"For me?" James asked as he ran the large feather through his fingers. "I don't know what this is for."

"I didn't get a good chance to ask," Christopher said, shaking his head. "She said it was all she had left to give you, something about you already having her heart."

"I wonder what that means…," James whispered.

"Maybe she likes you?" Kylie asked, sounding equally confused.

"Anyway," Christopher said, moving on. "Kylie, she wanted you to keep the cross, and she was sorry she didn't have time to give you a good memory…."

Kylie touched the cross around her neck, running the chain it hung from through her fingers. "I'm glad that we were able to help her."

"Me too…," James said, still carefully examining the big blue feather. "In a way, I'm really sad that this is all over…."

"Before I had to leave," Christopher said, "she said something about bad things coming. That, as the water grows closer and closer to the window, so do the bad things."

"What are 'the bad things'?" Kylie asked, very concerned at the thought.

"Bad spirits? Or bad people?" James asked.

"She didn't say…," Christopher answered. He really did wish that he had an answer to that question, though. It left him feeling rather frustrated, since he had no idea how to warn anyone or to even prepare for what might happen. It left him feeling helpless and frustrated. "I'm not sure if even she really knew," he said.

"What do we do then?" Kylie asked.

"I'm not sure if there's anything that we can do," Christopher answered quietly. "All she said that we could do was make choices."

The evening grew late as the three sat about the house, waiting for Bones to return so that they could tell him about the discoveries that they had made. Christopher and Kylie sat in front of the TV, their hands interlocked. The news was showing images of Saint Louis. Sections of the city along the Mississippi river were completely underwater.

"I didn't know it was that bad…," Christopher whispered, viewing the images of different neighborhoods that were completely submerged.

"I had no idea either," Kylie added. "My mom told me before she left that the entire Midwest was in danger of flooding."

"That's crazy," Christopher said as he shook his head. "And all this time I've been worrying about it being bad here. We haven't had it anywhere near as bad as they've had it."

"Bones is really late today," James said as he made his way out of the kitchen, a sandwich in his hands. "I wonder what time he'll finally decide to show up?"

"You remember last time," Christopher replied. "He came home so late, and had an entire trunk full of stuff. I had never seen so much new crap at one single moment in my whole life."

"Yeah," James said, shaking his head. "It was like Christmas in here."

"Aren't you worried, about him being gone so long?" Kylie asked.

"Well, the first time we were," Christopher said as he stretched his arms out in the air, letting out a brief yawn. "Then once we knew that he had been shopping and doing his own thing the whole day, we figured it was fine."

"Yeah," James said. "He's pretty much got his own agenda and does whatever he wants. I don't even think that he believes in keeping to any kind of schedule. Besides, none of the clocks in the house are even remotely right."

"I've come to notice that," Kylie said, a smile on her face.

Outside a vehicle pulled up in the driveway, the gravel underneath the tires crunching and grumbling from the weight of the vehicle. Christopher jumped up to his feet, happy that Bones was finally home. Even though he had expected Bones to be late, he couldn't honestly say that he hadn't concerned at all.

"About time!" James exclaimed as he rose to his feet as well, dusting the crumbs from his sandwich off of his shirt and onto the floor. "I wonder what he went out and did today…?"

A loud, demanding knock came to the door, and Christopher paused at the door for a moment. Bones wouldn't knock. He turned back to James and Kylie, giving the two a puzzled look.

"Maybe he forgot his keys," James replied, shrugging his shoulders.

"Then how did he drive the truck?" Christopher asked as he shook his head.

Kylie quickly ran to the picture window, peering out into the night to try and identify who was outside as the rapping on the door continued. "I think that's Jack Olen's truck—it should be all right."

Christopher unlocked the front door, cautiously opening it up to see who was behind it. He gulped deeply as he looked at the very big man at the other end of the door. This was definitely not Jack Olen. The man was bald, and had dark, angry-looking eyes. He wore a leather jacket that covered his large frame, and looked as though he would be able to knock down the door if Christopher had not answered it. *This is definitely...definitely not Jack Olen,* Christopher thought to himself. *Maybe this guy beat up Jack Olen and stole his truck, or—*

"Christopher?" the large man asked, pushing his way into the house, causing Christopher to step back nervously.

"Bill!" Kylie exclaimed, recognizing the large man. "You gave us one hell of a scare."

"Sorry," Bill said quietly, nervously eyeing everyone in the room. He fidgeted around for a moment, almost as though he was having difficulty piecing together what to say. Then finally, he just went and blurted it out. "Bones is in the hospital."

"Is he all right?" Christopher asked in shock.

"I don't know," Bill replied as he made his way back out of the door. "You're all supposed to ride with me though. I'll take you there."

"Where's he at?" James asked, following behind the big man.

"They've got him up at Lakeland Regional, in Springfield," Bill said. He opened the passenger door up for the three. "We should be there in about half an hour."

"Isn't it much farther?" Kylie asked.

"Not how I drive," Bill replied as he shut the door behind her.

Christopher's mind was full of terrible thoughts. Could this be one of the bad things that Alena had warned him about? He had really hoped that it wasn't. He couldn't deal with anymore tragedy in his life, especially with so many other things going on.

"Seatbelts," Bill said. He put the truck into gear, causing it to jump a bit.

James was sitting next to Bill. He turned to him and asked anxiously, "Bill, are you Jack's…?"

"I'm Jack's partner," Bill answered. He mashed his foot down on the gas, causing the vehicle to lurch forward, the tires spinning as dust and rock shot from the back tires. "The name is William Walker."

Christopher thought about the name for a moment. It was not the first time he had heard about Bill. However, it was definitely the first time he had actually heard his last name, Walker. Bones had always called him "Bill something-or-other."

"Do you know what's wrong, Bill?" Kylie asked, deeply concerned. She was sitting back in her seat, and was tightly gripping Christopher's leg in apparent shock at Bill's driving.

"Jack didn't say," Bill said quietly. "I'm sorry, I don't know more…. I'm kind of out in the dark on this one, you know."

Bill sped the truck through the forest, making Christopher almost nauseous at every turn and hill they took. He wondered if his stomach would allow him to make it all the way to Springfield, or whether or not at some point it would simply abandon his body in protest. He gripped onto Kylie's hand, hoping that he was not squeezing too tightly.

"I'm worried," Kylie whispered over to Christopher, squeezing his hand in return. "About Bones...."

"Me too," Christopher whispered.

Christopher looked off in the distance. The sky ahead was lit a dull red from the bright lights of Springfield. The closer they approached the more nervous and anxious Christopher began to feel. He wished he could be there already, and see Bones. However, on the other hand he wished he was farther away from the hospital, so the worry in his heart wouldn't be so great. Christopher watched through the window in silence. All around him were things so familiar, yet so alien to him now. Things like streetlights and gas stations passed by, and for once Christopher realized that he really hadn't missed all these busy things at all. The constant streams of traffic, all of the bright lights of industry and business, and the sounds of a city full of people. He had seemingly forgotten about this world, or had this world forgotten about him? Either way, he felt strange being in a city again. It looked so similar to Bloomington; it felt as though it could have been his former home. Yet at the same time this place felt as far away from home as he could possibly get.

"This is it," Bill said. He pulled the truck up to the hospital entrance. "Ask for room 504. I'll meet you up there after I park this thing."

"All right," Kylie whispered as she opened the passenger door, being the first one to step out.

"Thanks, Bill…," Christopher said as he stepped down from the truck and into the outside world. The sounds of the city were all around him and full in his ears as he followed Kylie into the main building.

James shut the door behind him, hurrying to catch up to the two, and once he did he said, "It's so strange being here."

"I know what you mean," Christopher said, looking around. It was strange for everything to feel so alien when it used to be so familiar. The noises of the city seemed way too loud, and the lights far too bright. It was as if he had been away from a city for years instead of just a week or so. Maybe it was just because he had gotten so comfortable in Pine Hallow. "It's so busy," he added.

The three quickly made their way into the hospital, searching for any kind of sign to guide them. After stopping for a moment to ask a nurse, they walked over to the closest elevator.

The strange smell of the hospital bothered Christopher. It was strange that even the smells here were so different and alien to him. As he stood in the elevator, he glanced to James and then to Kylie. They both looked as worried and concerned as he felt. Christopher wondered why he worried so much; after all, they didn't even know anything yet. Maybe it was not knowing that was most troubling.

"Are you okay?" Kylie asked, reaching out for Christopher's hand. She must have noticed that he was very nervous.

Christopher took her hand. "I don't know…."

"I'm sure things will be okay," James said, wrapping an arm around both Christopher and Kylie. "Let's go find him."

They navigated their way down the pale white maze of corridors and rooms, finally coming upon room 504. Standing outside of the room with a large cell phone to his ear was Jack Olen. He was dressed in his nice black trench coat, and underneath he was wearing some kind of business suit. He quickly nodded to Christopher, Kylie, and James, saying into the phone: "I'll have to let you go now."

Jack reached his hand out to greet the three, taking turns shaking each hand firmly. He finally said, "I'm glad you guys are here."

"How is he?" Christopher asked first, his hands sweaty and anxious.

“I don’t know how much you know…,” Jack nervously replied, rubbing his short black beard, “…but I don’t think it’s good.”

“We don’t know anything,” James said, a grim look washing over his face. “He never let on that he was even sick.”

“He is,” Jack quietly answered, shaking his head. “He has been sick for a while. I’ve known about it for about three months now or so. We didn’t expect it to ever get bad—at least not so soon.”

“It’s bad?” Kylie asked, sounding forlorn. “How bad is it?”

“The way it’s spread…,” Jack said, taking in a deep breath, “…they don’t think he’ll make it through the night.”

“What?” Christopher nearly yelled, in complete shock. Bones had never even hinted to anyone that he was sick, and now he wasn’t expected to make it through the night? It just seemed so unfair, and made him feel so angry and frustrated that he wished he could just tear the whole place apart in a rage he himself couldn’t quite understand.

“No…,” Kylie whispered, her mouth open and her arms slung across her chest as if she was hugging herself. “No….”

“Why didn’t he even tell us?” James asked,

sounding more angry than upset. "He should have said something! It's just not fair…."

"I'm so sorry…," Jack whispered as he hung his head down, eyes closed. "This is my fault, too; I was the one who helped arrange for you guys to stay with your grandfather. We both thought that there would be years of time, not days."

"It's all right," James said, kicking the hospital wall. "No one else in the family wanted us anyway."

"Don't think of it like that," Jack said, placing a hand on James's shoulder. "He felt so bad about what happened to you, and that he had never spent time with you when your parents were alive. He just wanted to make up for all the time he had lost."

"I just can't believe it," Kylie whispered. She reached over, drawing Christopher close to her. "He has been so happy lately."

"He's been so active that I couldn't even tell he was sick." Christopher quietly sobbed, and a tear came streaming down from his eyes. "I didn't even know…."

"Not knowing kept you all happy," Jack answered. He brought out a handkerchief from his pocket, wiping Christopher's tear away from his face. "He didn't want you to spend your time there worrying about him, or what might happen to him. He felt that you guys had been through enough, and had enough things of your own to worry about."

"Well, he's putting us through it now," James said, frustrated. "Telling us didn't help anything at all, now we're going to have to go through it all over again."

"James…," Kylie said, trying her best not to cry. "That's not fair. He didn't know."

"I don't care," James said as he stormed off. "Now we're just back were we started! We've got nobody left! Can't you see that?"

"James!" Christopher cried, going after his brother. He had never seen James act this way, it terrified him. "Don't…"

"I'll talk to him," Jack replied, holding Christopher close to him. "Don't worry, I'll talk to him. It's best if you see Mathias one at a time. You go first, okay? I'll go make sure James is all right."

Tears flowing from his eyes, Christopher simply nodded in reply.

"Here…," Jack said, handing a handkerchief to Christopher. "Don't let him see you cry. He is being as brave as he possibly can, so promise me you'll try to be your bravest as well."

"I promise," Christopher whispered, wiping away the tears from his eyes and trying to strengthen his expression.

Kylie gave him a hug, resting her head on his shoulder for a moment. Christopher could feel the wetness of her eyes as she cried.

Christopher opened up the door to Bones' hospital room. He paused for a moment to try and strengthen himself against the sadness that was deep within him, and then continued inside. In an almost dizzy, dreamlike state Christopher slowly made his way to Bones, who lay motionless in the hospital bed, tubes coming from his chest and an IV running from his hand. The sight alone was enough just enough to make Christopher almost lose it again completely.

"Christopher…," Bones whispered, slowly opening his eyes and turning his pale face laboriously in Christopher's direction. "I'm glad you could come."

Christopher took a deep breath. He was in a state of complete shock. Bones did not look even remotely like his normal self. He had seen Bones just that very same morning, and already Bones looked completely different. His skin was paler, his eyes red and dim. His voice, which was usually strong and deep, seemed brief and quiet.

"I'm sorry…," Christopher whispered, not knowing exactly what else to say. "I didn't know."

"Of course you didn't know," Bones said, attempting a smile. "I'm just sorry that I didn't tell you. I just thought that there was so much time left, that we'd have more time to talk about things later…."

"I know why you didn't," Christopher whispered. He carefully pulled up a nearby chair to sit beside Bones.

"I just wish that you weren't here. I just want you to be back home with us."

"I know…," Bones said quietly. He took another deep breath, releasing it with a loud cough. "I thought we had all the time in the world to become a family. I knew that one day this might happen, but I thought it was years, or even a year…a year is such a long time. Compared to this, a year is a lifetime…."

"I'm happy for the time we have had though," Christopher said, trying to think of something to say to comfort Bones.

"That's true," Bones said, trying to laugh. "What a strange week it has been, too, right?"

"Right," Christopher said, forcing a smile, although he felt as far away from smiling as one could feel. "We found Alena; she thanked us for what we did for her."

"Good…," Bones said, slowly nodding his head. "If it weren't for her, we might have died on that day in the storm. Although I may not have had a lot of time with all of you, I'm glad that I could have the time that I had. I'm content with what I was given."

"I don't want you to die…," Christopher whispered, his voice breaking for a moment. He could no longer hold it back. He quickly wiped away the tears forming in his eyes.

"I want us all to be together too," Bones said

with effort. Tears came from his eyes as well. "I'm just sorry that it won't happen. But I don't want you to be so sad for me; I've done a lot of things. I've loved, I've lived…I've gotten to know my grandsons, the two people that I've regretted not meeting for my entire life."

"Why didn't we ever meet before?" Christopher whispered with a hand at his eyes to hold back any tears that might come.

"Me and your father…we didn't get along," Bones said as he shook his head. "Pride—it was all pride on both of our parts. It was such a stupid thing for us to do. It was such a stupid thing for us to do to you and your brother…."

Christopher stood up and stepped closer to Bones' bedside. He reached down, careful of the IV, and held on to Bones' hand. He could no longer hold back any tears, and did not care to do so any longer. "I am glad that we met," he said. "I am so thankful for every moment and for everything that you have done for us. Thank you, grandpa…."

Bones brought his free hand up to his eyes to hide the tears that came streaming down. He let out a cry as he squeezed Christopher's hand tighter. "Thank you, Christopher…thanks for everything. Thank you for every moment."

Christopher slowly released Bones' hand. So many tears were streaming down his face that there wasn't even a point to attempting to hide them. He stepped back a few paces. "Are you ready…to see the others?" he asked.

Bones let out what could have been a short laugh in between his tears. "I don't know…I think this part is worse than the dying."

Christopher nodded, rubbing the sleeve of his shirt on his nose. "I'll be outside…," he whispered, painfully turning his back to Bones and walking out into the hallway. The weight upon his heart was so heavy that he worried that it might bring him crashing through the floor, but somehow, he kept walking.

James was standing against the wall. His face was red with anger, and he was scowling at the floor. Christopher shuffled to James, embracing him tightly as the tears came streaming down his face once more. James quickly returned the hug, squeezing Christopher so hard that it hurt his sides, yet the hug still didn't feel tight enough.

"James…"

"I'm sorry…," James whispered to his brother, fighting back his own tears. "I'm so sorry."

"Are you ready?" Christopher asked, pausing with each painful breath. "Are you ready to see him?"

"I'm not ready," James said between sobs. "I'm not ready to say goodbye."

James released Christopher and slowly made his way to the door of room 504. He looked back to Kylie and Christopher, who both nodded at him in encouragement. Nodding back, he took the well-soaked handkerchief from Christopher and then stepped into the room, shutting the door behind him.

Kylie embraced Christopher, bringing him as close to her as she could. "I'm so sorry."

"I just can't believe this is happening," Christopher whispered as he hugged her tightly. "I can't believe that in the morning Bones won't be here anymore. I wish that this was all just a nightmare."

"I know…," Kylie whispered, rubbing her hand against Christopher's eyes, clearing away the fresh coat of tears. "I wish none of this was happening. I don't know why we have to be punished like this."

"You're not being punished," Bill replied. Christopher had not noticed that he was standing next to Jack. The pair had watched in silence as the events had unfolded before them. Bill continued, "The world is just a place that really sucks sometimes. But you have each other, so at least hold on to that. The whole world can be the biggest mess possible, but as long as you three have each other in your hearts then it don't matter one single bit."

"He's right," Jack said quietly as he kneeled down next to the two, placing a hand on each of their shoulders. "Besides, you three have made Bones so happy. Look at it this way: if he had never met his grandkids, then who would be here to care about him when it was his time to go? Who would be here to see him off…?"

"Not to mention we've heard rumors of the strangest things happening lately," Bill said. "The rest of the area is flooding all around Pine Hallow, yet something is keeping us all from drowning in it. Then you guys all go and find that missing girl from that legend. I think it was fate that you guys were here. Bones needed you, just like that missing girl needed you all to happen upon her, and Pine Hallow is a better place for you all being here in it."

Christopher nodded in silence. These words were great and encouraging; however, they did not even begin to help with the pain within him.

"He should just be here to enjoy this. He should have been allowed more time," Kylie whispered, placing her head on Christopher's chest, her arms still firm around him.

"I think so, too," Bill said quietly, as though he had no more good things to say. "I really do."

The door to Bones' room slowly opened, and James emerged from behind it. His face was expressionless and blank, as though the whole world had fallen apart around him. He nodded to Christopher in silence as he went to sit against the hallway wall.

"Kylie…," Christopher said as he gently let go of her. "Do you?"

"Yeah…," Kylie whispered, letting out a small

encouraging smile. "Yeah, I do…."

Kylie made her way into the room, her eyes down to the floor as she firmly bit her bottom lip. She looked back once more to Christopher, gently shutting the door behind her.

Christopher watched as James sat against the wall, his head buried in his hands as he sat there, motionless. Then he suddenly looked up to Christopher, a strange look of understanding in his eyes. "We have choices…," he finally muttered under his breath.

"What?" Christopher asked, staring at James blankly.

"We have a choice," James said as he got to his feet and ran down the hallway. "We have a choice!" he yelled again, startling a nurse, who had to dart out of his way. He was running like a madman.

"Is he all right?" Jack asked, watching, a confused look upon his face.

"I don't know," Christopher said, thinking for a moment. We have a choice? What did James mean by that? It was what Alena had said before, but what did it have to do with this?

James came running around the corner; he was pushing a wheelchair out in front of him. He rushed up to the group and stopped before the door, his breathing heavy and his voice too shaky to understand. "We have choices…."

"What's this?" Bill asked, shaking his head.

"Please, just trust me," James said quickly as he turned to everyone around him. "You trust me don't you? We have a secret…a secret place."

"We trust you, James," Jack answered; intent on listening to what he had to say. "Go on."

"We have to get Bones there, to the cave," James continued, pausing for a moment to catch his breath in the midst of his excitement. He turned to Christopher and spoke: "Don't you see, Chris? This is what Alena meant by choices…this must be it!"

"Take Bones to the window?" Christopher asked, rolling the idea around in his head for a moment. It did seem like something that could be possible.

"Yes!" James exclaimed. "Don't you see? He doesn't have to die; he can live on in the cave. He can live on in his memories!"

James quickly rushed into the room, startling both Kylie and Bones as Christopher, Bill, and Jack quickly followed behind him. They were causing quite a commotion.

"What's going on?" Kylie asked, glancing around the room as though she was missing something.

"Bones!" James cried as he pulled the wheelchair up to his bedside. "Get in. We're taking you to the cave."

"What?" Bones asked, as he slowly sat up in the bed, surprised.

"You can live on, with Cat," James said as he went to Bones side, pulling on him in his bed. "You don't have to go. You can be with her again."

"Are you all right with this?" Jack asked, very confused at the current situation.

"Yeah…," Bones whispered back. "Okay, James…."

"Okay?" James repeated excitedly as he searched for some way to get Bones up and moving. "We can do this…."

"Bill, Jack…could you please step out for a moment?" Bones asked. "Please shut the door behind you."

"But…," James protested.

Bones quietly shook his head. "I really do appreciate it, James. Believe me with everything that I am."

"You aren't going to go…?" Kylie whispered as she tightly closed her eyes.

"Please understand, James…," Bones said as he reached out for his hand.

"I don't understand…," he whispered, the excitement gone from his face and replaced by sadness and tears once again.

"In the cave…," Bones began, his eyes heavy and red and filling with tears, "…in the cave that's just a memory. It's just a memory of me and Cat together…she's not down there. She never really was. While what you are offering me is very tempting, because at least I know for sure what would happen to me, I'll have to pass."

James fell on his knees. He hung his head down as tears came streaming down once more. "I know…," he finally whispered. "I know…."

"Wherever I go tonight…that is where she really will be," Bones said as he lay in the bed. "I'm so sorry; again…this is the choice that I make. But I thank all three of you for trying one last time. Thank you for this one last hope of an adventure."

"Bones…," Christopher whispered as he sat down on the ground next to James, "…you'll see her again, I'm sure."

A few hours later, in the early moments of the morning, surrounded by his beloved new family and the greatest of friends, Bones quietly died, releasing his hold on this world and slipping away into the next. He looked as though he felt no pain; he looked as though he carried over no worry. Christopher thought he looked at peace. He always liked to believe afterward that Bones had found what he was looking for.

Sometimes, he figured, the choices that we think we need to make are not ours to make. Sometimes the memories we have are shared memories and the dreams we have are shared by all. Sometimes the people we care about slip away from us, and sometimes we slip away from the people that we care about. Life is this, both good and bad. *It's the good moments that we have to remember,* Christopher had thought, *or else there isn't any reason to try. All the bad memories will take over, and everything in the world will always look grim and hopeless.*

Chapter 16: Last Day in Pine Hallow

If the sky can shed tears, and the thundercloud cry, then can the sunny day not beam as the ocean rolls with the wind in its heart?

The rain poured down from the gray sky so fiercely that Christopher wondered if the earth itself was saddened by Bones' passing. The morning hours had marched on, yet Christopher felt as though time had completely stopped. His body felt heavy, his mind exhausted, and his eyes were red and stinging with dryness.

Sitting in an awkward, sad silence, Christopher, James and Kylie waited in the hospital lobby, their eyes heavy and their gazes to the ground. There were no words that Christopher could bring to mind, no encouraging thought to break the mood around them, no jokes, and, worst of all, no words to express how sad he felt.

Jack Olen quietly approached the three with an umbrella in one hand and a suitcase in the other. "Kylie…," he whispered.

"Yeah?" Kylie answered, slowly lifting her sad eyes to greet Jack.

"I got a hold of your mother…," Jack said, setting his things down on the ground and kneeling before the three. "She'll be in around five tonight…."

"What's going to happen to us?" James asked as he rubbed his eyes.

"I've gotten in touch with Aunt Lynn…," Jack said, continuing with a hesitant look upon his face, "It's been arranged that you two will live with her now."

"No…," Christopher whispered. He shook his head in disgust. "Anyone but her…."

"Can't we just stay…?" James asked, although he already knew the answer to that question.

"I'm sorry…," Jack answered, reluctantly shaking his head. "Come on now, we'll go to the house and collect your things. We have all day to talk about what is going to happen from this point on."

Christopher nodded as he rose to his feet. He reached down, helping Kylie up as they followed Jack and James out of the hospital.

"Wait here!" Jack shouted, attempting to talk over the maddeningly loud rain. "I'll go get the car, you guys stay out of the rain!"

"All right," James said, nodding in acknowledgement.

Kylie reached out for Christopher's hand, gripping it tightly. She brought his head down to hers as she whispered into his ear, "Don't worry; things will be okay."

Christopher looked longingly into her eyes, the beautiful piercingly blue eyes that he had come to know and love. Then he slowly shook his head in disagreement, whispering into her ear, "I feel like things'll never be okay, not ever again. Today we'll be separated, and, in a small way, the world is ending for me."

Kylie looked to him, tears coming to her eyes. She shook her head, slowly wiping them away. She didn't have anything to say in reply, as though she could not think of a single comforting thing at all. Instead, Kylie reached for Christopher and embraced him fully.

Pulling up in the large truck, Jack quickly opened the driver's-side door and jumped out. Umbrella in hand, he circled around and opened up the passenger door, helping everyone into the large cab of the truck. It was James who went in first, and then Kylie.

Christopher stood alone as Jack held out a hand to help him into the truck. Christopher slowly turned away from the truck to look at the hospital one last time. Rain falling all around him, he slowly raised his head to look up to the fifth floor of the hospital, the floor that Bones had been on. He wondered where Bones was now, wondered if he could see him standing out there in the rain.

Jack rushed over, covering Christopher with the umbrella. "Are you all right?"

"Yeah…," Christopher whispered, forcing his eyes away from the hospital. "I was just saying goodbye."

"Let's get out of this rain," Jack said, sounding either touched or saddened by what Christopher had said.

"Right," Christopher said. He turned to the hospital once more, nodding at it as though it was a person he was talking to. He then slowly turned and made his way into the truck. His hair was soaking wet and his clothes cold and damp, and he didn't care at all.

Kylie reached over, pulling him closer to her. It seemed as though she didn't mind the fact that he was so wet either. "At least we got to say goodbye," she said

"Yeah," James agreed. "I wish that we had that chance with our parents. At least we got to see him one last time."

"Yeah…," Christopher replied. He stared out the window, watching the world through the rain-soaked glass of the truck window. Buildings rushed by, distorted in the rain, the lights of the cars in traffic lighting in each droplet of water with a brilliant red. Christopher saw people walking, umbrellas raised above their heads, busy making their way with whatever business they had at hand. He wondered as he watched them, slowly catching second-long glimpses of people who had lived their entire lives up to this point. He wondered it would be like, to be them and to live their lives. Would he not feel anymore sadness, or would he just be experiencing different kinds of sadness?

Christopher could feel his head becoming heavier and heavier, and the city was no longer visible from the window. He was returning home, or at least to what would be his home for the rest of the day. The ride, and the exhaustion, finally set in and he simply passed out, his head laying to rest upon Kylie's shoulder.

He didn't know how long it had been, as he was suddenly jolted awake.

"Stop!" Kylie yelled, her hands firmly pressed against the window.

Christopher jumped, realizing that Kylie was literally on top of him as she gazed through the window.

Jack quickly hit the brakes, causing the truck to slide for a few feet in the heavy rain. "What?" Jack said, sounding completely shocked, as if he had accidentally run someone over or worse. "What is it?"

"Is something out there?" James asked, his voice heavy, as though he had fallen asleep.

"I saw him…," Kylie whispered as she frantically scrambled to look out the back window. "I swear I saw him."

"Who did you see?" Jack asked, slowly turning around in his seat, attempting to get a better view out the back window.

"My father," Kylie said quietly, sounding as though she was a little unsure of herself. "I was half-asleep, and I was staring out the window. I could have sworn that I saw him. He just stared at me. He just stood there, staring at me."

"I didn't see anyone," Jack said. "Are you sure?"

"I don't know," Kylie whispered. "I was so sure at the time."

"Maybe it's the stress," James suggested, glancing out the back window.

Christopher scanned the area heavily with tired eyes, trying to make out anything or anyone in the rain. The entire area looked clear and undisturbed. If her father was there, perhaps he had already run off into the trees.

"I'm sorry," Kylie said, shaking her head and rubbing her eyes. "I must have just been seeing things."

"Not a problem," Jack said. He put the truck back into gear, rolling on ahead. "Don't be sorry about it, it happens under moments of stress and exhaustion like this. I remember one time, back when I was in school. I had stayed up studying so long that I was sure that I saw someone peeking in on me through the window of my dorm."

"Was anyone there?" James asked, clearly missing the point of the story.

"I lived on the twentieth floor," Jack said as he shook his head. "If someone was there, it must have been Spider-Man."

The group cautiously made their way into the house. The rain was still coming down strong all around them. Jack attempted to keep them dry as best as he could with his meager umbrella as he unlocked the front door and thankfully let the three in out of the rain.

"All right guys," Jack said as he hung his heavy black trench coat on a hook by the door, "have a seat."

Christopher, with Kylie in hand and James following behind, got to the couch. All three sat down with heavy eyes, and even heavier hearts. Christopher looked over to James; he looked as he did that first time in Aunt Lynn's car. He looked as though he was there, but really wasn't there, like he was back inside his own world in his head, blocking out all the pain of this one. Honestly, he couldn't blame him.

"Well…," Jack started, sitting down on the ground in front of them all, his hands folded in his lap, "…this is how things are going to work for a while."

"Are we staying with Aunt Lynn for just a short while?" Christopher asked, hoping that the answer was so. He couldn't imagine how his life would be if he was forced to go and live with her, especially with how burdened she had seemed on the way down there.

"No," Jack abruptly replied, bringing a hand up to his beard. "You will be staying with her until you are ready and old enough to move out on your own."

"Damn," James whispered as he shook his head. "Isn't there anyone else?"

"I know that she can be very difficult to deal with. I've heard some stories from Bones," Jack said. "You have to realize, though, that she was going through a pretty bad divorce, and she still is."

"Still…," Christopher said, shaking his head once more.

"I know she may or may not be a good person," Jack said, continuing, "however, I will make sure that you are both treated as best as possible. I will personally see to that."

"When will we have to leave?" Christopher asked, sounding very concerned. He had a small idea in the back of his head and feared that it was not just an idea but the cold hard truth.

"Tonight…," Jack said as he shook his head, knowing that he was saying something that was not going to go over well. "She wants to head back tonight."

Christopher turned to Kylie, his eyes growing heavy again. It just wasn't fair, it wasn't enough time. Besides, who knew how long it would be until he got to be with her again? There were too many things to say, and too many more moments he wanted to share with her. This news was just another topping on the crap-cake that was becoming his future. First he found out he was going to live with Aunt Lynn, and now he was losing Kylie. Christopher wondered what he had done to deserve all of it.

Kylie squeezed Christopher's hand tightly. She tried to let out a little reassuring smile, but failed and almost started to cry again. "I'm sorry," she said

"I'm sorry," Christopher repeated, wanting to say a whole lot more, but not being able to find the words.

"I don't want to go today," James said, sounding very frustrated and rather angry. "I don't see why we have to just because she wants to."

"Bones wanted you taken care of if this should ever happen," Jack answered as calmly as he could. He came off as though the whole situation was just depressing him more and more. "So, Aunt Lynn agreed to take you both in. Besides, she needs family too. Remember how Bones lived alone, and he needed you to be here to be with him? Just think of it that way. She's still a person."

"I bet Bones had to pay her," James replied meanly, shaking his head.

"Funny you should say that," Jack said. "She will get some help. I'm not sure if you were aware of this or not, but Bones was by no definition a poor man. In fact, he was rather well-off. So she will get a small amount of money. However, the rest of the large amount remaining will go to the both of you, when you are old enough."

"He left us everything?" Christopher asked, confused.

"He did," Jack answered with a nod. "I will take care of the house while you both are away, but this house is yours as well. When you are old enough either of you are welcome to take over, or sell the place. Whichever suits your needs."

"I can't believe he did that," James said.

"Can you really not?" Jack asked, rubbing at his beard once more. "After all, look how happy you being here made him. Think about it. He had this planned before you even got here."

"I wish we could just live here now," Christopher said as he sat back in the couch, amazed at all the information he was being given. Bones had left them everything. Just the thought of it completely dumbfounded him.

"I wish I could grant that wish," Jack said, "I really do wish that I could do that for you. But this is just how it is going to have to be for a few years."

"So three years," James said as he brought a hand to his mouth, as though in deep thought. "We can come back here in three years."

"Yeah," Jack said with a small confident smile on his face. "And Kylie..."

"Yes?" Kylie asked.

"Bones had it arranged for you and your mother to take care of Kate and Poppy," Jack said, "And, of course, he has left you quite a sizeable amount of money for their well-being as well as yours. Are you all right with that?"

"I would love to," Kylie said, both awed and shocked. "I had no idea."

"I know that there is a lot to be sad about right now," Jack said as he folded his hands in his lap once more. "I know that things don't look like they can be good again. It's a common thing to feel that way, especially after everything that has happened. I just want you all to know that your grandfather cared for all of you, and that he wanted every moment from this moment on to be as good as it could possibly be."

"Thank you...," Christopher whispered as he

took a few moments to go through everything that he was hearing. "Thank you, grandpa."

"Yes…," James whispered as he nodded his head in agreement. "Thank you."

"For everything," Kylie added.

Jack rose to his feet and picked up his suitcase and umbrella from the floor. He brought his hand up to his face and pushed the sleeve back with the other, revealing his silver watch. "So…," he said, examining his watch. "It's about two-fifteen now. Kylie, your mother said she'd be here to get you at seven."

"All right," Kylie whispered sadly.

"And Lynn…she should be here a bit after five," Jack said, walking to the door. "I'll be back to talk to Lynn, but right now I've got some pressing business to attend to. If there is anything that you would like to take of Bones', please feel free to do so. Other than that, just wait here and I will return."

"All right," Christopher whispered as he slowly got to his feet. There just didn't seem enough time left, and since that he knew the exact moment Lynn was expected to arrive there seemed even less of it. It was as though things were just moving too fast, as if this day would be gone and over before he knew it. Then, he and James would be gone from Pine Hallow, and Kylie would be on her way home, and then to Nevada. It seemed like such a bad ending to everything. Everything seemed to be so hopeful just the day before, now it had come to this.

After Jack left, Kylie, Christopher and James made their way nervously about the house. They did not know what they should do, or even what they could do. It seemed so strange to Christopher that Bones would not come walking into the door later, or that this whole house was now Christopher and James', or at least would be in the future. *It'll never feel the same,* Christopher thought. It would never even be the same without Bones there. He was like the heart of the house. He was what made it their home, even if it was just for a short period of time.

Christopher had decided on a few things to take with him. Nothing big really, just a few items that he had remembered—one of them being a pink oven mitt with small white jalapeño peppers on it. He remembered it back from that first morning there, with Bones' unsuccessful first attempt at breakfast. He took a few other items and small things, and then packed them away.

In his bedroom, Christopher scanned the area for anything he might have wanted. However, he found that all of the important things were the memories and the people involved in them. It had never been about material items; he had not even unpacked in all the days he was here. It was strange to think that he would eventually have to unpack, just somewhere else.

Confident that he had all that he wanted with him, Christopher looked about him room one last time. He had not spent much time there, yet that did not make it any easier for him to leave it. His heart heavy, he slowly shut the door behind him for the last time and quietly made his way down the stairs.

"Did you get all of your stuff?" Kylie asked. She was sitting on the couch in the living room, stretched out and exhausted from both sadness and lack of sleep.

"Yeah…," Christopher said as he pointed over to his suitcases. "Everything I own."

Kylie nodded in reply, her eyes looking heavy and sad. "How did it come to this?"

"I don't know," Christopher said as sat next to her. "We did so much; we figured so many things out. Yet, in the end…in the end we ended up losing so much."

"You haven't lost me," Kylie whispered as she drew Christopher forward, kissing him on the lips. "You'll never lose me."

"Then I'll never feel lost," Christopher replied, letting a small smile slip past his sad exterior. "I'll always think about you, and I'll always want to be with you."

"We'll always have this place," Kylie said, "Even if we're not here together, we will always have this place in our hearts to remind us. When we're older, it'll be here for us to come back to."

"That's true," Christopher whispered as he leaned in and kissed Kylie again.

"I'm all packed up," James announced as he made his way down the stairs, suitcases in each hand. "Oh, sorry…."

"It's okay," Kylie said quickly as she broke away the kiss, blushing.

James joined Christopher and Kylie, sitting down upon the floor and laying back, his head against the coffee table. "I can't believe it's going to go like this," he said.

"That's what we've been thinking," Christopher replied as he looked to the ceiling.

"It won't be too long now," James said, "She'll be here soon."

Chapter 17: In Conclusion

Christopher, Kylie, and James sat in silence as a firm knock came from the other side of the door. They didn't have to guess who it was, for all three knew it was Aunt Lynn.

James trudged over to the door, in no hurry whatsoever to see her again. He paused, as though readying himself for her presence, before opening the door to let her in. "Aunt Lynn," he said, greeting her disapprovingly.

Aunt Lynn rushed in, giving James a great big hug and confusing Christopher and Kylie, who both watched from the couch.

"I'm so sorry," Aunt Lynn said, although from past experiences Christopher had a hard time believing it. Maybe he was just so angry with her in the first place he couldn't even see any sign of sincerity in her. "I'm so sorry that he's gone."

After releasing James, who was staring at her in speechless confusion, Aunt Lynn quickly made her way over to Christopher, wrapping her arms tightly around him. "Christopher…I'm so sorry for your loss. I'm so sorry for everything that has happened. Now, who is this?" she asked of Kylie.

"I'm Kylie…," Kylie said, regarding the strange woman as she introduced herself to her.

"Christopher's girlfriend," James quickly added.

"Oh!" Aunt Lynn exclaimed, and then extended a hand. "Pleased to meet you then."

"Pleased," Kylie quietly answered, as though she had nothing more to say to this woman that Christopher and James had spoken so poorly of.

"So are we ready?" Lynn asked, eyeing Christopher and James' luggage. "You've got everything I see."

"We have to wait," Christopher said. "Jack Olen isn't here yet. He said he needed to talk to you. Besides, Kylie's mother won't be here until seven, so…"

"…not good to leave her all alone," James finished.

"Oh, right!" Lynn said, trying to sound more upbeat. "Of course we can wait then."

"Good, 'cause we weren't really asking," James said, sounding arrogant and rather rude.

"Right," Lynn said, confused. "Anyway, if we need to wait then I'm happy with that."

"Christopher, Kylie…," James said as Lynn sat down on the couch with a heavy sigh, "…I could use some help upstairs. I've got some stuff in my room I need to bring down."

"Yeah," Christopher said, noticing that James' suitcases were already fully packed.

"Sure," Kylie added.

The three of them bolted up to James' room, shutting the door behind them.

"What's up, James?" Christopher asked with his back to the door, a concerned look on his face.

"Oh, nothing," James said with a small, mischievous grin. "I just can't stand that woman. I didn't want our last hours here spent with her. Besides, we have the whole car ride back for that."

"Nice," Kylie said, letting out a little laugh. It

was the first time Christopher had seen her look the slightest bit happy the entire day.

"I can't believe we are going to live with her," Christopher said, shaking his head. "She's so damn fake all the time."

"Yeah," Kylie agreed. "I didn't know if she was really upset or just good at pretending to be. She's really hard to judge; in the way she acts, you can't tell what's real or not. I've never met someone like that before."

"You're lucky, then," James said as he folded his arms across his chest.

At that moment a small thumping came, interrupting the conversation.

"Is that the door?" James asked, his eyes straining as if he was trying to concentrate.

"It might be my mother," Kylie suggested with a tone of sadness. "I'll go down and check."

"Christopher you wait here…it'll give us a good excuse to come back up if it's just Lynn screwing around with stuff," James said with a little laugh.

"All right," Christopher said, plopping himself down on James' bed as he and Kylie left the room, shutting the door behind them.

Christopher waited around for a few moments, wondering what was going on downstairs. If someone was at the door James and Kylie would have quickly come to get him. He slowly got to his feet, pacing around the room. He stood before the window, and for a second he thought he saw a light out in the woods. That would be impossible, though; no one in their right mind would be out there in this storm. He strained at the window, searching the area outside. It was so difficult to see outside with the bedroom light turned on. He made his way to the light switch panel next to the door and shut the light off. He was halfway back to the window when Kylie came bursting through the door.

"Christopher!" Kylie exclaimed. She was out of breath and wet from being out in the rain.

"What?" Christopher shouted, grabbing Kylie's arms. "What's happened?"

"It's James," Kylie whispered, still trying to catch her breath. "He's run away!"

"What?" Christopher asked, as he started to make his way out of the room. "Why would he do that?"

"We were on our way downstairs to see if anyone was here," Kylie said, attempting to keep up with Christopher. "We overheard Lynn on the phone. That's what the banging noise was. She knocked it over trying to find it or something."

Christopher paused for a moment, and then turned to Kylie. "What did she say?"

"We caught the end, but it was something about

how she got all this money to take you guys in," she said, trying to get all the information out as quickly as possible. "She said Bones dying and leaving her that money was the nicest thing he'd ever done for her."

Christopher shook his head. He didn't believe what he was hearing. That just seemed impossible, and yet he expected no less, not from Lynn. "That monster," he whispered as he marched to the front door.

The rain was hard and pouring outside, some of it getting into the house and wetting the carpet. Christopher looked around for some kind of light source, and then, remembering his head-mounted light, he opened up his luggage. He rummaged around, throwing his clothes to the floor. When he found the light, he grabbed it and rushed outside.

"I tried to catch him," Kylie whispered as she and Christopher both ran out into the darkness and rain. "He wouldn't stop for anything."

Aunt Lynn was standing out in the front yard. She was desperately searching around, trying to catch some sign of James, as though he might still be in the area. "James!" she yelled, her shrill voice barely audible above the fierce thunderstorm.

"He's got his flashlight," Kylie said, "I think he might have planned for something else."

"Christopher!" Lynn screamed as she rushed over to him. "I'm so sorry. I didn't mean what I said. I didn't mean to drive him off. I was just *talking*, I didn't mean it!"

Christopher pushed Lynn away with all of his force and knocking her down in the mud. "You did this! What the hell is wrong with you? You're a monster! I don't ever want to see you again! I hope you die!"

"Christopher…," Kylie whispered as she reached for his shoulder. "Let's go find James."

"Please…," Lynn whispered, her hand outstretched to Christopher. "I'm sorry. I really didn't mean it."

"We're going to go get him," Christopher said to his aunt as he ran off, Kylie following closely behind. "You stay the hell away from us!" he added over his shoulder as he left.

Christopher grabbed Kylie's hand as he madly dashed through the wind-swept rain to Alena's Cave. He knew that it was where James was headed. Perhaps it was where he had planned on heading all along. It was no secret that James didn't want to leave Pine Hallow. Christopher just hoped that James didn't do anything stupid.

The ground was so muddy it was hard to keep a fast or steady pace. Every now and then he and Kylie would slip, almost falling to the ground. It seemed as though getting to the cave would be impossible, but soon they finally reached the entrance.

Christopher paused before stepping in. He

affixed the flashlight to his head, and slowly turned back to the direction of the house. In the distance he could see some lights that looked like they belonged to a car. "Jack Olen…," he whispered.

"I'll stay here," Kylie said as she gazed at the faraway lights. "In case Jack comes, I'll bring him to help."

"You sure?" Christopher asked, giving Kylie a quick hug.

"Yeah, I'll stay right here at the entrance," she said, "Just *please* come back to me, okay?"

"I will, I promise," he said, preparing himself for whatever was ahead.

"Go…," she whispered, nodding to Christopher. "Go find James."

Christopher nodded back, turning and stepping further into the cave. The water at the entrance was all the way up to his chest, and he worried that if it got any higher that he would have to swim through. The further he progressed to the back passage, the more the water receded. Luckily, it wasn't as bad as he thought.

Christopher waded through the knee-deep water at the back of the back passage, the sound of the nearby falls all that he could hear. He could feel his heart pounding in his chest, and he desperately tried to make his way through the water as fast as he could. It was his first time in the cave alone, and he was nearly sick with panic, and his stomach had long since knotted. He swung his head around wildly, trying to make sure he didn't overshoot the winding tunnel. Doing so would mean getting dangerously close to the falls.

He finally saw the tunnel, and, slowly, he stepped up the small embankment, catching his breath for a short time before he continued on, nearly running. The water here was up to his ankles and made the cave floor dangerously slick. With each footfall he worried that he would lose his balance completely and crack his head open on a rock. Luckily, he made it to the cave's main chamber exhausted and uninjured.

Christopher nervously splashed his way forward; the water in the room was almost up to his knees. He quickly made his way to the section of wall where the window should be. Taking a deep breath, he turned out his flashlight.

The light from the window slowly illuminated the water beneath his feet, causing the dirty brown water to glow a strange gray color. Christopher made his way to the window in the earth, which was already open. It looked as though water was pouring through the opening and into the room. Taking a deep breath in preparation for what lay ahead, Christopher leaned down on the ground, the cave water coming up to his face. He slipped his feet through the window and let them dangle out the other side, yet, strangely enough, he didn't feel cold or very different at all. It was as though the window he was sitting on was just a regular, ordinary window.

Christopher pushed himself forward with hands,

down and into the room. To his complete surprise there was no blackness, no strange feelings of falling. It was just a quick, short drop down to the ground. The water inside of the room was up to his ankles, and the walls no longer glowed or gave off sort of glittery brilliance. Instead this light was a dull, throbbing gray, almost as if the water was washing away any sign of the magic that had existed here once before.

"James!" Christopher shouted, finding it easy to actually talk beyond the threshold of the window this time. "James, where are you?"

A lot of different thoughts suddenly rushed through his head. What if James wasn't down here at all, yet somewhere off in the night, still upset over Lynn's comments? Perhaps he hadn't even thought about going to the window at all. Still, that didn't make much sense; James had brought his flashlight with him, after all.

Christopher made his way to the door at the back of the room, a feat made much easier by the fact that he no longer had to put any extra effort into getting there. If James was there, he had to be behind the door. He was sure of it. Christopher carefully placed his hand upon the doorknob, and turned it. Beaming golden light slowly filtered through, rising from the bottom to the top of the doorway. In half a second the light blinded Christopher, burning him slightly as it passed over his body. For a moment everything was hot and bright, and strange. Then, as before, it slowly seeped away, turning into a cool darkness.

"Not you too," Alena's voice came, chasing

away the darkness.

Christopher looked all around him as the world slowly materialized. He was at the Bait 'n' Tackle shop. It was early evening and the crickets were loud and all around him. Fireflies danced off in the distance and a swift breeze danced all about him. "Where is James?"

"He's here," Alena said. She walked gracefully toward the old bench where Christopher had first met Kylie. "He's inside, hiding."

"James!" Christopher shouted as he banged loudly upon the store's front door.

"You really shouldn't be here," Alena said, "Neither of you. The room is slowly flooding with water. Soon, you won't even be able to get back. Then you'll become memories, just like me."

"James!" Christopher shouted again, taking heed of what Alena was saying and adding urgency to his voice. "James, we have to get out of here!"

James slowly opened the door, his head hanging lowly in shame as he let Christopher into the building. "I'm sorry, Christopher. I just didn't want to deal with it anymore."

"I heard about what Lynn said," Christopher told his brother, giving him a quick embrace. "I know why you ran off."

"I just had to get out of there," James said,

shaking his head. "I didn't have anywhere else to go, so I came down here. In a way, I had wanted to come down here before I left; Lynn merely set it off inside of me. I had to come."

"I understand," Christopher whispered as he grabbed onto James' hand. "We have to get back. This place is obviously flooding."

"All right," James said. "I just wanted to say goodbye to Alena."

"Okay," Christopher said, leading James out of the store. "All right, do it, and then we have to go; we have to get out of here before it's too late."

"I'm sorry, Alena…," James said, turning to the bench and finding that she was no longer there.

"Lights in the cave," Alena's voice came, heavy and grim in the wind. "Bad things are in the cave."

"What bad things?" Christopher asked, the world quickly dimming around him. Christopher reached for James's hand in the dark, but instead fumbled around with nothing but empty air. He flung himself around wildly, trying to find something to grab on to—anything. He was alone in the dark silence.

"It's happening again, the memory is repeating…," Alena whispered inside his head.

"*What is happening?*" Christopher asked, very frustrated. Suddenly his thoughts turned to Kylie—he had left her out there on her own at the cave entrance. How stupid he was! What the hell was he thinking?

Slowly an image came into focus as part of his surroundings. He could see Kylie in the rain-drenched night, dimly silhouetted by a small beam of light that pursued her. She was running as fast as she could. He could hear her labored, rapid breathing, a small whimper, and then a loud cry for help, which he heard twice: once, right before him, and then again, faintly, from somewhere above. Kylie was in the cave now, and terrified of something, all right, but what?

"Kylie!" Christopher cried out, surprising himself. Either way, she did not respond. Was this a memory that he was seeing, like Alena's? If so, then Kylie was running down the back passage, and that could only mean…she was headed toward the falls!

His surroundings suddenly fell dark again. His eyes struggled to catch anything they could see, his heart drumming violently in his chest. He had to do something, yet what could he do? He caught a dim light from somewhere ahead in the dark, and it got bigger and brighter until he finally saw the source.

"James!" Christopher exclaimed. "Kylie…she's in trouble."

"Go, Chris!" James screamed as he pushed Christopher backward with all his might.

Christopher felt himself toppling back. He reached out for James, but he fell with such force that his brother was out of sight in seconds. Christopher landed roughly upon the flooded cave floor, water splashing up all around him. He quickly got to his feet, ripping the flashlight from his head and flipping it on. He used the beam to scan the entire chamber and, finding it empty, eventually settled the beam on the falls high above him.

Off in the distance he couldn't see anything—just the empty entrance to the drop-off above him. Maybe what he saw hadn't happened yet, maybe it was the future. That meant that he still had some time. He was about to run up the winding tunnel when someone shouted above him.

"Christopher!" Kylie screamed, gripping the cave wall near the rushing falls. "It's my father!"

"Kylie!" Christopher yelled back, as he started to run on ahead. "I'm coming!"

Christopher paused once more, now seeing a light shining down from the falls. He strained his eyes to see, and in shock he quickly fell back to his knees. He was too late. Her father had a hold of her and was dangling her over the falls. He would never be able to run up there and save her, it would take far too long. He really was too late.

"Christopher!" Kylie screamed again, this time in a deep state of fear. "Please!"

Christopher watched in horror as Kylie's father held her over the falls. Then, for a moment, he could see a twirling disc of light. Kylie's father had thrown down a flashlight, and it plummeted down the vast expanse of the waterfalls, skimming through the falling water and hitting the cave floor hard a few yards from Christopher and exploding into pieces.

He quickly brought his own flashlight's beam up, shaking in fear and unable to do anything at all about it. He watched as the Kylie's father, his body obscured in shadows, plunged something metal and gleaming into Kylie's side. "No!" Christopher screamed, realizing what he was seeing.

"NO!" Christopher screamed again, tears in his eyes. It was not happening, it couldn't be happening. He watched, unable to take his eyes away from the horrifying events. He knew they were real, and they felt real, yet he couldn't bring his mind to reason that these things were really happening.

Kylie's father dangled her over the ledge once more; blood could be seen dripping down her left side as she hung motionless in his hand. Then, without much ado, he released her.

Christopher was immediately at his feet. He knew that he couldn't catch her; she was falling from too high a distance. Still, he had to try. He had to do something or else she would die for sure. He couldn't stand it. Even if he was badly injured in the process, he had to at least try and get beneath her. Otherwise, there really wouldn't be any reason to go on.

Kylie plummeted down at him, growing large rapidly, the fragmented moments seeming completely frozen in time. Just as Christopher braced himself for Kylie's impact, he heard a loud booming sound behind him, and he watched as the entire room filled with a brilliant blue light. A huge puff of blue smoke appeared at the window in an instant, transforming into a huge, smoky blue bird. The bird zoomed off into the air above Christopher, catching Kylie in its large talons and leaving behind huge streaks of glowing blue smoke diffusing across the falls. The bird soared around the cave, slowly circling and then landing at the rocky ground near Christopher. As the bird released Kylie, he rushed to her. She was still breathing—thank God she was still alive! It looked as though she was bleeding pretty badly from her side, though; Christopher knew he had to do something, and quick.

Scooping Kylie up in his arms, Christopher watched as the bird dove into the window in the earth, exploding in a huge, expanding cloud of dazzling blue lights and smoke trails. Just as the bird disappeared, a great wave burst from the window and crashed against a faraway wall. It was James. He hovered behind the window, taking a huge breath and expelling another wave of water from the room with a mighty gust from his lungs.

"James!" Christopher exclaimed, as he struggled to carry Kylie. "I need some help. She's hurt really badly!"

"Go!" James screamed. He flew out of the room behind the window, landing next to Christopher and pushing him away, toward the passage that wound up to the top of the falls. "The room is almost flooded now, the cave will go next!"

"Let's go!" Christopher yelled as he turned away for a moment, heading back up. "I need help!" he said as he fell to his knees, almost dropping Kylie in the process.

"I can't," James whispered as he made his way back to the window.

"James!" Christopher entreated as he watched his brother leave.

Standing before the window in the earth, James shook his head and let out a little smile. "I'm sorry…Christopher," he said, and small wisps of blue smoke emerged and swirled about his lips as he spoke each word. One of the trails of smoke formed into a bird feather that rocked to and fro in a protracted fall, disappearing in a small puff as it came to rest on the watery rocks.

"No…," Christopher whispered as he watched, in a confused state of terror. "Please, James…."

"Promise me you'll keep in touch," James said, each word being followed by more and more blue smoke. "Even if it doesn't make sense right now, just promise me."

"I promise…," Christopher whispered as more tears came streaming down his cheeks. It was at that very moment he realized that James had chosen to stay behind for good. James had helped him and saved Kylie, yet in the process this choice had cost him.

"Alena needs me," James whispered as he turned to the window, his back to Christopher. "I love her, you know?"

Before Christopher could say another word, James quickly faded into the window, his exit followed by another huge explosion of brilliant blue smoke and bird feathers.

"James…," Christopher whispered once more. He looked down at Kylie, knowing the condition she was in. He had no time. James had done his part; the rest was up to him.

With Kylie in his arms, Christopher struggled his way up the winding passage, helped along somehow by a cool breeze from behind, and even at points where he thought his exhaustion and weakness had won, the breeze was almost magically refreshing, and gave him just that much more strength to continue on. He wondered fondly if his brother had something to do with it. Then, ahead in the darkness, he thought he saw something move ahead of them. *Kylie's father,* Christopher thought to himself, and felt horror creeping back into his heart. What was he going to do if it was him? Christopher lifted his flashlight up with a shaking hand, and there, with eyes gleaming like a madman and a bloodstained knife in his right hand, was Kylie's father. His face was pale and had dark, wet, matted hair hanging about his sunken, bloodshot eyes and shaggy beard. There were no introductions; he and Christopher just saw one another, and then reacted. Christopher tried to shield himself and Kylie with his arms as Mr. Leiter lunged at him with the blade, missing his head by mere inches and slicing deeply into his left shoulder and down his arm. Christopher screamed and, with all his might, threw himself and Kylie against Mr. Leiter, causing him to slip on the flooding cave floor and land on his back. Christopher was panting and bleeding as he gently laid Kylie in a dark corner behind him and whirled to face his attacker.

Mr. Leiter grunted like some kind of wounded animal as he flailed about on the ground and scrambled wildly to his feet. His breathing was inhuman, resembling a serpent's. He wetted his thin lips with his tongue and fixed his dark eyes on Kylie then shouted in a haunted, strained tone, "Alena, you stupid bitch… All you had to do was listen, you've ruined my life!"

"She is not Alena, she is your daughter! It's Kylie!" Christopher attempted, although knowing well that there was no reasoning with Kylie's father in his current state. It was apparent that he was fully lost to both his own madness and the abyss of darkness that the bad memory had shrouded his mind in.

Without reply, Mr. Leiter lunged forward, and immediately Christopher leapt back and to the right, barely avoiding the blade. Christopher knew he couldn't keep up the dodging for long, but what else could he do? Mr. Leiter brought his knife high above his head, ready to bring it slamming down on Christopher. However, just as he raised the knife, there was a sudden, jarring sound of meat tearing, and Mr. Leiter sunk to his knees, his mouth agape as he groped absent-mindedly at the paralyzing wound that had just been ripped into his back. The great blue smoke-bear, Face, stood behind him, his smoky claw wet with Mr. Leiter's blood. Mr. Leiter himself writhed about in agony, still trying in vain to reach the injury on his back. Face swiftly scooped up Kylie's father in its arms, and then, with a sickeningly loud thud, threw the full-grown man with bone-breaking force against the jutting rocks of the cave wall.

"Face…," Christopher whispered as he scooped Kylie back up. She was still breathing regularly and made soft, faint sounds as she did, as though she was simply sleeping. "…thank you." Christopher turned again to see Face sitting on the ground before Mr. Leiter's broken body. "Face," he said, "go, or you'll get left behind."

However, Face did not react at all. Christopher was worried for a moment that it was too late for Face. He hoped otherwise, and he looked back once more before he continued on ahead. He had to get Kylie to safety.

Christopher stumbled out of the cave entrance and was greeted by two flashlight beams, and their owners, Jack Olen and William Walker, who were both shocked to see him and Kylie. They ran over to Christopher and took her from his arms, planning on taking them both back to Bones' house. Luckily, fearing something was wrong, Jack Olen had already called the authorities, and an ambulance was already waiting there for them when they arrived.

That night, the police searched the entire cave.

Inside they found Mr. Leiter's body, gored and destroyed by what they believed to be some kind of wild animal. As for James, all they ever found of him were his shoes, and a single large blue feather floating in the cave's new pool, where the falls used to be.

The next day, Christopher visited Kylie in the hospital. She was doing fine and only suffered a small wound from the knife. Luckily, there would be no permanent damage and she would only be left with a scar as a memory of what had happened that night. Later that day, when Kylie was back on her feet, she and her mother left for Nevada. They had decided not to stay in Pine Hallow a single moment longer, not with all that had happened. It was just too painful. Christopher hoped that they would be able to stay in contact, yet had no idea if the distance would ever allow it to be possible. Saying goodbye was so difficult that Christopher felt as though he would never really get over it.

Christopher stood at the house, his suitcases in his hands as he made his way to Aunt Lynn's van. He stopped for a moment, looking back one last time at the old Janes house and remembering all the memories he had made there, and all the people he had loved and lost before, after, and in-between. He wondered if he would ever see James again. Just thinking about it all made him feel as though everything had been so pointless. Bones was gone now—James, too. Kylie and her mother were in Nevada, and Kate and Poppy with them.

Jack Olsen quietly made his way up the Christopher. He looked downright exhausted. After getting back from the hospital he had helped with the search for James.

"Christopher…," Jack said as he held out a hand to say goodbye.

"Jack," Christopher answered lightly, returning the firm handshake.

"We will keep looking, I promise you," Jack said, placing a hand on Christopher's shoulder. "If he's still on this earth, we'll find him."

"I'm not sure that he is anymore," Christopher said quietly. "Though, I don't think he minds."

"Someday you'll have to let me in on this," Jack whispered as he patted Christopher on the back. He picked up Christopher's suitcases and helped place them in the back of the van.

Christopher paused for a moment as William Walker towered over Aunt Lynn. He could hear him yelling something like, "If you don't straighten up your ways I'll break you into little pieces and straighten you up myself," and then he mentioned something about lighting her on fire afterwards. Bill quickly became silent when Christopher walked up to the car.

"Bill," Christopher said, nodding.

"Have a good trip," Bill said, and then opened the back door on the driver's side for Christopher. "If you need us, you know how to get a hold of us."

"Thank you," Christopher whispered as he watched the two oddly coupled men walk back to their truck.

Christopher was about to step into the van when he felt something strange brush up against the back of his leg. "Stinky?" he asked, looking down at the gray-and-white cat.

He carefully picked up the feline, examining him closely. The cat let out a low little meow, followed quickly by the tiniest wisp of blue-colored smoke. Christopher hugged the cat to his chest as he climbed into the van.

"What's that?" Lynn asked as she looked back to Christopher and the cat.

"It's my cat," Christopher whispered, rubbing the animal gently behind its ears. "I'm not leaving without it."

"That's all right…," Aunt Lynn whispered, knowing she had no choice. She slowly put the keys into the ignition, started up the van and then began backing it out of the driveway. "So…what's the cat's name?"

Christopher stared at the cat for a few moments, and then smiled. "Face…."

"'Face'…?" Aunt Lynn asked. "What kind of a name is 'Face'?"

May 31st, 2002

James Janes
The Cave at the Janes House
Pine Hallow, Missouri

Dear James,

I'm sorry. I know it has been a long, long time since I have written. Please don't think that I've forgotten about you after all these years have passed. I would never feel right if you ever thought that way.

I just wanted to write to tell you everything that has happened, and things that might happen. I don't know if this letter will ever reach you, but I just want you to know about these things that happened after you disappeared.

I'd like to say that everything was just fine after leaving with Aunt Lynn, but life was hard adjusting to the new school there. It was as though I was adjusting to a whole new world entirely. Aunt Lynn and I ended up settling down in Troy, Illinois. It's a pretty small city that's about half an hour from Saint Louis, and was far enough that the great flood of '93 never came our way.

About two weeks after you disappeared, I made it down to Pine Hallow for Bones' funeral. I had really hoped to see Kylie there, but she wasn't. I don't know why she wasn't there, and I had lost contact with her completely at that point. I remember I was so saddened by it all, just seeing the house and the cave again. I wanted to go in, but couldn't bring myself to do it; I knew that you weren't there anymore. You know they actually buried your shoes in a coffin? I thought you'd get a kick out of that.

I went to college in Bloomington, at Illinois State University. I was happy to finally get out from Aunt Lynn's house and free of her. She wasn't a bad parent, but she just was too irresponsible. I'm glad that she never saw any of the money that Bones had left for us.

Two years ago, I finally got in touch with Kylie, on the internet of all places. Can you believe that? I invited her to come up the following weekend and stay with me for a week. Upon getting my address, she arrived the very next day. She never left. We were married shortly afterward. We are actually expecting a child of our own soon. Me, having a child. Can you believe it?

I'm thinking about getting into story-writing, and maybe one day writing about our story, and what happened that short week during that unforgettable summer. I don't know if I'll ever follow through with it, though.

I don't know what else to add. A lot has happened, but in the same way not much has happened. Stinky, that stray cat from Bones' house, he's still with us. I don't think he's a normal cat, as he has lived an unusually long time. I've actually named him "Face," because I believe that at one time that was what he was called. Alena once said that Face used to be "one of the bad memories." I think I finally understand that now. I think Face was a bad memory that Alena turned into a good one. Sometimes in life that is just what you have to do. I will keep you updated as things happen. Hope to hear back from you someday.

Sincerely, and with love from your brother and sister-in-law,

Christopher and Kylie Janes

58681973R00201

Made in the USA
Lexington, KY
16 December 2016